Paramnesia

A Grendel Press Horror Anthology

Edited by Susan Russell

GRENDEL PRESS

Copyright © 2023 by Grendel Press LLC

All rights reserved. No part of this publication may be reproduced, distributed, or transmitted in any form or by any means, including photocopying, recording, or other electronic or mechanical methods, without the prior written permission of the publisher, except as permitted by U.S. copyright law and author-publisher agreements.

This is a work of fiction. Names, characters, businesses, places, events, locales, and incidents are either the products of the author's imagination or used in a fictitious manner. Any resemblance to actual persons, living or dead, or actual events is purely coincidental.

ISBN: 978-1-960534-00-2 (Paperback)

Cover art by Susan Russell
Story art by Dany Rivera
Edited and typeset by Susan Russell
Proofread by Rachael Swanson

Contributors:
Hark, Now I Hear Them by Brandon Ebinger
Without You by Clarence Carter
Running In Circles by David Lee Zweifler
Real Estate by Gordon Grice
THIS SHOULD BE THE PLACE by Stuart Freyer
A Nook Obscure by Thomas Bales
A Little game of Hide-n'-go-seek by Thomas Stewart
Mol of the Plague by M. W. Irving
I Am Monster by Christopher Beck
Changeling by Christopher Yusko
Rogue Taxidermy by Dustin Reade
Dr Marcus by Terence Waeland
House of Reverie by Susan L. Lin
End Bed by Paul Melhuish

Contents

1. Rogue Taxidermy — 1
   by Dustin Reade

2. Real Estate — 17
   by Gordon Grice

3. I Am Monster — 41
   by Christopher Beck

4. Running In Circles — 71
   by David Lee Zweifler

5. End Bed — 81
   by Paul Melhuish

6. Mol of the Plague — 103
   by M.W. Irving

7. A Little Game of Hide-n'-go-seek   133
    by Thomas Stewart

8. Hark, Now I Hear Them   159
    by Brandon Ebinger

9. A Nook Obscure   181
    by Thomas Bales

10. THIS SHOULD BE THE PLACE   207
    by Stuart Freyer

11. House of Reverie   225
    by Susan L. Lin

12. Changeling   239
    by Christopher Yusko

13. Dr. Marcus   261
    by Terence Waeland

14. Without You   295
    by Clarence Carter

Par·am·ne·sia

A psychological state involving distorted memories or the inability to identify between fact and fantasy, also known as confabulation or déjà vu.

Rogue Taxidermy

by Dustin Reade

Martha Maxwell lived alone in a small pink house beside a diminutive patch of wilderness. If you were to stand in her soft blue kitchen, from a rectangular window, you would see a small pathway carved into the woods, the trees bent inward at the tops as though the trail had happened rather suddenly, and they were still staring in silent surprise at the lacerating fissure between them.

In the backyard, in a spot just before the grass ended and the woods began, there was a single, gnarled willow tree. Various animal feeders hung from the many branches, and a wide variety of traps lay strewn about the tree's base. From the kitchen window, Martha l could sip at her coffee and watch as a small parade of raccoons, foxes, badgers, and the occasional deer ventured into the yard to nibble at the apple cores she had tossed around the traps. When a fox might get its foot caught in a claw-toothed snap-and-grab, she could push her own foot on the bubble where the linoleum was cut too long against the sink counter. Grabbing a butcher knife from the wood block, she could slip into her slippers, walk outside, and slit the animal's throat before it had the ingenuity to gnaw its own leg off.

On this particular day, a bluebird had become ensnared by its tail feathers in one of the many hanging traps. Martha shrugged into her favorite cardigan, tattered and gray like herself, and waddled excitedly out back. The acquisition of a fresh carcass made the days go by faster and more pleasantly. She smiled as she ran the knife along the bluebird's neck, whistling as the blood drained over the apple cores.

Martha knew there was something ghoulish to her delight, but she never allowed her conscience to overwhelm her collecting. Each creature was a sort of prize; a cadaver full of flowers, gems, imagination, and inspiration, and the obtaining of a fresh work of art was prized above all else in her long, simple life. Martha loved these little works of art, and the backyard provided a steady stream of her favorite decor: taxidermy.

Her living room was full of little treasures, but it was far from the only display room in the house. Over the years, she had acquired quite a collection of buffed, tanned, and stuffed critters, all lovingly displayed from near the front door—where she kept her earliest attempts—to the entryway of the kitchen where the latest animals were displayed. On all the walls, various heads gazed down through glass eyes, mouths in perpetual snarls, teeth glazed with nail polish to appear drenched in saliva. On every countertop and bedside table were humorous dioramas of crickets playing tennis with rackets made from toothpicks, a crow smoking a cigarette, and several hummingbirds staring forever at a television screen glowing out from a walnut—the screen a piece of tin foil.

After stuffing the bluebird into the icebox, she made her way slowly, dragging her hand down the wall, to the living room.

Martha's favorite chair was a wide leather number, with the stray hairs of a thousand dead animals clinging to its static-heavy surface. Beside the chair was a three-foot stack of *Taxidermy Monthly*, a trade magazine for those in the 'Stuffing Game'. Martha had been a subscriber since March 3rd, 1979. Flipping through the magazines, one would see articles with titles like "How to Flesh Capes With Precision Using New Tools Designed by Modern Taxidermists," "Tricks with Antlers and Horns," and "The Importance of Novelties."

It was while sitting in this chair that Martha happened to glance out the window and notice a wall of dark storm clouds—heavy, black, pendulous—moving slowly over the tops of the trees. With a sigh, Martha walked outside to roll up the windows of her beat-up Ford truck, when something caught her eye.

It was a fox. Stuffed, clearly one of her own, hiding under a miniature pine tree. She could remember stuffing it several years ago. Laying the fox down on its belly over an old sheet, feet outstretched. She had made the incision from between the ears, along the back, to the base of its bushy tail. Then she peeled back the hide and stripped out the tailbone, being careful not to tear its delicate, orange-red skin. She even remembered how she had rubbed the inside of the hide with borax.

The memory caused a giggle to rise up from her chest. Borax, she thought. How young I once was! Still, she thumped her temple with her index finger, pleased she could remember such an insignificant detail as that. Her mother had gone soft in the brain fairly early, barely stepping into her fifties before confusing names and places. Her father was always mentally sound, but even so, Martha had a deep fear of slipping away into the darkness of senility, and she thanked the Gods every day for the—seemingly—solid nature of her mind.

Borax...
Borax...
Ah, yes.

Nowadays, of course, she used a specialized tanning/preservative blend of her own design. No one used borax anymore. Martha scoffed at the thought, picked up the stuffed fox, and made her way back into the house, closing the front door just as the first pelts of rain made their way to the grass and pavement.

Martha knew instinctively where the fox belonged. It had held the same spot atop the television for the last fifteen years. It sat beside a stuffed rabbit's head, cut off just below the forehead so that only the ears remained, forever bent in a ghastly pantomime of antique antennae. Carefully, she wiped the dust from the set and returned the fox to its natural habitat. She did not wonder as to how it had come to be outside, a one-time occurrence and certainly nothing to worry about.

Besides, there was a two-week-old badger in the vegetable drawer that would not allow for any more waiting.

Stuffing a badger is better than stuffing a buffalo. There is no smell in the world quite like an ice cream scoop full of buffalo brains. Smaller animals are no less pungent, but the smell is... well, different. There is something less vile about the fragrance of death on lesser creatures, more like a food item than a corpse.

Every creature has its own unique scent of decay. Ask a vulture.

After skinning the badger and preserving the hide with her special rubdown, Martha pushed a handful of clay into each of the four legs to fill out the toes, feet, and forelegs. She then slipped the skin onto the mannequin. Starting with the feet, she pulled the hide in the same way one would pull on a pair of pants. She then sewed the head in place and inserted two glass eyes, painting over each with nail polish to give the appearance of life. She then turned the mannequin onto its back and began sewing up the underbelly seam.

As she did so, she heard a soft thump come from the living room.

In the home of a taxidermist, soft thumps are to be expected. Animals often fall from weak stands, or head mounts fall from the wall as the supporting nails are pulled from their holes, no longer able to hold the weight of a full-racked buck.

Martha finished sewing the underbelly of the badger, wiped her hands on a stiff red rag, and walked into the living room. Scanning the floor, she saw that no mounts had fallen. She checked the windows and found they were all shut firmly. She then noticed the fox mount was again gone from the television, as were the two pheasants that hung over the front door. Looking to her right, she was surprised to find the front door was open, closed only enough to create a convincing illusion.

Pulling it open, Martha saw all three of the missing animals out on the lawn, piled one on top of the other beneath the miniature pine tree. Martha looked around the yard and then stuck her head back into the living room and shouted, thinking perhaps there was some stray cat or dog that had made its way inside and was now pulling her mounts outside for whatever reason. The house remained silent, save for the buzz of the kitchen light and the ticking of the clock.

Was it possible she hadn't really brought the fox in the first time?

But then, how would that explain the pheasants now beneath the tree? Flashes of her mother wandering the halls of the nursing home in nothing but her tan underthings fought for position in her mind. A frightening blue confusion shook down her spine as she stood in the doorway, staring at the stray mounts. What was happening, exactly? If she watched long enough, would it move? How would she react to such a thing? Was there more saliva in her mouth? Was that feather dust under her nails?

No. No, surely she had brought in the fox. The television set was freshly shorn of dust, and she could still see her finger marks along the surface, as oblong and obvious as fresh carrots.

"Well," she said, running out into the rain and retrieving the animals. "I'll just have to put you somewhere you can't escape!"

A joke...
    A joke...

She put the fox in the hall closet beneath the stairs. The closet was tapered off in the back and had little in it save a few jackets hung up in front. She walked the fox to the back of the closet, thinking to herself that it was a rather ratty-looking thing and that she could surely pull one of the more lush foxes from the kitchen walkway that would look much better on the television.

The two pheasants were nailed to the wall by their wings.

Over the next two weeks, the closet under the stairs became filled with an exotic menagerie of animals stuffed, buffed, polished, waxed, mounted, dried, tanned, and fiberglassed. It seemed every other day, another animal found a clandestine path to the outdoors, as if—once they reached the wilderness—they would be reanimated, thrust into life like Pinocchio. At first, Martha found it almost funny. The novelty quickly wore off.

Before long, the fear set in.

Martha took to chewing her fingernails down to splintered nubs. The dark hours of the late night were spent huddled under heavy blankets, listening to the imagined chorus of paws beating the closet doors, of mounts falling from the walls.

One night, the mounts fell like raindrops. The windows rattled with each large thump as the specimens fell from the walls. More than that, Martha swore she could hear dozens of smaller thumps: the sounds of her mounts somehow hopping along the floor. She lay, blankets almost to her eyes, as all her little treasures broke free of their chains and limped towards liberation. A picture flashed before her of a wide, moonlit field littered with taxidermy animals, each reared up on their wire-and-clay haunches to howl at the moon. She saw the eerie blue glow of the Sea of Tranquility reflected in a polecat's eye and almost smelled the glue melting from its teeth, the jaw flexing, snapping shut.

With a courageous inhale, Martha leapt from the bed, pulled the flashlight from the nightstand, and raced down the hall, grabbing every animal still hanging and throwing it with a scream into the closet.

The closet...
The closet...
It haunted the house like a ghost. Martha became nervous whenever she had to walk by it to get to the kitchen. She knew the animals were angry. Not because she had killed them, and not because she had thwarted their escape attempts, but because she had thrown them in with others not of their kind. They had become something more than mere animals. They were specimens, things to be classified. She often thought of straightening them all out, lining them up in proper order, but she could not. The chaos in the closet remained as foxes stuffed and mounted in 1972 could be found atop raccoons mounted only a few short months ago. The tennis-playing crickets were crushed beneath the upper torso of a fully matured black bear. The bear's paws were outstretched as if reaching for the fiberglass blowfish hanging from the rafters over its head.

Soon, the walls of the living room were completely bare. The house became less a museum of eccentric hobby and more a graveyard full of disquieted ghosts. Martha patrolled the headstones of closets and cupboards in a tattered nightgown, listening to the scratching and hissing of the innumerable mounts filling up the various downstairs closets, including the thin cupboard in the bathroom. Once, that cupboard held a few spare blankets, helpful in getting her through the long winter months. Now, the cupboard housed her rather extensive jackalope collection.

Sitting in her favorite chair, Martha looked around at the bare walls, chewing her fingernails to bloody points.

The walls...

The walls...

White spots showed where deer mounts once hung, the rest of the wall having grown gray and dusty over the years. The blue paint was like ice, and it made the room feel colder somehow, a morgue, a coroner's office. Martha remembered her mother's body in the basement of the nursing home. She remembered how her skin had seemed too loose, like stretched animal hide cut loose from the tanner.

She's gone to a better place, Martha thought, surprised by the bitterness in her mind. The truth was, her mother had been dead for years, and someone had simply forgotten to tell her body. It had been a constant emotional strain to see her talking to strangers as if they were old friends, the embarrassment she felt as she apologized to shopkeepers, waiters, paramedics, and nursing home staff. Then she had finally let go, dying fully clothed in the bath with a purse full of shredded paper and half-eaten food. The horrible sense of relief she felt when she got the call, "I'm sorry. It's finally happened. We did all we could. If you could just come down and sign a few things, have one last look, make sure everything is in order." And so on.

Anger, sadness, desperate hope, it all came to an end when she saw her on that slab, every inch her mother, and yet strangely less so than ever. Martha bit down hard, pulling the last of her fingernail from its root. The memory warped as she remembered her mother's flesh stretching out, pouring from the sides of the stretcher and flattening out, surrounding her, choking her, hardening around the edges until they were as blue and dusty as living room walls...

With no air-conditioning, the house quickly filled with the stink of death.

It had been weeks since Martha had the time to stuff anything. The traps in the backyard were empty. She had not baited them since all of the strangeness began. The electricity had gone down days ago, the result of a jackalope puncturing the generator. In the absence of power, the carcasses in the deep freeze had begun to rot, but even so, Martha could not bring herself to throw them out. Indeed, she could barely even enter the kitchen anymore. The birds in the freezer squawked as she approached. Martha had moved whatever dry food she had into the living room and lived most hours in her chair, talking to herself to drown out the pitiful dirge surrounding her.

It was on a Sunday afternoon that she happened upon an article in the latest issue of *Taxidermy Monthly* titled, "Rogue Taxidermy." She had ignored the magazines for weeks, the animals making it too difficult to read. Had she not happened to drop a box of Cracker Jacks between the chair and the books, she may well never have read an issue again. The animals were quiet at the moment, so Martha started reading.

Rogue taxidermy was the creation of stuffed animals that did not have real, living counterparts. Many taxidermists, she read, did not consider it to be true taxidermy. They may represent hybrid creatures such as the jackalope or skvader. The jackalope is a jackrabbit with horns or antlers and a pheasant's tail. The word jackalope is a portmanteau of "jackrabbit" and "antelope," an archaic spelling of antelope.

In 1918, taxidermist Rudolf Granberg created what he called the "skvader." On display at the museum at Norra Berget in Sundsvall, the skvader has the forequarters and hind legs of a hare and the back, wings, and tail of a female wood grouse. It was later jokingly given the Latin name, *Tetrao lepus pseudo-hybridus rarissimus L*, meaning extinct.

Extinction is the biological end of an organism or group of taxa. Extinction can be considered to "begin" the moment the last creature of any given species dies. Because a species' potential range tends to be quite large, determining the exact moment it goes extinct can be rather difficult and is usually done after the fact. This difficulty leads to phenomena species, mythical creatures such as dragons. Dragons feature in the myths of many cultures, much like chimeras.

In Greek mythology, the Chimera was a monstrous fire-breathing creature of Lycia in Asia Minor, composed of the parts of multiple animals: the body of a lioness with a tail that ended in a snake's head, and at the center of her spine was a goat's head. The Chimera was one of the griffins.

The griffin was a legendary creature which had the body of a lion and the head and wings of an eagle. Traditionally, the lion was considered the king of the beasts and the eagle was the king of the birds, and therefore the griffin was an especially powerful and majestic creature. Griffins are normally known for guarding treasure.

A unicorn is likewise a mythological creature. While the modern image of the unicorn is that of a horse with a horn coming out of its forehead, the traditional unicorn also has a billy-goat beard and cloven hooves—further distinguishing it from a horse.

Most examples of rogue taxidermy are made from parts of more than one kind of animal, or they may be artificially created. Rogue taxidermy is often seen in sideshows like the Ten-in-One.

The "Ten-in-One" was a program of ten circus or sideshow acts under one tent for a single admission price. Typically the ten-in-one contained a freak show featuring human oddities, though they would often include "working acts" who would perform stunts or magic tricks. Made popular near the end of the 19th century, dime museums were designed as centers for entertainment and moral education for the working class. The museums were notably different from the more highbrow entertainments found in urban centers like New York City, where many immigrants settled among genuine freak animals.

Martha again read the line, "made from parts of more than one kind of animal." An idea began to form in her mind like a lump of chewed food in her mouth. She slowly rose up from the hair-coated chair and made her way over to the main closet. She could hear the animals wiggling around inside. There was a series of bumps that somehow managed to sound dry, stale. She reached her hand out nervously, feeling the chipped paint against her palm. Something kicked at the door, and she felt it as a baby moving in the womb.

"You'll have to be big," she told the animals. "You'll all have to work together. It'll be hard... hard for all of us, but it's the right thing to do."

The right thing to do...
　The right thing to do...
She worked all night. The animals fought her initial attempts, fizzling holes in their hides where she applied her tanning solution. It was as if they were willing their own decomposition, somehow speeding up the process, so they dissolved right there in her hands until she finally resorted to borax and felt the flesh relax like a sleeping child in her arms.

Borax...
　Borax...
How young she once was.
Several times, she had to pull away from her work, plopping down in her chair and sleeping for a few hours before returning to the task at hand. The black bear growled as she stripped the mount. It was a gentle sound, deep and soothing, and for a moment, Martha felt like her old self again. She remembered the joy she felt, fleshing the bear all those years ago, the power she had felt even in its dead body as she bent its stiff knees and severed its ligaments with a serrated blade. She smiled as she worked.

It took two days to complete, and in the very early morning of the third day, Martha bit the last bit of thread and stood back, admiring her work. She took in everything, almost eating the monstrosity with her eyes. The powerful hands, twice the size of a grown man's, connected to the muscular arms, the barrel chest, and the fur... everywhere the fur.

Neither animal nor man, but something in between.

Martha patted the beast on its leathery chest, feeling a surge of electricity beneath, and then... was that? Yes. It was subtle, buried beneath layers and layers of pelt, but it was there: a heartbeat.

Martha pulled her hand away slowly, letting it brush against the various bits of bloated body before retiring to bed. The stairs creaked heavily with each step. Her fingers left thin, bloody streaks where they made contact with the walls. In her brain, finally, all was calm.

She had only been asleep a few minutes when she heard the first thump. She sat bolt upright in the bed, the blankets pulled up to her chin, knuckles white, breath cold, fast. Would this really work? She wondered. The fear, again, like a caterpillar boring a hole in the back of her head. Another thump sounded, and Martha was back in the nursing home basement, her mother's corpse before her on the stretcher.

"That's her."

"I'm sorry. If it's any consolation, she most likely didn't suffer at all. When they're that far gone, they tend to just fall asleep."

"Thank you." But she knew differently, now. It was never peaceful; madness. Madness was frantic, frenzied, clutching forever at your own throat while imagining invisible threats. It was like swimming in the ocean at night and catching glimpses of writhing things beneath you.

Downstairs, something fell, something that, unlike everything else, was not supposed to fall. A slithering noise. It took Martha a moment to realize it was her stack of *Taxidermy Monthly* being knocked over, the copious issues sliding smoothly over one another. Back in the morgue, her mother opened her eyes. Martha took a deep breath, startled, but there was nothing sinister on her mother's face. She smiled softly, raising a hand and caressing Martha's cheek.

"Don't worry, sweetie," she said. "Your father will take care of you."

The thing had found the steps now. Martha listened, feeling her mother's cold palm against her face as it climbed awkwardly closer.

"I'm sorry," her mother told her, closing her eyes. "I wish I could have been there for you."

"You're here now," Martha said.

"So is he," she said as the bedroom door began to open.

So is he…

    So is he…

About the Author

Dustin's Amazon Author Page

Dustin lives and works in Port Angeles, WA, and spends the bulk of his time reading about and looking for Bigfoot. He is the father of a gender-fluid child, and an avid record collector. He is also the author of several books, the most recent being the short story collection "Songs About My Father's Crotch" and "The Secret Sex Lives of Ghosts," both released through Planet Bizarro Press. His short stories have appeared in numerous anthologies, and online at Bizarro Central, New Dead Families, and Sideshow Fables.

Other Works From This Author

The Secret Sex Lives of Ghosts
Bad Hotel
Under the Dusty Blanket
Songs About My Father's Crotch

Real Estate

by Gordon Grice

"What I love about this one is the façade," Clint said as he guided the Davidsons up the walk on Rockland Circle.

"What kind of stone is that?" Mrs. Davidson said, shoving a mass of dark curly hair out of her eyes for a better look. "Granite?"

"Yes, and locally mined, I believe," Clint bluffed. The house looked saleable enough—stone halfway up, the foundation free of cracks, snug forest-green shingles. Clint couldn't remember showing it before, though it certainly felt familiar. His facts came from his company's listing, which he'd consulted on his phone while waiting for the Davidsons.

He unlocked the door and swept it open for them, taking care to make it look effortless. As he passed in, he took another glance at their minivan, four or five years old, its paint chipped around the wheel wells. Not a lot of money here, he thought, but then a house like this shouldn't take any great feat of financing.

The Davidsons paused in the entryway. Clint eased around them. Something seemed to have darkened their mood. He didn't see anything amiss with the entryway, but he judged it best to guide them past that and help them focus on the better features within, if there were any. He took a second to imagine the floor plan he'd seen online, then led the way.

"The family room's there," he said, gesturing to the left. Mr. Davidson stiffened a bit; his wife almost cringed. So that's where they'd spotted the problem, whatever it was. "But let's save that for last," Clint went on, pretending not to notice their reaction.

"This is nice," Mr. Davidson said as they entered the kitchen. "Lots of walnut." He had a watery kind of face, not fat but seemingly made without bones. Clint felt he was faking his enthusiasm. This will not be a sale, he thought; something has really turned them off. He had other houses to show, but doubted any were in the Davidson's price range.

"And it doesn't darken the room like you get with some walnut," Mrs. Davidson added. She didn't sound any more enthusiastic than her husband did. Clint had met prospects like this before, too shy to say they didn't like a house. As if it were his, and he'd take offense.

"It's the vertical windows," he said. "They let in plenty of light." This was probably the wrong thing to say; he couldn't imagine why he had. If you know the customer doesn't want a house, you only make them resent you by pushing it, and that makes it harder to sell them the right one later on.

"It'll be nice in the mornings," Mrs. Davidson said. It was late afternoon now, and sun glared from windows and the built-in range-top.

"This little area could be kind of a breakfast nook," Mrs. Davidson added. "With Grandma's old table." Clint began to feel confused. He was almost certain they hated the place, but they were putting extraordinary effort into giving the opposite impression.

They moved on. There were two bedrooms for the children and then two steps down to the master bedroom, which featured a fireplace. Clint enumerated such features as they went, using phrases like "nice little extras." He would go on performing his role, he decided, for all the good it was going to do him. Or them.

The house was built into the side of a hill, and they eventually looped to the lowest room in the place, the family room they'd skipped at first. Clint led the way in, down three steps, with both Davidsons uncomfortably close behind him. Were they scared to be left behind? The carpet, a utilitarian green-brown, seemed unusually clean; Clint saw the telltale whorls that meant it had been shampooed recently. The seller must have worked hard to remove some stain. He glanced around for any sign of it and found none.

He ought to say this color of carpet wouldn't show dirt, but it looked like pond scum. He could almost smell it—something revolting under the faint chemical odor of the shampoo. He simply stood in the center of the floor.

The Davidsons hadn't come very far into the room. "The shelves are nice," Mrs. Davidson said at last, indicating a full wall of built-ins, but rather than approach them, she stayed beside her husband, holding his upper arm with both hands.

"Aren't they, though?" Clint said with as much enthusiasm as he could muster. "My wife is always telling me you can't have too many shelves."

"You know what?" said Mr. Davidson abruptly, almost interrupting. "I'd like to get another look at that kitchen."

"Absolutely," Clint said. Once they were out of the family room, the feeling of disgust drained out of him. Maybe it wasn't disgust.

They stood in the kitchen and, despite what Mr. Davidson had said, made no further effort to look at anything. Instead, Mrs. Davidson asked whether Clint had children. He admitted he had a boy and a girl. So did they. Anecdotes followed. They were all, Clint realized, attempting a conversation so that they could avoid rushing from the house. He did not especially like mentioning his children in this house.

Before dinner that evening, Clint stood smoking on the patio. The sun was setting. On the cement, he thought he saw an insect walking in drunken ellipses. He wondered where it imagined it was going. Maybe it was not an insect, not outside his body at all, only one of those bits of stuff that float inside your eye.

A wind ruffled the hedges. He folded his arms and pulled hard on the cigarette to finish it. Its orange tip pulsed brighter. The tree line across the road seemed sinister tonight, as if it harbored someone. He felt himself reaching down to palpate his conscience, to see how he was doing, and he felt a sudden revulsion.

There were the small unkindnesses. People he'd crossed in business. Losing his temper with the kids. Things he'd done in bedrooms. Surely everybody has skeletons, he thought, but the image of a neighbor named Beth wouldn't leave him alone—Beth grabbing her clothes and rushing out of the bedroom in tears because of something he'd said in a moment of fantasy. She'd never let him come near her again, had left his things on the patio in a cardboard box. He tried to explain, and she hung up. Her last email said, "I'm sure you can't help it, but please don't call me again." Thank God he'd never said anything like that to Sabrina.

Without thinking, he ground the bug beneath the toe of his shoe. When he raised his foot, nothing was left. If it had been there at all, it must be stuck on his sole.

"I showed the strangest house today," he said at the dinner table.

"Like the one with the indoor merry-go-round?" eight-year-old Tyler said.

"Nothing like that," Clint said. "It just seemed a little creepy."

"Did it have dead bodies in the closet?" six-year-old Maisie said.

"No, no, nothing like that either." He wished he hadn't mentioned the house in front of the children. "Just an ugly carpet."

"Boring," Maisie said. "Can me and Tyler go watch TV?"

"After you put your plates in the sink," Sabrina said. When the children had gone, she brought coffee. "Ugly carpet, you say?"

"It looked like a festering pond."

"Uglier than ours, even?" She laughed.

"The couple weren't too interested."

"Well, you tried," she said, pouring a drop of half-and-half into her coffee. As always, she paused to notice the pattern it made.

"I don't even know why I brought it up. It seemed really creepy at the time, but maybe I imagined the whole thing."

"Did the couple say anything about it?"

"No, actually. Everything they said was positive."

"Well, there you go. They probably thought it was perfectly nice. Maybe they'll call in a day or two and want to follow up."

"Maybe." He traced his finger around the rim of his cup, then touched the surface to see how hot the coffee was. Too hot. "The thing is, I would have sworn something bad must have happened in that house."

"You're just having one of your moods," Sabrina said. "What hideous thing could have happened in the 'burbs?"

"Murders," he said and was surprised to hear himself say it.

The new phase of his life began the next day in the afternoon rush. Raindrops seemed to pop into existence on the windshield without falling, as if by perspiration, and the wipers smeared them with a squeal. The sound disagreed with the music on the radio. He was uneasy. The morning's phone calls and ordinary matters of business had felt strained; hypocritical. He felt as if he were floating down to disaster.

The soggy mood had nibbled at him all afternoon. He wondered whether Sabrina really loved him. Of course she did. But she hadn't slept with him for weeks. He was alone in his troubles. Her face was still beautiful to him, but its stony silence masked something. Or maybe it didn't; maybe his depression was crowding in, making him see things askew, the way it had in college.

His lust stirred within him and was complicated by the memory of Sabrina's blood in childbirth, the immense pool of it on hospital tile looking silver under fluorescent light. That had been the first real rupture in their love life—her long recovery after Maisie, and the way her wounds made him feel.

Something shifted within him. There was a sensation of popping—not a sound, exactly—and his head felt suddenly as if someone had driven an ice pick into it beneath his right ear.

"Don't you have some appointments?" Sabrina said the next morning, fastening her earrings by the little mirror in her jewelry box. She was dressed for work in her dark blue skirt suit. He'd never liked that one much; she looked bony in it. When he didn't answer, she turned to look where he lay. He heard her, of course, but words wouldn't come. He was beginning to feel alarmed, but the sensation of alarm was itself slow to unfold. Nothing worked right. He looked at her, and his eyes began to brim. He couldn't blink.

"Honey, what's wrong?" she said. She rushed to him across a shaft of morning sunshine. He must look as bad as he felt; her tone told him that much. Suddenly his head was free to move. He turned it and vomited onto the sheet.

"Go ahead and turn on your side, honey," a nurse said. Clint lay in gauzy little booties and a gown. The paper under him crackled as he turned and curled like a fetus to allow access to the interstices of his spine. He felt her lay the flap of his gown aside; then the scrubbing started. The ice pick of pain in his head joggled with each movement.

A technician advanced with a frank smile. He steepled his fat fingers as if for prayer. "Our whole procedure today should take about half an hour," he said.

Sabrina took Clint's hand and held it firm. He didn't look at her. It was harder to block the pain if he saw it reflected in her eyes.

"You'll feel some coldness as I swab your lower back," the tech went on cheerily. A chill, a pause, and then the hard textured smell of the surfactant. Clint's pulse surged. Each blood vessel in his skull seemed individually aware of its own pulse.

"Little pinch here, and then you're going to feel some discomfort for just a few seconds. This will numb you up," the tech said. He felt a tug at his hand and realized Sabrina had turned her head aside.

"OK, and now you're going to be aware of some pressure and maybe just a little discomfort," the tech said. Before he had finished speaking, Clint felt he'd been kicked in the back. Sabrina winced. He must have squeezed her hand tight enough to hurt her.

A month into the inconclusive tests, with more scheduled, Clint returned to work. A morning of paperwork went fine. Lunchtime found him at his desk with a sandwich. He felt paper-thin. Without exactly falling asleep, he began to dream.

 He was lost in a stony landscape. Scraps of mist met him with unexpected resistance. He tried to take another step, but it clung to him with moist tenacity. He took hold of it with both hands, this bit of mist, and it tore audibly. He fell, wounding his hands and knees on the stones. He groped and touched a smoother stone slick with dew. His hand traced letters. All around him, headstones loomed in the mist. They were simultaneously human bones protruding through mossy flesh: and when his hands moved on them, he could feel the answering sensation in his limbs.

 On a granite slab stood a pool of rain. In it, toads mated and twitched. And his own body, the real body outside the dream, spasmed to cover itself, to cover its genitals.

 He looked around in shame. He was in his office, fully awake now, and around him, his co-workers looked up at him and then turned their heads awkwardly away.

"Dad, the closet's full of dead bodies." Maisie held his left hand in both of hers and tried to pull him off the sofa.

"Make her stop saying that, Dad." Tyler pried to loosen her grip on Clint. Their little fingers, fumbling among his, gave him a nauseous image of tentacles.

"Pipe down, both of you, or I'll lock *you* in the closet." Clint reached for his lighter. It tumbled out of his pocket and lost itself in the couch.

"Stop it, Clint," Sabrina said with controlled fury. "You'll give them nightmares."

"I never get nightmares," Maisie said. But Tyler ran to the corner behind the recliner, shrank himself small as he could, and dwindled like a singed spider. His eyes looked out huge and terrified.

At him, at Clint.

Sabrina watched him too, watched him with burning eyes. Obviously, something else had happened while he was at work. Beth had talked to her; that must be it. But which parts had she told? Once the kids were in bed, Sabrina would make a scene.

"I keep thinking of that house on Rockland," Clint said at the breakfast table.

"Rockland? Where's that?" Sabrina said, setting two cups in front of him—one with his coffee, the other with his meds. It seemed to him she set them down with a bit too much force, as if the fight last night and the lovemaking afterward, such as it was, had solved nothing.

"Rockland Circle. The house with the ugly green carpet. The one where the Davidsons acted so weird."

"I'm totally lost. Who are the Davidsons? Clients?" She was trying not to be impatient.

"Yeah, and we all three felt like there was something wrong with the house. I told you about it at the time. Like something bad happened there."

"You must have already been getting sick," Sabrina said. "Maybe that was the first sign of it."

Or the cause, Clint thought. Chemicals in the carpet, maybe. He noticed suddenly that he'd been pondering this idea for a long time. Sabrina shuffled out with the breakfast plates. He grabbed his car keys. Sitting in the driver's seat, he felt only a little woozy, certainly able to drive.

He took the turn onto Rockland. Three houses down, coming into view beyond a mass of blackberry bushes, was the forest-green roof and then the half-granite façade. A man next door paused in watering his petunias to look as Clint pulled to the curb. The fleshy stink of the flowers reached him as soon as he opened the car door. He leaned on the car to steady himself.

On the porch, he paused to fish out the key he'd picked up at the office. The receptionist there had looked at him strangely. He wondered exactly what he'd said that day the week before, when he dreamed at his desk.

He had fretted enough about that, however. Now was the time to confront this house. The key slid into the lock.

He didn't turn it.

Something else had occurred to him. He had thought of Maisie asking in her serious little voice whether the house had dead bodies in the closet.

Nothing like that, he had told her. But now he realized that the Davidsons had not opened the closets. Especially not the one in the family room with the green-brown rug that smelled so suggestively beneath the orange-scented cleaning fluid. These details came back to him with great force.

Ridiculous. What could be in the closets?

He forced himself to enter. A coat closet was almost the first thing he saw. He looked inside it.

Nothing.

In the kitchen with the walnut cabinets and the vertical windows, he found a broom closet. It contained nothing except, to his surprise, a broom.

He could go through the entire house looking in closets, and it wouldn't mean a thing. All that mattered was the family room. That was where he and the Davidsons had felt such dread. That was where something had touched him—some dangerous chemical, perhaps, or air riddled with black spores.

He found his way there, descending the three steps. It still smelled bad; maybe that was the petunias from next door. He had, after all, left the front door open.

There was no closet in the family room. He could have sworn he'd seen one. Perhaps the paneling made its door hard to see. He could grope along the walls.

He preferred to leave.

As he locked up, the man with the petunias shouted to him.

"Hey, neighbor. Haven't seen you in a while."

Clint sized him up. Glasses, moustache unevenly trimmed, polo shirt, shorts. He was holding a leather jacket, though this was hardly the season.

"I can't quite place you," Clint said.

"It's been a while. Say, I kept wanting to return that stuff you lent me, but I never could seem to find you."

"But I never lived here. You must be thinking of someone else." The petunias stood glistening, purple ones mixed with marigolds. The smell was making him dizzy.

"Here's the jacket. The thing is, my wife put most of your stuff in her garage sale. I'll be happy to reimburse you, though. Do you think a hundred would be fair?"

"A hundred?"

"I guess I could go a little higher."

"No," Clint said. "A hundred is fine." He said this because he could see the twenties already clenched in the man's hand. Taking them seemed the fastest way to escape. But the man wasn't done yet.

"Listen," he said. "Do you suppose you could get me more of the stuff we did that night?" And as Clint strode down the walk to his car: "I'd only need a little this time."

"Go on," said the doctor, fingering the flesh beneath his own eye. He didn't seem particularly interested in Clint's dreams nor in his addled memories.

"The point is, I was awake, but dreaming."

"Nothing to worry about," the doctor said, swiveling a bit on his stool. "The pain's interfering with your REM sleep at night, so you're compensating with micro-naps in the middle of the day."

"But I don't fall asleep. I still know what's going on around me."

"It's called lucid dreaming. I'll give you something to help you sleep. You should see this clear up pretty quickly." He reached for his prescription pad.

"They're more vivid than normal dreams."

"Nothing to worry about once we get you on some meds."

"And in the dreams, I can taste the colors. Green is bitter, it almost makes me vomit. Like overripe limes. Sometimes I wake up, and I do vomit. Orange is sweet and watery."

The doctor paused in mid-scribble, looked thoughtful, tore off the unfinished prescription, and ripped it in half.

"Synesthesia," he said slowly. "That might suggest a different kind of neurological involvement." He scribbled on a fresh sheet. "I'm going to try you on a different family of analgesics," he said. "These have an anti-depressant component as well. Don't expect results right away, but this should make a difference over the long run."

"Are you cold?" Sabrina said, looking at the leather jacket. The sight of it sprawled on the sofa made him a little nauseous. It looked like a hollow copy of him. He wondered if she could smell the petunias.

"I was just trying it on earlier, to see if it still fit."

"You have lost weight."

"Do you remember where I got it?"

"You had it when we met," she said and bolted through the arch into the kitchen. What was that tone of voice for? He thought a while. Memories lay like discarded laundry, out of reach, inert. The medications seemed, if anything, to make these symptoms worse.

Her tone was suspicious, even jealous. Maybe she smelled something more than flowers on it.

He sat in his car, paging through his daybook.

Obviously, he could still drive. No one had honked at him. He hadn't wrecked. That part of his brain must be working fine.

The problem was his sense of direction.

He had set out to visit the house on Rockland Circle. Half an hour into his trip, he realized he didn't know where it was.

It wasn't like him to forget addresses. His job had made him develop a good memory for that sort of thing. He could picture the house, with its new forest-green shingles and its half-granite façade. He could picture the blackberry bushes crowding the street, so you couldn't see the house until the last minute. He could picture the corner where you turned onto Rockland, its twinned junipers pruned high. They would be pocked with blue-green fruits at this time of year.

He just couldn't find any of that. His daybook showed appointments going back to January. Already he'd found two old dates with the Davidsons, to show them different properties, which they'd canceled at the last minute. "Sick," he had jotted across the first, and across the second, underscored twice as if in a rage, "SICK AGAIN!!!" But the addresses jotted on those dates were not on Rockland Circle. He couldn't find an address on Rockland.

It wasn't that he didn't remember. He remembered perfectly well that Rockland branched off 43rd right after Quinn. It was alphabetical: Olivier, Prentiss, Quinn, Rockland, Surdick. Except that it was no longer an unbroken alphabet. He cruised along 43rd and ticked them off: Olivier, Prentiss, Quinn, Surdick. Then he remembered it was Rockland *Circle*, while the others were avenues. That seemed for an instant to explain something. The explanation evaporated before he'd grasped it.

The ice pick behind his right ear made an electric connection with his left eyeball. This was the sensation that struck him just as he pulled into the garage. The wire through his skull felt like a strained tendon, like wet gristle. His body jolted; the gristle twanged and vibrated.

"For God's sake, take your foot off the gas!" Sabrina shouted from a distance. No, not from a distance. She was standing right beside him, right outside the car, with the window between them.

The wall in front of him buckled into spider-web cracks. Fine sheetrock dust speckled the red hood of the car.

The vibration grew louder. He felt her hand on his shoulder, shoving him. It was a great relief to fall sideways. The pressure in his head drained away the instant he fell over, diminished almost to the buzzing level he was used to. He saw into some cranny in the dashboard. A miniature world began to unfold within it, a tableau. A waking dream, obviously, but he wanted to concentrate on it. Sabrina came crowding in to fumble with the brake and the gearshift. She made it hard to focus on the cranny world, where a blond goat had got loose in a doctor's office and gone strolling. Its hooves clicked on the tile.

Some room cleared in his ears. Sabrina had switched off the engine. He struggled to sit up. The gristle in his head flapped and whined like a powerline in high wind. He managed a sort of diagonal slump. Now he was looking into the new cracks in the sheetrock wall, but the goat's little world seemed to be there too, uninterrupted, the goat clicking along, defiling the pristine tiles, nosing into things, gouging with its horns to widen the cracks. Gouging to get out.

"No more driving," Sabrina sobbed. She tucked his keys into the ashtray. As if he wouldn't notice that. As if he'd have any trouble finding them later. She found a tissue in the pocket of her sweater and blew her nose.

"It's only drywall," Clint said. "I can replace it myself."

"I always said you'd go too far one day," Sabrina said, trying to laugh. It was true. She had said it often, sometimes when he lost his temper, sometimes in bed. At the sound of her voice, the goat seemed suddenly to notice her. It turned to look at her through the haze of drywall dust.

The vividest dream yet took hold of him in the waiting room of a specialty clinic he'd been referred to. Clint was gazing at the wallpaper, noticing its intricate folds, its flaking gray valleys. A clinic should smell clean, not like this. Clat, clat, clat. Hooves on tile. It came into view then, threading its way between chairs and shaded floor lamps—an enormous goat, its hair luxuriant and blond. It smelled like his leather jacket after that time he and Beth had rolled in the flower bed making rough love. Her husband had watched from his bedroom window, pretending to disapprove, leaning forward so far his glasses clacked against the window pane.

"Can me and Tyler pet the goat?" Maisie tugged one of his fingers with each of her little hands.

"What are you doing here, honey?" Clint said, and only then realized he was dreaming. The goat should not be in the same place as Maisie. He tried to wake. His pain made an orange buzz.

"Look at this Rembrandt on the wall, honey." He realized his dream-self was trying to distract Maisie so she wouldn't touch the goat. "It shows a surgeon cutting into a guy's brain." It did; the patient's blood welled from the canvas and dribbled down to accumulate on the frame. Too much blood, and the receptionist would probably blame him. He herded the children out of the room and into the corridor—for Tyler had appeared too, trembling by an end table.

"Sabrina, why did you bring them?" he whispered, so the receptionist wouldn't hear. "This is no place for kids." No point talking to her, though; he could tell by the way she slumped across two chairs that she was dead.

"I want to look at the brain-cutting," Maisie protested.

"It's too bloody." Clint shoved her ahead. He felt the bones of her shoulder, delicate as a hatchling bird's.

The goat shambled into their path, its hooves clattering on the tiles. It turned its shaggy blond head to gaze directly at Clint. He heard it shushing him. No. The shushing was only the buzz of his pain. It lowered its head. He knew it would charge; already the valleyed texture of its horns seemed to weep red.

He woke. Someone was speaking to him—had, he felt, been speaking to him for some time. It was a gaunt woman with dark curly hair, leaning on her walker—a fellow patient, it seemed. She went on saying something he couldn't immediately make sense of. He wanted to interrupt, to tell her he couldn't understand her language, but soon he realized she had been speaking English all along. It was only the timber of her voice that confused him—a forceful, laryngitic whisper.

"Of course my husband was sick, too, before he passed," she was saying. "They never did settle on a diagnosis." She told him about her flight from the West Coast, and he heard himself say "a little turbulence" in return. The suspicion dawned on him that he was speaking with Mrs. Davidson, the woman he had let into the house on Rockland Circle. Could disease have changed her so? It had certainly altered him. He was aware of the painful proximity of his bones to the surface of his skin.

How exactly his thumb stumbled on this string of old messages, Clint didn't know. One message was simply a photo of the house on Rockland. Below that was Mr. Davidson's response: "Those blackberry bushes will have to go! Still, we'd like to take a look."

Clint sat in his car, scrolling.

He shouldn't be in his car, according to Sabrina. She said his fine motor control was gone; in fact, she had added, all of his self-control was gone.

Here was a message containing the address. It occurred to him that he could have his phone give him the directions, turn by turn. Even though he knew where it was supposed to be, right there between Quinn and Surdick.

"Start out going south toward 65th Street," the phone said. The goat, gazing out from the power port in the dash, looked restless. Clint turned the key in the ignition.

"Turn left onto Rockland Circle," the phone said pleasantly. Clint turned, and as he passed the twinned junipers on the corner, he could see all the way to Beth's yard, crowded with flowers. It was getting too dark to tell their colors.

"Arrived," his phone said, but that wasn't quite true. He was just now passing the ragged stand of blackberry bushes. He'd meant to have them removed ever since the night Sabrina had stepped out from behind them to confront him about something or other. Probably about Beth. And her husband.

He pulled to the curb.

Inside, the carpet gave a chemical smell, inadequately masked with orange and floral. It was enough to make you sick, if the color didn't. He should have it replaced. Not just here in the family room, but in the closet too, where the rug was just some remnant he'd tacked down. You didn't need nice carpet in a closet. If it got dirty, you could tear it out. Replace it. Have your neighbor burn it.

"Don't ask Beth to do anything else," whispered the man who tended petunias. He stood in the doorway with his arms crossed, pretending to disapprove. "Because she's been asking me to help."

"And did you do it?" Clint asked.

"You can smell it," the man said. "You know we shampooed the carpet and cleaned the walls and everything."

"You're not finished. Somebody's going to notice the smell. They're going to find what we left in the closet."

"I would have cleaned that up already, but how am I supposed to look at them? Or put my hands on them? Beth's already so depressed she can't get out of bed."

"There are a lot of unhappy couples in this town, Petunia," Clint said.

The man flinched, retracted like a slug sprinkled with salt, but he smiled too. His eyes positively glistened. He liked it when Clint talked that way. He liked it even better if Beth heard Clint talking to him that way. "I can't believe we did it," he breathed. "I always wanted it to get rougher, but I never dreamed we'd take it that far."

Clint's head hurt worse than usual. He needed to sit down. He staggered out to the patio. The junipers loomed, pendant with blue-green fruit. He gazed at his home on Rockland Circle, granite halfway up.

***

About the Author

GordonGrice.com

Gordon Grice's stories have appeared in ChiZine (honorably mentioned in Ellen Datlow's The Year's Best Fantasy and Horror), Aurealis, and Metaphorosis. His nonfiction books include The Red Hourglass: Lives of the Predators. He occasionally remembers to post at GordonGrice.com.

Other Works From This Author
"If Gold Runs Red" in Metaphorosis, November 2022
"Wet Weather" in The Cryptid Chronicles
A Bowl of Beer" in Unfading Daydream 3
"In the Mountain Valley" in Aurealis 119
"Three Fathers" in Musings of the Muses

I'M A MONSTER

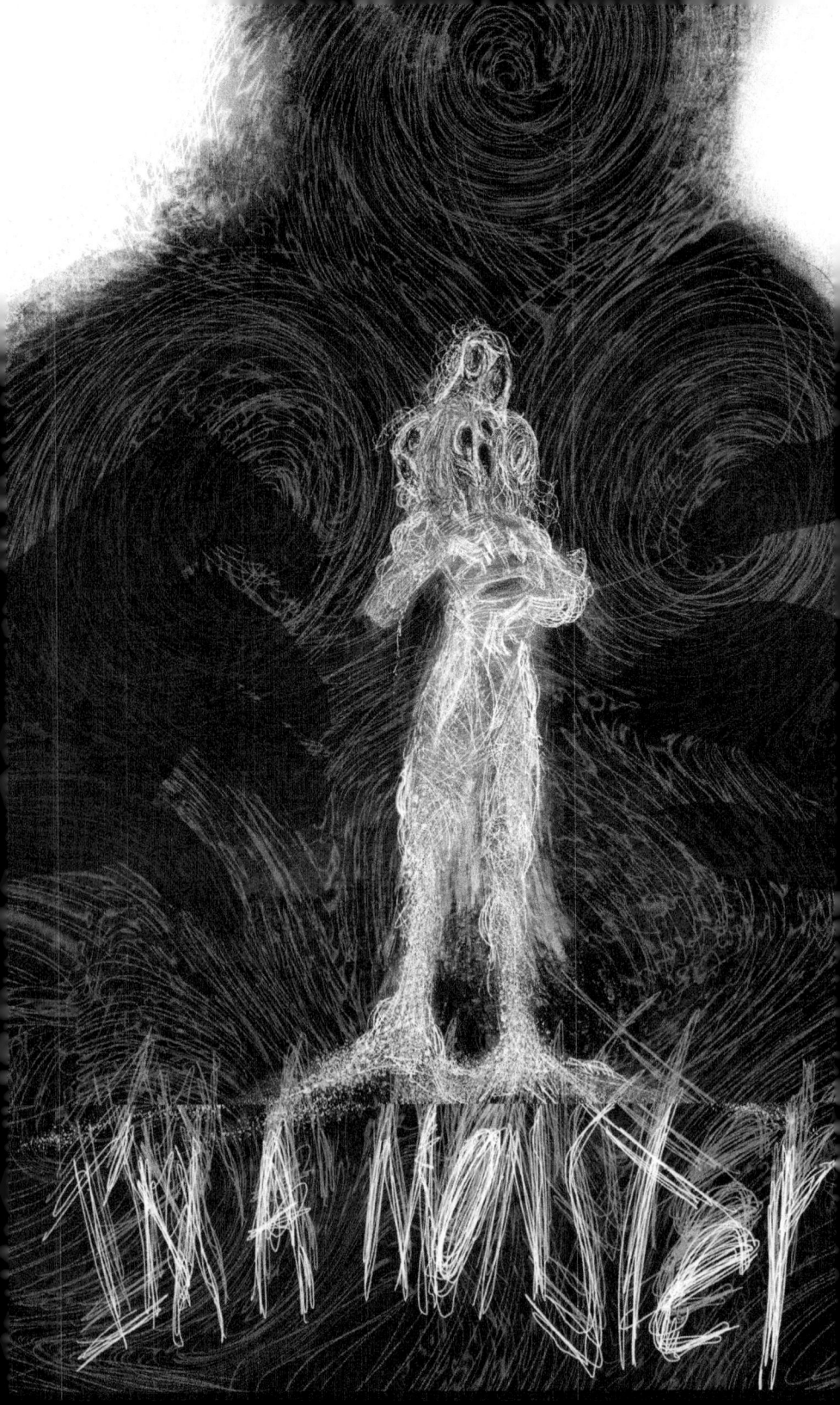

I Am Monster

by Christopher Beck

3 /4/95

"Do it. Shoot him in his stupid face and burn the fucking house to the ground."

These words, my son, were in my head; spoken by the voices that had begun to torment me night and day. Maybe the voices were always there, I don't know, but this was when they moved to the front and looked to take over.

"Do it, you cunt!"

I was huddled on the bed, knees to chest, shaking and sweating, with your father snoring next to me. I was terrified. Thought my heart was going to explode.

The voices spoke in unison but also separately.

"That's what he likes to call you when he's angry, right? Cunt?"

"Yes, he likes to knot your hair in his hand, bring his face close to yours, and scream the word."

"But sometimes, he'll whisper it and smile as if it's his favorite thing."

The voices weren't wrong. Your father... wasn't always a nice man, and, for a moment, I wanted to obey them. The gun cabinet was right there, across from the bed. It was never locked. The 20 gauge always had a shell in it. There was always a can of gas in the garage.

"You've fired that gun dozens of times."

"You've even put a couple of deer down with it."

"Surely you can do the same to the fat old man next to you."

I will not lie to you, my son (I have before, but I won't here), but I almost did it. The shakes stopped, and my heart settled. A special kind of darkness drifted over and through me. It felt good. I rose from the bed. Shouldered that shotgun. Flipped off the safety and pointed it right at your father.

The voices cheered so loud that I shushed them. I didn't want them waking your father before I pulled the trigger.

"Yes"

"Do it."

"Kill him."

"Burn it."

The voices cackled.

And I was close to following through with it all. My finger tightened on the trigger. Slightly pulled it back. The hammer moved, ready to strike.

Then I thought of you and said, "What about my boy?"

The voices didn't have an answer. They fell silent.

I let the gun fall to the floor, went upstairs, and woke you, and we left.

You were confused and disoriented by it all. As you know, we didn't grab clothes or toys. I just ushered you out the door into the car. Told you we were leaving your father. You stared back at the house as we pulled out of the drive and cried.

It broke my heart. Left me feeling cold and selfish.
You didn't understand, and I couldn't explain then.
You were too young.
And now you know.

There's more to say, but this has already been emotionally exhausting, and I need to rest. I'm sure this hasn't been easy to read. Just know: I'm not the monster you think I am.

3/5/95

Everyone wants me to write, whether it be stories, poems, or whatever. The doctors are hoping it'll help me to remember... things. And, as it's all honesty here on these pages, I would like to remember and fix my brain. There is a lot I do recall, but when I try to dig up the repressed memories, everything shakes, and the shadows rush in to pull them back.

So I'm writing, but to you, my son. Maybe I'll remember things forgotten, maybe I won't, but you deserve to know and, hopefully, understand why some things happened as they did.

You were always my baby. Still are. Always will be. I wish I were there to hold you. It's been so long since we embraced. I can still feel your hair ruffle under my hand, your arms around me; your face pressed tight against me.

I would give anything to feel one of your hugs again.

But not my mind, 'cause I'm already crazy.

Ha.

Ha. Ha.

It's lunchtime, so I have to run for now.

3/6/95
Missed yesterday, but back to these pages again today, Son.

Yesterday was just bad. Had a seizure at breakfast, and while my brain was going nuts (more so than it already is... haha), death visited me. In the darkness, he was only a silhouette, but I could see the edges of his robe and the blade of his scythe. He told me my suffering would end one month from today. And then he was gone.

I would be okay with that.

I've not become close with anyone in this shithole of a boarding home, yet they were all staring at me when I came to. I guess some may have been actually concerned, but I told them to all mind their own fucking business.

Anyway, where were we? Let me go back...

So, I didn't kill your father or burn down the house, and I probably was—no, I *was* sick before then... this was just when the steep decline started.

What fucking fun!

An elevator drop that never comes back up.

Remember when, not long before I came to this home, we walked down to Clark's Pond at night to go swimming? We splashed and laughed, and I pulled that little leech off your baby toe. Remember that? I do. That was the last fun thing we did together.

Then the shadow man came and turned the evening to shit. He was following us, dipping behind trees and parked cars every time I turned to look at him. I tried hard to play it cool, but you asked what I kept looking at. I told you, and you looked at me like I was some two-headed monster. You said there was no one following us, but you were wrong. The shadow man was there, the blade of his knife reflecting dull moonlight.

"There," I said. "Right behind that telephone pole!"

"There's no one there, Mom!"

"He is! He wants to carve us up, taste our blood!"

You screamed, "What the hell is wrong with you!" and then took off running.

After that night, the distance between us grew substantially. And it tore me apart.

You are and will always be my baby. I love you and never meant to push you away.

The clouds fell that day.

3/7/95

When Clouds Fall

When the clouds fall around you and I, all I see is nothingness.
Hold on to my hand. Please don't let go. I can't see you.
I feel you slipping away. Please hold on.
Your fingers slip away, and I feel nothing.
When the clouds fall, the nothingness is more than nothing.
It has powers hidden within its white walls.
Lightning strikes a blow to my head, knocking me down.
Where are you? Are you around?
Lesser bolts push and shove me 'round and 'round.
Then another forceful blow slams me down.
When the clouds fall, there are hidden doors within the nothingness.
Booming thunder from fierce lighting cause the doors within the white walls to open.
From the doors, scurry termites, ants, and spiders, crawling up my hands and my legs.
Oh. Please, please, where are you?
Can you take my hand? Save me from this awful land?
Mice and rats bite at my toes. Crickets tear at my clothes.
I see a figure come this way. Is it you?
No. It's the Shadow Man.
Who wants to take me away with the big, bright, shiny coins he throws my way.
When the clouds fall, they have the power of the winds.
When the lightning strikes me down,
When the insects and rodents eat at my soul,
When the Shadow Man leads me astray,

The winds begin to blow.
Please, please help me. I can't find you.
Take my hand if you know where I am.
The wind is spinning me 'round and 'round.
The lightning is knocking me down into nothingness.
The Shadow Man is holding me.
I can't get up.
I can't see my body for the number of spiders and termites and mice covering me.
I hear a voice say, **do it.**
It's *easy.*
You can do it. Just give up.
It's *easy.*
I feel one hand take mine and the other hand place a potion on my tongue.
Two arms wrap around me and hold me tight until what's done is done.
Everything is nothingness.

3/9/95
Write. Write. Write. Every day it's "How's the writing coming?" or "Where's your journal?" or "Any new poems?"

They want repressed memories. They want to know why I'm so fucked in the head. I wanted to remember, too, at first. But remembering is painful. Reliving the past is painful.

I've already been through this shit; I don't want to relive it again. I just want to be me; the me I used to be before I lost my smile and had a daily smorgasbord of medications. The thin me with nice hair and a sparkle in her eye. The me that slept at night instead of pacing and biting her nails. The me that you loved. The me I was before you thought I was a monster.

3/13/95

Friday the 13th. Today isn't Friday, but remember when we first watched the movie? You were probably too young to be watching it, but we had a good time nonetheless. We laughed and ate popcorn, just like a normal mother and son would do.

Remember the movie Arachnophobia? We put my houseplants outside to soak up some of the afternoon sun before popping it into the VCR. It was a good flick; made us both jump. Then, before heading out for dinner, we brought the plants in, and when we came home, there were spider webs all over the plants and the walls. That was some creepy stuff.

Fun times, though. I wish we had more of them… I wish we were still having them.

Being here, in this home, with these people, it's no fun. Being sick is no fun. Your mind betraying you is no fun.

Being away from you, my son, is no fun. Maybe I can come see you soon.

3/14/95

I remember the day I came to this boarding home. I was sent here by my own mother with nothing but a pillow and some clothes. Not that I owned anything more than that at that point.

The week before, I remember, was a bad week.

I had a seizure early on, the first you had witnessed, and it terrified you. You didn't understand what was happening and ran off before I could fully come back to my senses, and you refused to talk about it after the fact.

A day or two later, the Shadow Man came for me. I was out on the front step listening to Guns N' Roses on your Discman when he appeared behind a tree across the street. It was light out, but he made sure to stick to the shadows. In one hand, he had a knife, and in the other, a coin. He wanted me in the shadows with him; he wanted to pull me into the nothingness.

His minions, with their tattered clothes, broken teeth and fingernails, and soulless eyes, burst through the ground in front of me. They snarled and groaned, and black saliva dripped from the chins of their rotting faces. I screamed, jumped up off the step, and ran into the house. The storm door slammed against the railing, and I tripped over the threshold, falling hard against the floor and dropping the Discman. You came rushing into the living room to check on me.

Then I told you that he was out there and to lock the door, and your demeanor changed. The concern left your face, replaced by shame and disappointment.

"There's no one out there, Mom," you said. "And you broke my cd player," you said, pulling the headphones from my neck.

We were sharing the spare room at grandma's then, and that night, I managed some sleep but with some terrible dreams. I was thrashing about, yelping, and you tried to wake me, and I slapped you. You didn't yelp or cry. Just touched your cheek, stared at me for a moment, and turned away.

It wasn't intentional, Son. Hopefully, one day, you'll understand that. Never would I just hurt you like that.

Anyway, that week was the final straw for grandma, and she said I was too much for her to handle and that I had to go. So I was shipped off to the first boarding home that would have me. When that ugly van came to collect me, you were there. I tried to hug you goodbye, but you pulled away.

"I hate the way you breathe," you said to me.

3/15/95

This place is dumb. The mental wards were better.
The other tenants are dumb and are plotting to poison me.
I'm all alone here.
Never did care for being alone.
My mind is dumb.

3/16/95
Oh Mother
Oh Mother
Can't you see what you're doing to me?
Oh Mother
Oh Mother
Why did you bump me out while on bended knees?
Oh Mother
Oh Mother
I always made sure there was pudding and tea.
Oh Mother
Oh Mother
Can you not see that now I'm on bended knees?
Oh Mother
Oh Mother
The waves are crashing down on me. Why won't you take my hand and pull me from this raging sea?
Oh Mother
Oh Mother
Pull me in with your protective wing and help take care of me, for I am in need.

3/18/95

Did I ever tell you about Ron? Probably not. I've always remembered his face but, apparently, have boxed up memories with him and shoved them to the back of my mind.

Last night, the old tape on some of those boxes began to split, allowing the flaps to pop open.

Ron was before your dad. Before you. Before New Jersey even. I met him while still out West, when I was barely out of my teenage years.

Grandma and grandpop—his time in the army served—moved back East (home), but I decided to stay in sunny California. I was young and dumb but having a great time partying it up out there.

Ron came along when I was still waitressing. I didn't serve him, but he saw me taking plates to another table and called me over.

He was handsome and charismatic and had me from hello.

It was fun at first: cruising around together in his convertible, spending his money on strippers, booze, and coke, but things took a turn after that first month or so.

His money came from dealing drugs and pimping women, and he told me that I needed to take up one or the other. I told him I was his girl now and that I should be exempt from those things. He laughed and told me that's not how it worked.

Of course, by now, I had stopped waitressing and basically had moved in with Ron.

So I told him to teach me how to sell "the goods." He said I was too good for that. Too beautiful for that. And that my body would make more money than selling the drugs would. I told him I wasn't a whore. He said it wasn't being a whore if you earned money from it.

I still resisted.

But then he tricked me.

He agreed to let me sell "the goods" but said I needed to experience them all in order to be good at pushing them. Grass and coke were already daily staples for me, but I had yet to even go near heroin. I didn't really want to.

Ron said, "It's either this or that sweet, young ass."

So I caved and let Ron put that tube around my arm, that needle into my flesh.

I could feel the tar enter my vein and spread through my body, and once it fully took hold, I was gone.

I was still aware but not, and once I was flying, Ron helped me to take my clothes off. He sat me on the couch and said, "Enjoy."

He opened the front door, and a line of guys came marching in. They passed Ron wads of cash and then fucked me while I was fucked up.

It wasn't the only time.

3/19/95

Write. Remember. Write. Remember. Write. Remember.
Maybe some memories should stay boxed up.
They don't know what it's like to have a sick mind.
They don't know what it's like to have twisted dreams.
They don't know what it's like to see monsters.
My monsters are real.
Fuck them.
More boxes have opened.
This is draining.

3/21/94
Drain
One drop shed at the time of conception
One drop shed at the forming of the heart
Two drops shed at the forming of the brain
One drop shed at birth
One drop shed learning to walk
Two drops shed at cutting of hair
Two drops shed losing lady
One drop shed at the drunken state
One drop shed for the loss of days
Two drops shed for being left alone
Two drops shed for the puddle of daddy's blood
One drop shed for all the lighting going on
Two drops shed for the pistol shoved down my throat
Two drops shed for being touched in secret places
Two drops shed for pissing on me
Two drops for the holding of my legs
One drop shed for leaving home
One drop shed for the birth of my son
One drop shed for the start of my marriage
One drop shed for being held prisoner
One drop shed for the drugs
One drop shed for the booze
One drop shed for all my clothes being ripped off me
One drop shed for all the walls I was slammed into
One drop shed for all the objects thrown at me
Two drops shed for all the knives held at my throat
Two drops shed for my poisoned blood
Two drops shed for the birth of my son
Two drops shed for the beating of my son

Two drops shed for the touching of secret places
One drop shed at the time of my marriage
Two drops shed for the heart attack before me
Two drops shed for intimate times with paper towels
One drop shed for all the degrading words
Two drops shed for the beatings
Two drops shed for the loss of my independence

3/22/95

I don't want to remember any more.

3/23/95
The silhouette came again this evening.
He reminded me that peace, blissful peace, was but two weeks away.
I asked why peace couldn't be had now. And he simply said soon.
I said okay.
He said to ditch the meds.
I asked why.
He said to make it easier.

3/26.95

My monsters are real, but my mind is free.
My monsters are real. My mind is free.
Monsters real. Mind free
My monsters are free.

3/2796

I don't know if any of these words will help you, or even make sense, but I hope that they do. I am sorry that I have written them and I am sorry that you have to read them.
I am sorry for everything.
I love you. So much.
I have only ever wanted what is best for you.
I hope you live a healthy life. I hope you live a happy life.

Don't be fucked up like me.

32896

no more floors
elevator all the way down
madness comes

30.96
your father here so is ron should have killed them both whe I had the chance

9.331.6

monsters monsters monsters
everywhere

monsters monsters monsters
over here

over there
free free free

monsters monsters monsters
I am not one

496
shawdom man came
stabed him with a pencile
I found it funne
he did not
I laughedand laughed
wasnt him
was a tenant
oops
haha

2-96/4
peace tommor
no more
monsters
no more remembering
no more pain
son
please rmember
I
am
monster

***

About the Author

Christopher's Author Page

Born in California but raised in New Jersey, Christopher, the author of THE CORN WITCH, THE BIRTHDAY GIRL AND OTHER STORIES, as well as numerous short stories, enjoys spending his free time hiking and searching for ancient evils.

What inspired the idea for your story?
Real life. My mother was very ill, and this story is very muc hers. She passed when I was 15 years old and there is a lo that I don't know about her past, her mental illness, and this story was an exercise in trying to understand a small part of what she went through. I Am Monster was based o memories and a few journal entries written by my mother. This story is 90% real life.

Other Works From This Author Links
The Corn Witch
The Birthday Girl & Other Stories (Short Sharp Shocks!)

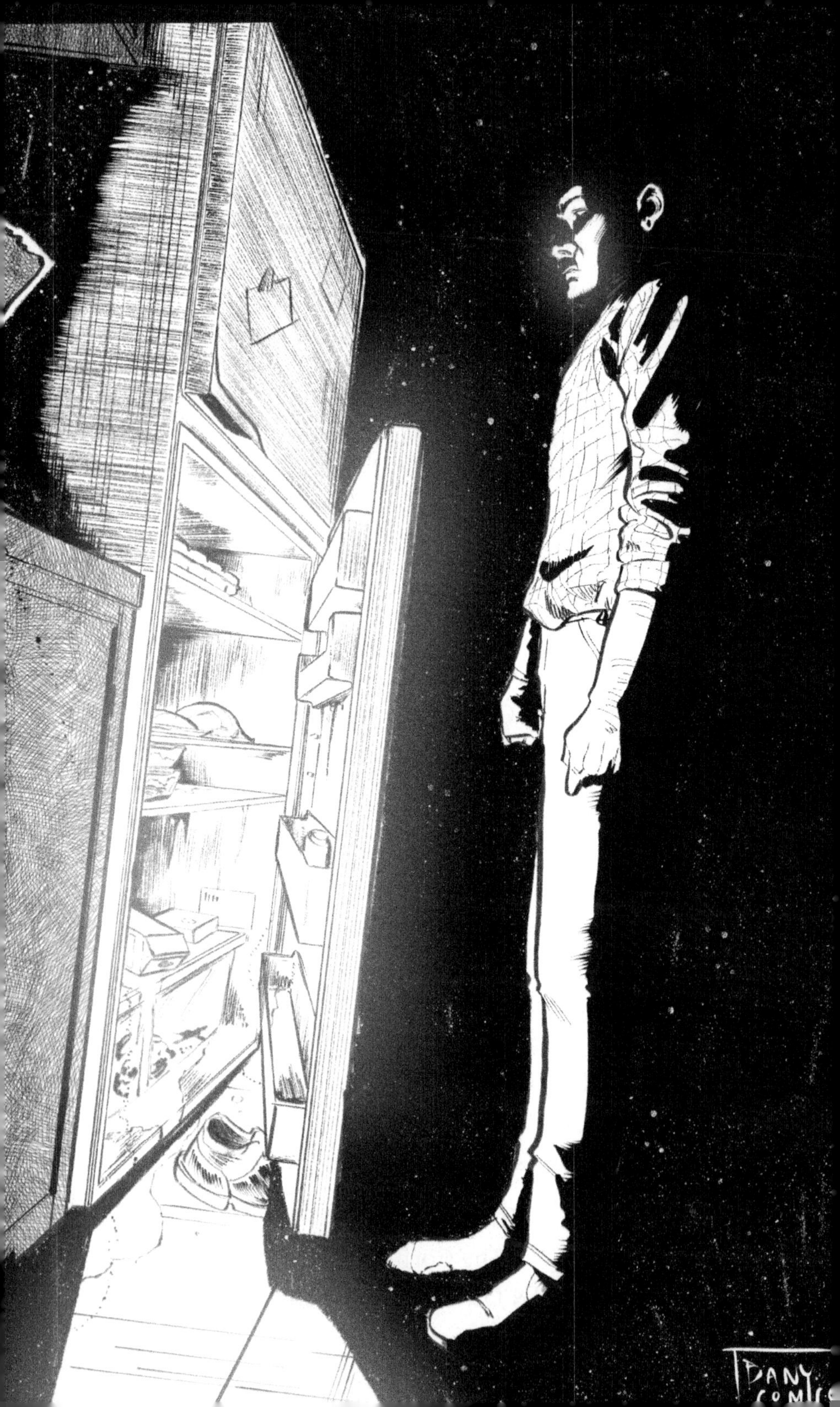
DANY

Running In Circles

by David Lee Zweifler

Viola Securus.

An elegant name for a musical instrument, perhaps, or a Greek poet or a wine. But not for what's happening to everyone now.

The door to the garage from the kitchen closes behind me, and the first thing I realize is that, good Christ, I am hungry. Nothing unusual there because I'm always stuffing my face. I thought keto was supposed to help with this.

Speaking of faces, mine is wet, which is odd. And my throat is sore, which is also odd. Neither of those things are symptoms of VS.

Anyway, there's no time for snacking. I'm just in and out. Just going to pop upstairs and grab my bug-out bag.

I know. "Bug-out bag." I sound like some kind of doomsday prepper. Yes, I do have a bug-out bag—a knapsack filled with a few days' worth of rugged clothes, beef jerky, a knife, a small pistol that I've taken to the range a half-dozen times, and an assortment of molle-webbed, black tactical crap.

My bug-out has been packed and ready to go since Trump was in office. (Mental note: don't eat the beef jerky.) Given everything that was going on then and during Covid, it just seemed prudent to have a bug-out bag, even before Viola, which everyone is calling VS now because nothing that crappy can have such an elegant name.

I've already got the boys packed. Just need to grab my bag and their raincoats for the storm outside, and we can hightail it downtown to pick up their mom, Lilly, at the office.

Google Maps is down, along with internet and cell services, and the cable TV is out, so I don't know what traffic looks like.

I'm banking that everyone is going to be heading *out* of the city, and we'll be the only idiots heading in the other direction. Hopefully, we can pull off a reverse commute and get Lilly before there's a lockdown.

In my last call to Lilly, before the phones went out, I said, "Stay put. We'll get you." Like I'm off-brand Daniel Day-Lewis or something, but by Christ, that's what we're going to do.

Finn came down with a fever right after that. Poor kid. He's sleeping in the front seat of the car. His baby brother Asher is in the back. He's fine, but he's hungry. Crying. The garage is hot, with lousy ventilation, but I won't take long in here, and I'll give him his sippy cup in the car.

I just need to grab my bag, and we'll get the fuck out of here, although I'll be goddamned if I know where we're going after we pick up Lilly.

I'll grab some cold drinks from the fridge—maybe a Diet Pepsi to take the edge off the hunger—then go upstairs. Man, I'm really hungry. But I just ate, like, an hour ago, so I'll suck it up and wait until we can stop and grab a bite.

"Someone left the fridge open!" I yell back at the garage.

It looks like the fridge has been open for a while. Finn must have grabbed something on the way out—he's always leaving the door to the refrigerator open.

The light in the fridge is on, but the cartons of milk feel warm.

None of that matters now. I have a feeling that once we leave, it will be quite a while before I'm sitting down enjoying a bowl of Apple Jacks, or their disgusting keto equivalent, at my kitchen table again.

Is it breakfast time? Maybe that's why I'm so hungry. The sun is coming up over the Hudson now. That's east.

I feel like I need to move fast because things are moving fast here. It was just yesterday—maybe two days ago—that we saw the squirrels running in circles. Not lazy squirrels-playing-in-the-grass circles, but tight, crazy pinwheels on the ground, on the sidewalk, and even in the streets before they were inevitably squished by cars. First, they ran fast, then slow. Then they went to sleep.

Viola Securus.

Not a violin or a wine, but a roundworm. A parasitic worm that causes neurological damage in squirrels, resulting in loss of coordination and perception, making them run and run, endlessly in circles.

That's what the Wikipedia page said, anyway. I read it for the first time—yesterday, I think—along with, maybe, a billion other people.

I saw it once when I was a kid without knowing what it was. A big fat squirrel, running a tight loop on the sidewalk even after I walked up to it. Or maybe it was just rabid.

This was different, obviously, because this wasn't one or two squirrels or one hundred. It was every squirrel. Every single one. All at the same time.

It hit fast. Faster than VS is supposed to. So fast, that the CDC and all the scientists on TV didn't even pretend to know what was going on.

I notice one of the milk cartons is on the floor, and it's leaking. Did I knock it over without realizing it? No—I just got here. It must have been Finn before he went to the car. What the heck was that boy doing in here?

The light in the fridge is off now. It must have just burned out.

I recall that, pretty soon, the local station was cutting to the weather every few minutes, with the attractive, black... weather woman? Is that a word? Meteorologist. There you go. The meteorologist was giving the same weather report. Over and over. Not a recording, but live.

"Clear," she said. "High of seventy. Low of forty-five."

How the fuck do you even dress for that? Jesus, that's a twenty-five-degree difference. I guess you have to layer. Listen to grandma, kids. She knows what she's doing.

That was yesterday. Right? Or maybe two days ago. I remember the last time the TV had a signal, I was still seeing the pretty meteorologist, not-so-pretty anymore, standing in front of a blue screen without an image up, her makeup bleeding onto the collar of her yellow, perspiration-stained dress. Between the automated announcements coming through on the emergency broadcast system, she'd come back, talking about clear skies with a high of seventy, low of forty-five, with the rain coming down hard outside.

Now the TV is just static.

I look out the window. It's brightening. It looks like the rain has stopped. Suddenly. We've been getting a lot of weird weather lately. I'll take it; the sun is overhead, and it's shaping up to be a beautiful day.

Wait, I'm skipping ahead. After a while, it wasn't just squirrels.

Poor Olivia, our dog. A little boxer mix. Still a puppy, with her brindle coat and her little white paws.

She is the cutest, sweetest dog that ever lived. So, of course, if *she's* going to get a brain parasite, she needs to develop the cutest, sweetest little brain parasite symptoms ever.

She was running in circles too. She would head out of the room and then run back in and jump all over me, licking me as if she hadn't seen me in hours. Over and over. It was very sweet. It got annoying real quick, so I had to put her in her crate upstairs.

The CDC said that VS might affect pets. Bigger animals, with bigger brains, get it slower. Bigger circles. Longer loops.

I don't know what the fuck to do at this point except to keep the family together, so I'll pick up Lilly, but first, I need to get Olivia, then my bug-out bag, and the kids' raincoats—do they still need raincoats? It's overcast again, but I can almost see the outline of the sun setting in the west through the haze. Better stay on the safe side and grab the jackets. And then I'll grab a sippy cup of milk from the fridge for Asher. And then we'll get on the road, so we can get some distance, pick up Lilly, and figure this all out.

I head up the stairs, past the rows of photos on the wall arranged chronologically, past marriage pictures, to baby Finn, then, round the turn midway, to shots of him holding a newborn Asher. I try to think through the list of additional things I need to bring that aren't already in the go-bag. Extra aspirin? A blanket? I have no idea. This is my first apocalypse.

I walk into my bedroom, and the first thing I notice is that the go-bag isn't where it's supposed to be in my closet. The goddamn cleaning ladies must have moved it again.

The second thing I notice is that Olivia is in her crate, but now she's sleeping. Then, the third thing I notice is that her eyes are open and all cloudy, and she's not breathing, and I want to cry, but I don't have time because I have to get the fuck out of here because the kids are in the car in the hot garage. Because this shit is getting serious.

Also, we're getting more weird weather. Now it's dark outside.

I think maybe a storm has rolled in, but when I move to the window, I see that it's just night. Cool and clear, with stars.

Maybe nature has a fucking brain parasite, too. Maybe the whole universe is running on a tight little fucked up loop.

Then I realize that I should just forget the fucking go-bag and get the fuck out of here. Finn is in the front seat of the car. Sleeping. Asher is in the back. It's hot in the garage. It's very hot. But I didn't take long.

I run down to the garage. Down the stairs and past the photos. When I get there, the first thing I notice is that Asher has stopped crying. Then I see the go-bag is in the front seat.

Then I smell those smells. First, sweat. Then, the smell of shit. Then, another, more subtle, but once I smell it, it's in the car, the garage, and everywhere. Something rotten sweet, like spoiled fruit or corn syrup in an overflowing trashcan that's been sitting in the summer heat.

That's when I realize that the boys were waiting for me for a while. Waiting for me for a very long time.

Now, I'm screaming. Screaming until my throat hurts. I can't see because the only light is the yellow overhead in the car, which seems dimmer than usual, and a little sliver coming from the door to the kitchen, which is open just a crack, wedged ajar by one of Asher's Crocs. It's all dark and blurry inside the garage because tears are falling out of my eyes and down my cheeks.

I'm running and screaming. For a moment, I don't know where I am. I'm heading toward the sliver of light. Back to the house. How long have I been screaming?

Viola Securus.

It almost sounds like... a violin, or something. Or... maybe wine.

My hands are shaking. I bring them up and can feel cheekbones when I touch my face, which is odd because I turned into a fat fuck at fifty, and now I look like some cartoon dad with an egghead and a double chin. But my skin is tight now. I guess I've lost weight, which would be a great silver lining to this ordeal, even though I'm still feeling like shit.

Then, I realize my face is wet, and my throat is killing me. Like I swallowed broken glass. Still, it's all good because those are also not symptoms of VS.

Someone left the fridge open, and the fridge light is off. All the power is off. Finn probably left the door open. The kitchen smells of sour milk, which is covering another, worse smell which is probably food rotting in the fridge. That Finn. Leaving the door to the fridge open. He's a little savage.

I stop to listen and, thankfully, Asher stopped crying. Finn is still sleeping in the front seat.

The garage is hot, but I won't take long. I'm in and out. I just need to grab my bag.

***

About the Author

davidleezweifler.com

David Lee Zweifler spent decades writing non-fiction in jobs that took him around the world, including long stints in Jakarta, Hong Kong, and New York City. David has work published in Freeze Frame Fiction, Little Blue Marble, and Wyldblood, and has stories in the current and upcoming issues of The Dread Machine. He resides with his family in New York's Hudson River Valley.

Other Works From This Author Links
Getting Better
Do You Know Why We Stopped You?
Early Rise
I Like To Be Hit
The Inevitablist

D3

End Bed

by Paul Melhuish

'So, Mr Dixon. I'm going to ask you a few questions to test your memory. Is that okay?'

Mr Dixon was sitting up in bed. He smiled. Slightly unshaven, a tangled moustache and a fringe of grey hair curtaining his humorous eyes. He wore one of those hospital gowns with a split up the back that exposed your arse to the entire hospital as you walked along. Not that Mr Dixon had done any walking since he'd been admitted. He'd refused to walk with any of the nurses or us therapists. He'd also given up on eating and drinking. The doctors were considering administering IV fluids as a Best Interests decision. Before doing this, they had to establish that he wasn't in charge of his mental faculties. It needed to be confirmed that he was confused or delirious before they gave him the needle.

That's why I was here. To carry out a simple test to assess his memory and processes to find out if there was a problem with his overall cognition.

Mr Dixon was in bed D3 in ward sixteen. There were three other men in the bay. Two days ago, D3 had been occupied by a 93-year-old called Mr White, who'd died. As I sat there next to his bed, I wondered how I was going to get through this test with all the noise in the ward. A woman in the next bay was shouting for a nurse, and the beeping of a chair sensor alarm in the opposite bed kept activating as Mr Khan (97, UTI, dementia, high risk of falls) kept getting out of his seat. In the bed next door, a nurse took an ECG using a machine that sounded like a fucking disco whilst talking loudly to her deaf patent. The phone by the nurses' station kept ringing and ringing and ringing. It took all my mental energy to blot this lot out and hold at bay the avalanche of stress fracturing my overworked brain as I faced another day of impossible deadlines and high patient numbers, all of them needing urgent assessments today.

'So, what's this for?' he asked in a clear, bright voice.

'A memory test.'

'I'm an accountant. I should be able to manage it,' he said and gave a sweet little chuckle. I was warming to Mr Dixon. He was clearly a nice man.

'Right, let's start. Where are you?'

'Stevenage.' (He wasn't. This was London.)

'What day is it today?'

'Thursday.' (It was Monday.)

'What month is this?'

'May.' (It was November.)

'And what year is this?'

'Fudge cake.'

'No, what year are we in?'

'Year?'

'Yes.'

'Err...well...is it Tuesday?'

I gave him a score of zero for that one on the sheet.

'How's your maths?' I said.

'Very good.'

'What is one hundred take away seven?'
'Sorry?'
'One hundred take away seven?'
'Forty.'
'I'm going to say five words, and I want you to repeat them back to me. Ready?'
'Okay?'
'Face. Church. Daisy. Red. Train. Can you repeat them?'
He gave me one of his sweet smiles but didn't reply.
'Those five words I said, Mr Dixon. What were they?'
He shook his head. 'What words?'

The rest of the test didn't go well. I asked him to draw a clock, put the numbers in and set the time at ten past ten. He drew a triangle. I asked him to copy the drawing of a cube in his own hand, and he just sketched three wavy lines. At that point, I abandoned the test. He scored zero out of thirty, indicating serious problems with his cognition.

'How did I do?' he asked.
'Nothing to worry about, really,' I said.
'Oh, okay. Good to see you,' he said. I thanked him and said goodbye, and he sat up smiling in his bed, looking like he didn't have a care in the world. I went to the nurses' station and slipped into the doctor's office behind to tell the young registrar, Annabelle, that he'd failed the cognitive test. They could put the drip in now. Annabelle was typical of a lot of junior doctors passing through ward sixteen. Posh, thin, very good-looking with a nervous haggard look about her.

I fetched his medical notes from the trolley and wrote up the results of the test. When he was up and walking, maybe I'd get him to perform a functional task. See if he can get himself washed and dressed or make a cup of tea in the kitchen. That's if I had time. I had 15 other patients to see today, and I was due to finish at five but probably wouldn't see my front door until eight tonight. His confusion may just be the result of a Urinary Tract Infection. His urine had been tested for a UTI, and they were just waiting for the results. I didn't feel comfortable writing him off on the basis of just one paper test. If he did have dementia, then he could possibly go home with carers, or maybe social workers would find a residential home for him. It all depended on how at risk he would be on discharge.

Just as I was planning his future, I noticed that in bay D, the nurses were pulling the blue curtains around the bed, shielding Mr Dixon off from the rest of the world. He'd been washed earlier, so I wondered what they were doing to need to pull the curtains around.

A squat, blonde nurse approached the nurses' station from the bay and spoke to the consultant, Doctor Hussein, who was checking something on the computer screen.

'Mohammed.' She was senior enough to call him by his first name. 'Death certificate for Mr Dixon. He's just passed away. P.E., we think.'

I sat in the lavatory, head in my hands, trying to absorb the shock. P.E. (Pulmonary Embolism). Fucking hell. I'd only been talking to him a few minutes earlier. He'd been smiling. Not a care in the world. No sign that he was going to die. With some of the palliative patients, you can tell. They lay in the bed, pale as paper, mouths agape, skeleton thin, but Mr Dixon wasn't like that.

Ward sixteen is an elderly ward. People die all the time. The sheer clinicism of the place desensitises you to death, but now and again, one gets to you. I wasn't crying, and I wasn't sad, but my brain refused to process the event. How can a man be here one minute and dead the next? Where had he gone? Where was his soul? What was he seeing, feeling, and experiencing now? Was he floating around the ward, disembodied, watching us? Was he being ushered into the presence of God with angels singing and peach-arsed cherubs blowing trumpets? Or was he entering the dark space, the wailing and gnashing of teeth loud in the gloom, about to spend eternity in that lost, dark place? The image of that sweet smile triggered in my mind's eye.

'No. No. Fucking no.' I couldn't stand the thought of him going there. A sick feeling crawled across my stomach.

Perhaps he was just dead. Perhaps there is no soul. You just...well...stop working. Mr Dixon was a machine that stopped working.

He had two sons and a daughter. How the hell were they going to process this information? Their shock would be more intense than mine. It would also include grief, that poisonous mixture that flavoured loss like rotten yeast in bread. Fuck. How were they going to cope?

I was up against it today. I had 15 more assessments and a home visit before the close of play. I had no time to waste being maudlin in a hospital toilet. I flushed, got up and washed my hands. On exiting the toilet, the porter pulled a trolley, a human-sized rectangle covered by blue tarpaulin-type material. They were taking Mr Dixon's body to the morgue.

Another fucked up night. Went to bed without eating. Weird dreams followed by being wide awake at 3 AM, staring at the ceiling. Getting to sleep at 05:45, only for the alarm to sound at six.

I fell asleep at the traffic lights driving into work again. The guy behind me woke me, honking his horn in outrage. Fuck him. Fuck them all. Fuck them all to hell.

The next guy to occupy bed D3 was an overweight man called Mr Daniels. His girth filled a bariatric chair by the bed. He'd been admitted due to leg cellulitis, which had caused immobility. He calmly and rationally explained that he used to be a normal size, but problems with his heart meant that he became short of breath easily, and so moved around a lot less. This meant he'd put on weight, and now he was obese. I really liked Mr Daniels. He was a man you could reason with. I tried to get him to stand to a frame, but his legs were in such pain that he just couldn't. I asked one of the healthcare assistants to help me hoist him back to bed. We fitted a large-size sling around his girth and then wheeled the hoist over. The crane designed for humans lifted him easily, but halfway through the transfer, the battery died, and he was left hanging there.

'Sorry about this Mr Daniels,' I said as he hung like a huge baby in a hammock.

'Don't worry,' he laughed. 'It's quite comfy. It's quite safe, is it?'

'Oh yes. It has a two hundred kg limit, and you don't weigh half that,' I replied and instantly felt bad for mentioning his weight.

'Doesn't feel that way sometimes,' he said. The HCA fetched the battery from the other hoist we kept in the treatment room, and the hoist powered back up. We lowered him onto the bed and removed the sling.

I went to see him two days later, and the cellulitis had decreased due to the antibiotics doctors had given him intravenously. His legs were a lot less painful, and he could walk a few steps with a large fold-out walking frame I'd broken out of the stores. I was really pleased, and it brightened my day. I vowed to return the next day and see if he could go further and gave him some leg exercises to be getting on with. Another job for my growing list of things to do. My brain began to throb with the worry of getting through it all.

When I returned the next day, the bed had been taken by a very ill-looking woman. I went to the nurses' station to see where bedflow had moved him to. Before I could even log in, one of the nurses collared me.

'If you're looking for Mr Daniels, he passed away last night. Brain Aneurysm.'

How does death enter the hospital and claim his victims? I imagine he pulls up in a big black Bentley, parks across two disabled bays and his very attractive blonde undead lady chauffer opens the rear passenger doors for him. There he is, sliding out of the smooth leather back seat, immaculately dressed. He wears a long coat - not too long, calf length- and a tall top hat. His face is covered by black material. He doesn't need to see. He can smell dead meat. He knows the stench of death like a crow smells the exposed guts of roadkill. Death just follows his nose.

The NHS issued him with a special pass for every door to every hospital. He wears a lanyard around his neck with a square identity badge. The picture is blank because you cannot take his picture, and has no name or position inscribed on the front because he has no name or position. Death arrives at the door, bends, and presses the ID badge barcode side to the little red light by the side of the door, and the door opens.

Death strides unchallenged onto the ward. The night nurses greet him, buxom women in black uniforms. They lead him to the bed of the deceased, where the poor sod waits, shivering in fear, standing looking at his lifeless carcass lying in bed with disbelief and incomprehension. When the dark, thin collector emerges through the doors into the bay, he suddenly realises. His time is here.

Some simply follow, accepting the inevitable. Others try to resist, but he just grabs them by the hair or wrist with his thin, skeletal fingers possessing supernatural strength. He drags them out of the bay, out of the ward and into the darkness.

I wake; darkness all around. Light from a moribund streetlamp cast a thin beam of light through the curtains. It's 03:30.

Buxom night nurses? Where the hell did they come from? This is what happens when you're too busy to wank out your sexual frustrations. They get mixed up with the nightmares and morbid realities of acute care.

'So, Mrs Tiles.'

'Ms Tiles, if you don't mind,' said the next victim, I mean, the next patient in D3. She was a spirited posh woman. The kind of patient that wasn't going to let illness and old age beat her. She'd come in with an exacerbation of her Chronic Obstructive Pulmonary Disease. The doctors had changed her inhalers and increased the dose, and this seemed to have worked. She still needed oxygen but was able to function for thirty to sixty-minute periods without it. She was keen to go home. I was keen to get her home, away from bed D3.

'Sorry, Ms Tiles. You've been declared medically fit for discharge, so I just need to ask you a few questions and then see you walk.'

'I can walk all right. I've been going to the toilet by myself this morning. Using that walking frame contraption, of course. I can use one I've got at home that they gave me when I had my knee done.'

'So, do you live in a house or a bungalow?' I said.

'A bungalow.'

'A bungalow. No stairs then.' This was looking good. She might make it twenty metres on the flat without oxygen, but stairs were a different matter for a patient whose lungs were so clogged up with shit they failed to process the oxygen into the blood properly.

'Do you have a bath?'

'Of course I have a bath.'

'Right.' Again, this might cause her a problem.

'I don't use it, though. My son fitted me in a walk-in shower.'

'Excellent. Any problems getting out of bed?'

'No.'

'Chair?'

'No, I have one of those ones that lift you out. My son bought that for me too.'

'A riser-recliner. Excellent. Any problems getting on and off of the toilet?'

'I find it a bit low.'

This may be a problem for discharge. I'd need to see if she could get on and off the crapper, having spent a week in bed. If not, I could issue a raised toilet seat and frame from the stores. Her kind son could pick it up for her, and she could be out of this place by lunchtime.

'Okay,' I said, standing up and moving the wheeled table away. 'I need to see you walk to the bathroom, and then I need to see you get on and off the lavatory.'

'Whatever for?'

'If you can do it here, then you can do it at home.'

She sat up in the bed. The sidebars were up, and the profiling action lifted her upper body into the sitting position. Perhaps, I wondered, after she'd walked, then she might be able to sit in the chair. How far did the powers of this bed extend? Hopefully, only the range of the mattress. She might be safe in the chair. If she could sit in the chair by lunchtime, the doctors could quickly write her prescription, the pharmacists prepare her meds, and her son could pick her up. She need not even get back into the bed.

I checked myself. What the hell was I thinking? This was a mass-produced hospital bed made from plastic and metal, not the Altar of Satan. I couldn't believe I was even thinking this way. Still, the drive to get her out was imperative.

'So, before we go walking, I'll just take your pulse.' I walked over to the observation machine. It reminded me of a robot from a sci-fi film. A small oblong screen on a stand and a wheeled base. I brought it over, switched it on and took the sats monitor. The little machine took temperature, blood pressure and blood oxygen saturation. In the future, I imagine they'd make a robot version that could wheel itself around and do it automatically.

'I'm just going to put this over your finger,' I explained, taking the white finger monitor, which looked like a futuristic peg, the plastic jaws gently clamping onto her finger, a little red light shining out under the skin of her finger.

'They've done this so me before,' she said. 'Do you think I'll be going out today?'

'Yes, if I can help it.'

I expected her blood/oxygen saturation to be low due to her chronic condition. Normal range in people is 95 to 100 percent.

I studied the screen. There was a register that indicated pulse, a moving bar of little lines which went up and down with the pulse. She was at 89. Above, the large numbers on the digital display flashed the number 89. It stayed at 89, but the display below it changed. I'd seen lower sats on Mrs Tiles. The display below began to slow. The bar was falling, decreasing in height at each wave until it died, didn't flicker, and didn't move. She had no pulse anymore. It had gone.

I looked at her face. Her eyes had rolled back into her head, her mouth agape, her head lolling to one side.

'Mrs Tiles, sorry, Ms,' I said out loud. 'Mrs Tiles!'

I hit the crash alarm, a triangular red button above the bed.

In under a minute, three nurses, a physio, and a junior doctor arrived with the crash trolley, a bulky wheeled affair with oxygen, defibrillators and other cardiac paraphernalia. We all looked at the obs machine, the funny little droid, and knew none of this would be needed. She was dead.

This place was an abattoir, a meat factory where the cattle were fetched from outside to be stunned, disabled and dispatched. You can see this cancer factory from the motorway. It's a hulking, rotting palace built on a plague pit to deliver souls to darkness. So sterile but utterly stinking with every virus, contagion and poison known to man. Sometimes I gagged on the stench of the place.

Sleeping was out. When I closed my eyes, I saw a wall of necrotic pornography, Mrs Tiles' mouth agape, soul standing by the bed waiting for the reaper to pull up. The bed. The Deathbed. The End Bed. All who lie in it die in it. Maybe it was cursed. How was it cursed? Perhaps the metal, foam and plastic had become conscious and lusted for death.

My mind was fractured. I slept at the traffic lights again and was woken by the beeping of the car behind me. I hardly ate when I got home. Meat just reminded me of rotting corpses, so I stuffed biscuits into my mouth while the death of Mrs Tiles played on the TV before me. Fuck it, she'd been so determined to go home. She should have been at home that afternoon watching Bargain Hunt, her son sticking Wiltshire Farm Foods meals in the microwave for her. Getting up on the frame to go for a piss, safely and easily transferring on and off of the toilet with the raised toilet seat and frame combination I'd given her. She should have been looking out of her bungalow window at her scruffy, neglected garden, watching robins flit from the fence to the shed roof, seeing the next door neighbour's cat walk perilously along the fence until it got dark and then she'd close the curtains, go to bed and sleep peacefully.

Now she was in darkness. He had taken her. Used his special card to come in after the curtains had been pulled, after the nurses had washed her corpse, and he'd taken her. Had he dragged her, or had she walked behind him like a tired, battered obedient wife? Would she be buried or cremated?

I was losing my mind. There were two things I needed to know.

1. What happens after death?

2. Was bed D3 a death bed?

In the darkness of my sleep-absent night, I figured out what I must do.

I crossed the corridor, and an old woman glided by, but a nurse shuffled her carcass to the lavatory, her mind fucked beyond repair by dementia, existing in a perpetual hell of confusion, disorientation and loss. I'd looked at a CT scan of her brain an hour before as the nurse had the software open on the PC. Instead of a healthy brain filling a skull, it looked like a shrunken walnut that had been chewed by rats.

 She repeated the same phrases. Where am I? Who are you? Where's Geoff? (Husband, dead, brain tumour, 1997). She was sleeping on the death bed. She'd be cold meat by the morning. She was the last to die in that bed for a while. An outbreak of Norovirus cleared that bay until only she was left. She died at 03:57.

The journey in was slow, The big red sigh over the highway burst into light. A big number 40
flashed up warning that we all needed to slow down and, as one, the cars stood
still. I slept until the aggressive horn of the lorry behind me woke me to the fact that traffic was moving again. I pulled off at my junction, my head humming with thoughts of the day's impossible tasks ahead. One of my tasks would be to assess Mrs Braintree in Ward sixteen. I got into the office, told my line manager I'd make the time up, and add it to all the other time I owed due to lateness on the fucking motorway. She insisted I stay late that evening. Internally I wished the rotten cunt a painful, lingering death, then hit the wards.

 Time ran like water through skeletal fingers. I worked through dinner (I couldn't face another half hour staring from the canteen window at the motorway, wishing I was on it), and as the afternoon turned to evening, the sun fell from the sky like a stone plunging the hemisphere into darkness.

Ward 16 at 18:00 felt like midnight. I barely registered the sister's warning not to go into bay D as I entered. Four empty beds met me. I didn't have to ask. Mrs Braintree, the patient I'd come to see in D3, was dead. The bay was closed to Norovirus, and I shouldn't have been in there.

The nurses were having handover at the nurses' station. The Philippine cleaner didn't give a shit that I was in there as he sauntered past with his mop. The lights were off, but the bright lights of the corridor shone across the blue floor.

There it was.

The death bed.

The metal hospital bed looked functional. Clinical, to the casual observer. A metal base and plastic head and footboard. The bed rails on each side were down, giving access to the bed. They were also known, rather morbidly, I thought, as cot-sides. I didn't like that term. It conjured images of entrapment or injury. The bed had an inflated mattress. The air cushion mattress usually inflated one cell at a time, giving the air-filled mattress ridges all the way up the bed. The mattress was deflated now. The pump hanging from two hooks at the bottom of the bed switched off now that no one was in the bed. Wires snaked under wheels.

As no one was there, I wondered what it must be like to be a patient laying on the bed, dying. Was it really the death bed? I decided to lie down on the bed to see if I could feel anything. Get a sense of what it must have been like for them. I was curious, and that curiosity pushed me towards the bed. I'd lay here. Just for a minute. Just to see.

I sat down on the metal frame, and it creaked beneath my weight. I felt nothing. In one swift movement, I swung my legs into the bed so that I was lying on it. I felt the hard metal beneath my buttocks under the deflated mattress.

I'd been on the go for twelve hours. I could do with a bit of sleep. I laughed, thinking that the ward sister would go nuts if she found me snoring there. Besides, I really didn't have time for this. I had three more patients to see on this ward and another three to see on eighteen. I was wasting time. Besides-

'Shit!'

The left-hand cot-side snapped up into position on its own. I stared at the three bars beside me then the right-hand cot-side flew up and clicked into place as if pulled up by invisible hands.

I gripped the bars to pull myself up, and all the strength in my hands left me. I could hardly grip, my fingers slipping from the metal, and fine motor movement ceased to function.

My breathing became shallow, and I struggled for breath. Not just from shock; my lungs felt heavy, struggling to process air. I thought of Ms Tiles and her COPD. I tried to lift my head and look over into the bay. Darkness framed my vision, and my sight was occluded by some mass obscuring my central eyeline.

Cataracts, the word entered my mind. I'd suddenly developed cataracts in my vision. This was not happening. I tried to scream, but the noise only erupted as a croak. Every joint and bone ached, and I was acutely aware that I'd just pissed myself.

'Oh, God!'

In the dimness, figures, pale, thin, emaciated visitors, watched me. I angled my head. One of them was Mrs Braintree. The other was Mr Daniels, the happy hoist guy who'd had an aneurysm. They flanked a central figure whom I recognised from my sleep-deprived hallucinations. I knew him by the lanyard he wore about his neck. The shadowed face under a tall pallbearer's top hat. He moved forwards. This was Death, and he'd come to take me to darkness.

I thrashed and screamed as best I could in my geriatric state. I wouldn't follow passively. He'd have to drag me along the corridor as I resisted. My pathetic, weak body would be no match for the Father of the Grave.

Nooo. Fucking Noo. NNNNNNOOOOOOO............

He stood over me now like a doctor. In his hand, he held a syringe. He was going to put me down here and now like a cancerous dog at a vet.

I pushed away, up the bed, as he studied the syringe. His black-clad nurse was ready with a needle taken from a metal kidney dish.

I was aware of another figure on my left. Behind me, the cot-side on the other side of the bed from the Father of the Grave popped down. Two kindly hands took my legs and pulled them over the side of the bed as I was still unable to move them. The same soft hands took hold of my shoulders and pulled me up into sitting. I looked into the smiling face of a man in pyjamas who had bright eyes and a shining comb-over of hair.

'Come on, son,' said Mr Dixon. 'It's not your time yet. You need to stand up.'

He helped me, and after three attempts, I was standing, my vision clear, my strength back, and my joints pain-free.

The room was empty. I was alone. The cot-side on the far side of the bed was still up, but I was alive.

The door opened, and the ward sister entered. She scowled, and said, 'What on Earth are you doing in here?'

I screamed and belted out of the bay, out of the ward and out of the hospital.

I know that had been an illusion. A week later, I had a full mental breakdown. The car park security guy found me in my car where I'd been sleeping for two days, having taken twenty paracetamol. That attempt on my life was my ticket out of one hospital and into an entirely different one. Hammond Ward in the Mental Health unit next door. No caseload, no wards to cover and no commute up and down the motorway.

I was the sanest fucker on that ward. You know why? Because I know that what I saw in bay D3 was a hallucination. No, I can't explain how the cot sides snapped up. Maybe I did it myself and just imagined they'd snapped up themselves. The rest of it? Death, the black-clad nurse, the other dead patients and Mr Dixon rescuing me were all an illusion.

They were not real, understand?

There is no spectre of Death waiting to take you to darkness.

There is no afterlife.

There's nothing after death, understand?

Nothing.

***

About the Author

paulmelhuish.wordpress.com

Paul is a 52-year-old Occupational Therapist and writes in his spare time. His latest novel DarkChoir was published by Silver Shamrock Press in 2020, before that, his previous novel, High Cross, was published by Horrific Tales in 2018, along with other short pieces published in magazines and anthologies. He remains a proud member of the Northampton Science Fiction WritersGroup.

Other Works From This Author Links
Terminus (2008) published by Greyhart Press. (UK)
Do Not Resuscitate (2009) Murky Depths Magazine
Choice Hill Farm (2010) Horrified Tales magazine
Necroforms
High Cross
Fearworld
Dark Choir
"The Last Economy"

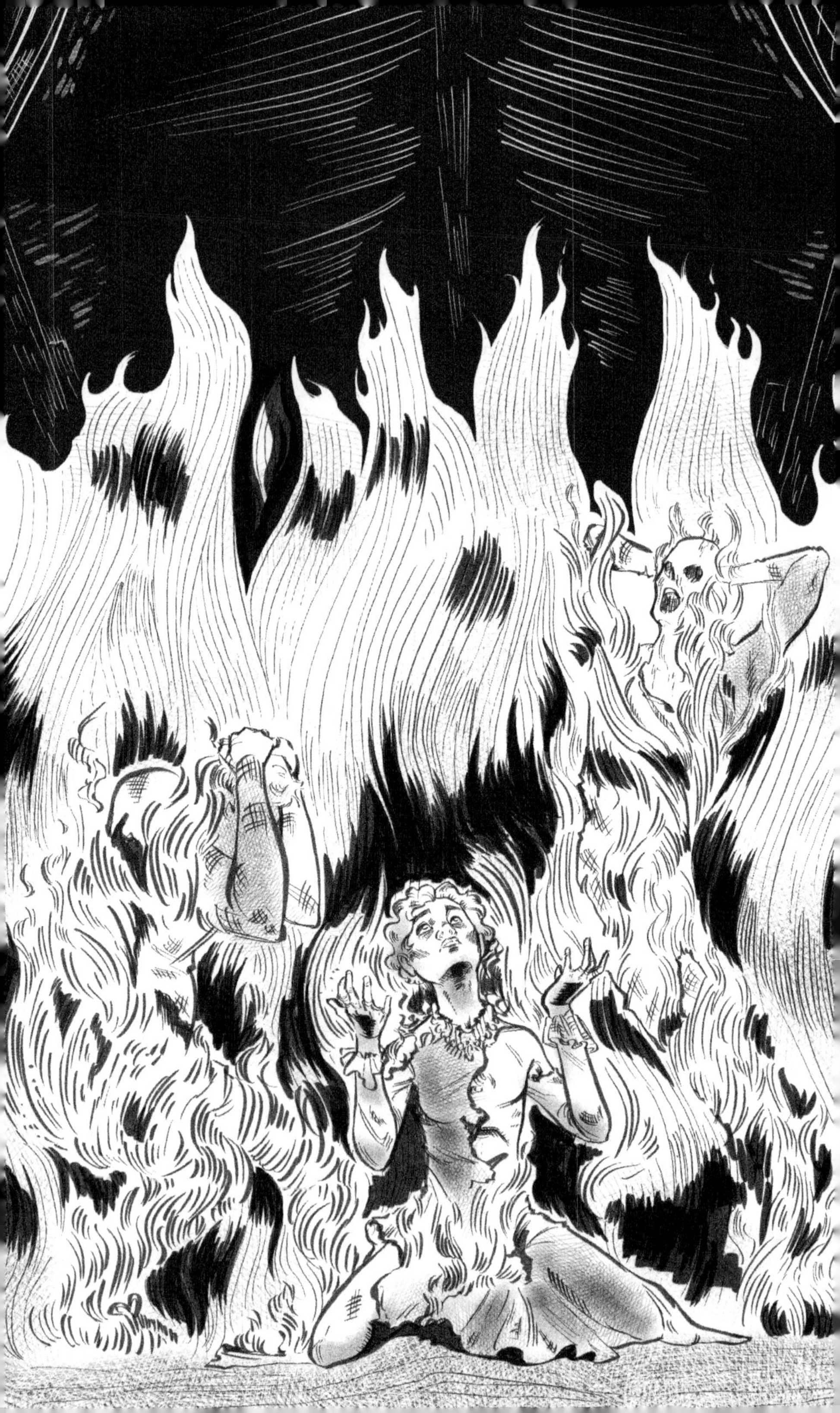

Mol of the Plague

by M.W. Irving

Mol did not look like a fiend. Far from it. He was the most beautiful child you could imagine, perfection itself. Perhaps I would have recognized him as the creature he was if the horrors of the plague had not numbed me so. For months the streets had been lined with yellowed, leathery corpses that grinned with their shrunken lips at the misery of those left behind. Or perhaps it was my desperation; the theatre closures had left me destitute. By the time the crown had decided it was safe to stage plays in crowded playhouses again, I was on the doorstep of debtor's prison. I needed a performance that could draw people out from the safety of their homes and that depended entirely on my Cedric—the rising star of my troupe. He had the ability to command audiences. They would sigh, laugh, gasp, or weep as he saw fit. He carried the play, and puberty took his voice just as the plague began to loosen its grip. Its coming was heralded by the honks and squeals of his shattered voice.

We were at the end of the first dress rehearsal to revive *Theseus and the Minotaur* when I realized the situation needed to be addressed. The stage crew had begun snickering, and when Cedric heard, he ran offstage in tears.

"I'll handle it," I said, patting the air to the rest of my troupe. Half appeared concerned, the other half wore faces pinched by frustration.

I was dreading this talk with Cedric. I had hoped to get one more season out of him, but boy players are ephemeral creatures, and he was nearly fifteen. I chased him into the dressing room and found him lit by a single candle, strewn across the floor and staring at himself in a hand mirror. His eyes were glazed with tears, his dress slumped off one shoulder, and his wig had been abandoned in a heap at the door. I nearly tripped over it as I approached.

"I'm hideous," he said through sobs.

"You're as beautiful as ever, Cedric. You're magnificent, but your voice."

I lit the sconces and brought the room into a warm, flickering glow.

"I know. I'm sorry."

"It was bound to happen, dear lad. You're a tremendous actor, and once your... situation clears up, I will have countless leading roles for you. Ariadne, though, will have to be played by someone else."

His bottom lip slid out, and tears trembled on the edge of spilling again. In the candlelight, his eyes were two copper pots brimming with gold. They had looked that way in our last performance when Theseus abandoned Ariadne at the end, after she had helped him kill her brother, the Minotaur. Every heart in the house broke, as mine broke then. In secret, I worried that I would not be able to keep him. Burbage and his ilk were always prowling, looking to snatch up real talent, and their purses were heavier than mine.

"And what will I do until then?"

"You can do some stagehand work until next season. Krebs will find something for you," I offered. He pulled away with a jerk, outrage splayed across his cherub face.

"*Krebs?*" He squeaked. "Krebs is a brute. He smells like a dead dog and hits me whenever I come near him."

"I'll talk to him. Everything will be fine."

"Everything will *not* be fine. I want to play *her*, Thomas."

He didn't have to say who. She was to be the centrepiece of our next show. Cedric was wonderful as Ariadne, but as Bathsheba, he would be transcendent. Together we had written her just for him, and it was nearly finished. He would have played her magnificently, too, had he not begun to sound like a goose in a girdle.

"I don't want to play leading men," he complained after a long, sullen pout. "Nobody weeps for them. Nobody falls in love with them."

"You can change that. They will cry for you, Cedric. You know they will."

"Fine," he said, and this time his voice didn't break. "But Krebs better not lay a finger on me."

"He won't," I promised with my best reassuring smile.

I broke the news to the company that rehearsals would be put on hold until we found a replacement Ariadne. I wish I could say they reacted with disappointment. I had let the tension of Cedric's changing voice build for too long, and everyone was relieved to have it out in the air. I was left nauseated, knowing it could be weeks and even months before we found a boy to fill the role. Longer still for him to memorize it. My hand was forced. I wrote the letter I had managed to avoid even during the darkest depths of the plague. I dipped my quill and scraped the words onto a page as quickly as possible, bile rising.

Dear Mr. Burbage, I am willing to reconsider your offer, should it still stand. Please meet me at the Prospect of Whitby Pub at ten o'clock tomorrow morning.

Yours in earnest,

T. Lockerby

I hurriedly folded the letter and pressed my seal onto it. Writing the letter had been bad enough, I was not about to hand deliver it. I went in search of someone to deliver it for me and found the troupe had abandoned The Curtain, leaving the new girl to finish the grunt work. I beckoned her to me with a call and flourish of my wrist. Her deeply pimpled face went pale, but she dutifully trotted over.

"Take this letter to the residence of Mr. Richard Burbage. I trust you know where he resides?"

The girl nodded without a word, swallowing hard. "Good, and for the love of God's wounds, tell not a soul I sent you."

"Right," she said, her voice barely leaving the back of her nose.

Then she was off like a kicked rat. I sighed. Tomorrow's meeting with Burbage would make my conversation with Cedric seem like a dream. Losing my theatre and going to debtor's prison, however, would be worse still, but only barely. The situation called for a deep, dark drunk. I grabbed a bottle of wine from my room tucked away at the back of the theatre. The bedroom had been mine for nearly twenty-five years, ever since I was an apprentice to Old Burbage, Richard's father. As it always did, thinking of Richard enflamed old scars. I flinched away from them and took a couple steps towards my writing desk. Reconsidering, I grabbed a second bottle and resolved to drink myself to sleep. A knock on the door interrupted my grand designs. It was Cedric.

"I know a boy," he said flatly. His eyes were dark, his face slack. "His name is Mol, and he is beautiful. He sings for scraps outside St. Paul's Cathedral with a voice bequeathed by God. He has a countenance and speech refined by some education, so he's likely able to read. My guess is his parents died in the plague."

"Mol," I said, savoring the way the name felt in my mouth. The vibration of the "M" on my lips and the way it finished on my tongue. "That sounds promising. See if you can have him come by."

I figured Mol would be the first in a long and tiring line of candidates and thought little more of it. Cedric nodded at me and left. Alone once again, I recommitted myself to my darling bottles, savoring the curve of them. There would be no need for glasses. I took them by the neck to bed.

The chill of the morning woke me and froze a headache behind my eyes that I knew would be slow to thaw. Shivering, I changed out of the clothes I'd slept in and into a doublet that bore fewer stains. When I stepped out into the late morning air, it was thick with a fog that left my face clammy and the city heavy with shadows. Clanging church bells and clattering hooves drove hammers into my skull. Before I had taken a dozen steps, the tilted silhouette of a man materialized out of the mist in front of me. The arrow-straight set of his body and the ridiculous brim of his hat made the figure of a high cross, sharpening as it drew closer. He wore the garb of a Puritan. Beneath the hat's edge, I could just make out a long and pallid face. With lips tight in indignation and his finger thrust to heaven, he called out a righteous voice,

"Though there are many players in your troupe parading sin across your stage, Lockerby, there is only one who performs there. His name is the Devil. You court him openly—dressing young boys as harlots, luring them to transgression and perdition. This behaviour makes a mockery of the laws of both God and man. It shall be borne by neither you, sinner! Prodigal behaviour! Immodesty! Drunkenness! Sodomy!"

As the list of sins grew, his voice went shrill. Screeching echoes chased me as I hustled away and left him to the fog's purgatory. Blasted Puritans. They were corpse flies buzzing around the husk of my life's work. Before the plague closures, they had driven away dozens of my patrons. They had gathered at The Curtain's entrance to describe the methods by which my patrons would be tortured for an eternity in Hell for attending my plays. They were relentless and ultimately effective. I was certain I felt the familiar touch of Burbage's hand in it.

I arrived at the Prospect of Whitby Pub late, yet he was nowhere to be found. I purchased two cups of ale with what scant coin I had and escorted them past the dimly lit faces floating in the gloom. I pictured Richard's face as I imagined it had looked when he received my letter. He would have laughed after reading its contents, his father's laugh. There was so much of Old Burbage in him. They shared that strong, jutting brow and high-arched nose. Richard inherited his father's greedy hands as well. I knew better than to let that snake in; he wanted nothing more than to see me ruined. Even more, he wanted The Curtain. He hobbled me at every turn, poisoning the ears of London's most influential. No matter one's talent and determination, success always depends on who you know, and Richard Burbage knew everyone who mattered.

I'm uncertain how long I waited, but the ale I bought for him was empty, and I had started on mine. Finally, I caught sight of him sliding in through the door of the pub. The pale, stony light from outside lit him from behind, so he was little more than a silhouette. Falling in ringlets about his shoulders, his dark hair danced a lively caper as he searched for me. I made no motion to catch his attention, delaying the inevitable misery. Finally, his impossibly green eyes found me prompting his disarming grin. It brought his face from handsome to exquisite.

It had been long years since I saw him last, and I could see them in his face. Wrinkles pushed into skin where none had been before, yet he was all the more attractive for it. He appeared every inch the champion of the stage he had been when we first met. I put my head down and drained a sizeable portion of my ale. My head throbbed.

"Lockerby," he said, drawing out my name and oozing amiability. "It has been too long."

"Burbage."

I lifted my cup. He swept his coat out from beneath him and sat. Taking quick stock of me, he gave me a series of short, disapproving head shakes and tutted his tongue.

"It must be lean times indeed, judging by the look of you."

"Yes," I confirmed.

"You should have reached out sooner. You needn't have suffered so."

"Perhaps."

"Let me get the measure of you," he said, leaning in and gazing into my eyes. I was satisfied to see that a ring of grey had appeared around the emerald pools. "Yes, yes, I can see Julianna in you still."

He reached to cup my cheek and ran a thumb over my skin. I shrank away, cursing my inability to grow a proper beard or hold his gaze. Burbage chuckled.

"We truly were something back in the day, weren't we? I still remember the sighs the audience gave us every time we kissed. All of London was in love with your Julianna."

"That was some time ago."

"It feels like yesterday."

I stared at the table and made no reply. He went on after a protracted silence.

"I can see you are eager for me to get to the offer you made. Let me remind you that my offer was made. I'm afraid I am no longer in a position to accommodate that particular arrangement. You're not the only one light in the purse after the closures. The Black Death has hit us all hard."

He reached out a hand to touch my arm. I jerked away.

"Please, Richard. I'm desperate, and it will save The Curtain."

"Call me Roderigo once again." His lip curled into a malevolent smile.

"No."

"Beg me, Julianna. Beg your Roderigo." He grabbed my hand and held it aloft. "Beg, and I shall yield to my Julianna once again, as I did all those years ago."

"Please, Burbage," I begged.

"In her voice," he said, growling now. His grip on my hand became painful. I swallowed hard on my rage, then spoke in a high and lilting voice.

"Please. I'm a fortnight away from foreclosure."

"Call me Roderigo," he whispered, his grip tightening further.

"Roderigo," I said in Julianna's voice. That voice. The one Richard's father liked having me put on.

"Of course." He relented, releasing my hand. The blood had been squeezed out of it, leaving my fingers yellow and pale. "But the arrangement will have to be amended. I'll need seventy-five percent of your earnings until the balance is paid. I'm hardly able to keep my own theatre running as it is, I cannot afford further risk."

"The original offer was fifty percent."

"That was before we all withered beneath the plague. It is the best I can do, Lockerby. The amount owing on The Curtain is no paltry figure. I have shareholders who would crucify me if they knew of this arrangement. I cannot think only of myself. As you well know, one's legacy is everything."

I finished my ale.

"I cannot live off a quarter of my earnings," I said. The ale threatened to come back up for a curtain call.

"And I do not believe you'll be able to produce anything worth a damn!" He was shouting, up close and slamming his fist upon the table. I winced back into my chair, nearly knocking it over. "I'll be lucky to recover half of what I'm handing out to you!"

"I have a new play. It's nearly finished. It will be ready in mere weeks. It's called *David and Bathsheba*. Richard, it is the best thing I've ever written. It will earn back the sum and more."

Burbage regained a measure of his composure before going on.

"I have a new proposal I believe will be more than fair. I will forgive the debt entirely if you sign The Curtain over to me." He fixed me with a wild gaze, and I caught a glimpse of the old cruelty I had known so well in our youth. "I could wait until you lose it, of course, then gather the dregs of your ruin, but I don't want to do that to The Curtain. She should not go dark because of your failures."

This again.

"Your father left it to me, Richard. It's mine, and it is not dark yet."

"Ah, yes. I suppose he knew you would need the leg up, and you got one, didn't you? Only to squander it. To bring it to the brink of ruin. My father bequeathed you a theatre, *my* theatre. I grew up there. I was raised by The Curtain, and he left it to *you*. Now look where we are, where you are."

"I'm doing my best," I said. I could think of nothing else.

"That's what I'm afraid of, Lockerby. Now listen closely." He pulled me in across the table by the collar. "I will accept half your earnings, but if you fail to pay me in full after the run of this next play, you will give me what should always have been mine. You will give me The Curtain." He twirled a ringlet around his finger, an old habit.

I had no choice.

"Yes. Alright, after the next play," I said through clenched teeth.

The fog had lifted by the time I left the pub, yet the gloom remained as thick as ever. I walked through it, blind with the lingering shame and dread cast upon me by the contract Burbage had hurriedly written, and I had signed. Mercifully, my way back to The Curtain was free of Puritans, and I arrived home prepared to plunge myself into another lake of wine.

I heard the voice even before I entered. It danced up through the open-air top of The Curtain, beckoning me in. Its resonance doubled when I opened the doors. I walked in through the pits, and there, standing above my gathered troupe, stood Mol. He sang with his hands clasped one over the other in choir boy posture. Thick, ruby lips parted, and a diamond voice picked up the air, lifting all who heard. It was an aria I hadn't heard before, and when it ended, I was weeping. The boy looked down, taking me in. I felt naked under his gaze.

"Thomas Lockerby," he said with a voice like the chimes of a church bell. "You are the one Cedric spoke of?"

"Yes."

"It is a pleasure to meet you. I am Mol."

"You are here for... to read for Cedric's part?"

"Yes."

"Have you acted before?"

Mol made no answer. He was dazzling, yet gaunt. Half-circles, the colour of bruises, dipped beneath his eyes, and his cheeks clung to cheekbones. His lips, though, were thick and pouting with youth. He seemed to soak in the gaze of those standing around him as a stone warmed by sunlight. Cedric approached him, script in hand.

"The part is for Ariadne."

"No!" I shouted, surprising myself with the volume of my voice. "Have him read Bathsheba."

Cedric's eyes narrowed; he didn't move.

"Now, Cedric!"

He glared before storming off to fetch the unfinished script and returned in an instant. Or perhaps it was longer. I couldn't tell as I stared up at Mol, who stood still and silent until Cedric delivered the script. Mol's eyes flicked over the words for a moment, and then he became Bathsheba. Her shoulder dropped, her hip swayed out, and her chin lifted. Mol's gaunt features lent her a beautiful vulnerability I hadn't realized she possessed. When he began to speak, it was with her voice. There was a collective breath from those of us beneath her when he was finished. Cedric brooded with crossed arms. Then I noticed Krebs, standing just offstage. He slouched deeper than usual; his thick bear's arms hung limply before him. Wearing a loose smile, his lips were wet and sagging. A slow string of drool reached the middle of his chest before it broke off. His eyes were mirrors that shone with Mol. They shone and were black.

The first performance was a week later. Mol memorized Ariadne after a single reading, and he took direction instinctively. Within days he was molded into my character completely. I was awe-struck. Every one of the smattering of people who attended on opening night returned for the next performance to see if such perfection had been the stars aligning, just that once, to imbue the Earth with a dose of their radiance only to disappear thereafter. But Ariadne drew them in again. She took them, and then they were

Mol's. Word spread, and by the fifth performance, we were turning people away.

Mol began to change, show by show. Ariadne's cheeks filled out, her costumes fit better, and the plum colour beneath her eyes melted away. She became more beautiful, agony to behold, while those who watched her began to appear more and more like living dead just before the pestilence claimed them—shambling, pale, and hollow. Still, they turned up in droves, desperate for more. The first bags of their coin I brought to the bank were so heavy I had to bring Krebs, whose thickset bulk bore them easily. He could singlehandedly lift set pieces that would otherwise take a trio of stagehands to move, and he followed instructions with empty-headed accuracy. Together, we stepped out of The Curtain, and I brought up the issue of Cedric with him. I'd forgotten to warn Krebs off mistreating him, and the boy had received a few bruises as a result.

"You're going to have to be kinder to Cedric," I told him, after a bit of hesitation—Krebs could intimidate anyone. He grunted and made an eye-rolling expression of distaste at me. "He is going to replace David as our lead actor, and I need to be sure he will stick around. He'll be incredible playing opposite Mol."

With the mention of Mol's name, the muscles in Krebs' face and neck loosened.

"Lockerby!" a voice shrieked at us. It was the Puritan from the week before. "I have warned you enough. You mock God openly. Rot and ruin are all you offer. Lechery and sin!"

"You should write plays," I muttered. "You have a poetic tongue."

Krebs took a quick step in towards the man. His broad fist drove savagely into the birdlike ribcage. The robed Puritan bent double, gasped, and crumpled to the ground. The wide brim of his hat caught on the breeze and tumbled away, revealing a bald scalp. I looked up at the massive fellow beside me.

"Effective, if a bit excessive, Mr. Krebs."

If he heard me, he gave no sign. His face remained slack, as though he had fallen asleep with his eyes open. It was then I noticed the blade in his hand, dripping blood. I watched a crimson drop collect and drop from the knife's tip. My throat thickened, and hot dread rolled through me. My legs continued walking, turning corners and past people, but I had shrunk away. It was a trick I had perfected long ago; one I hadn't needed for years, allowing the world to affect me no more than a passing shadow would. When we returned to The Curtain, the collapsed shape of the Puritan remained exactly as we had left it. Krebs didn't so much as glance at it, nor did anyone else who passed by. The sight of a corpse on the ground had become an unremarkable set piece on London's streets. The stain of the plague lingered.

On one of the murkiest days, just before a performance, a man stepped out of the fog and attempted to kidnap Mol. I was at the theatre when it happened, overseeing preparations for the next show as I always did, when Krebs went rigid. Though Mol was some distance away, the hulking man bolted from the theatre and went straight to where the kidnapper struggled with a gnashing and writhing Mol. I followed and was there when Krebs killed the man dispassionately, crushing his throat with one hand while taking

Mol in the other. The thickness of Krebs' arms enveloped the boy's slender form completely. Krebs wept and knelt before the angelic child. Mol showed no emotion, allowing himself to be held with indifference. He began to lick at the tears streaking down Krebs' face, running a pink tongue across his stubbled cheek. A tear would pool and fall, and Mol would catch it with his mouth. I decided then that Mol would live at the theatre, with me. I didn't know why I hadn't thought of it earlier.

Or perhaps I had.

There seemed to be some part of me resisting the idea, driving it from my mind before it could take hold. After nearly losing Mol, however, whatever resistance I felt was wiped away.

"I will stay there as well," Krebs said when I told him the plan. I could feel the rumble of his voice in my chest, and his tone said there would be no argument on the matter.

I put Mol in Richard Burbage's old room. It had once been his father's before Old Burbage senior died and left The Curtain to me. Richard had taken his father's bedroom without a word to me, and I did not fight him on it. He remained there, burrowed like a tick, for five long years before he went and got himself his own theatre. The room had been vacant ever since and somehow seemed a fitting place for Mol. I did not have to show him the way. He strode without hesitation to the master bedroom. The boy had no clothes with him aside from what he wore and kept no possessions to speak of. Nobody knew where he had been sleeping before The Curtain, and nobody thought to ask. Perhaps we knew better.

When I showed him the room, he took a pair of strides inside and stopped abruptly. He drew in a long, searching breath through his nose. Then, as though he detected something sweet in the air, he smiled. He turned to regard me.

"There are deep memories in this place," he said.

I hesitated a moment before turning to leave and closing the door behind me. I had expected something more but could not for the life of me think what. I retreated to my own much smaller room to collapse into my bed. The stale straw mattress wrapped me in its prickly embrace, and I lay awake. It was Bathsheba up there, in Old Burbage's room. I recognized her from the scant lines Mol had read. It was her, exactly as I'd imagined her. The tilt of her head, the turn of her wrists, the posture of her legs. It was perfect. It was Bathsheba.

My left hand was raised and knocking on Mol's door as though drawn by invisible strings. I hadn't even realized I'd gotten out of bed. Gently, gently I knocked. In my other hand, a candle burned and set haunted shadows dancing in the corner of my eye, warning me away. Waving me off stage. The darkness beyond my candle's reach was nearly perfect, but I had traversed the worn floors of The Curtain since childhood. It was my home.

I needed no light.

"Bathsheba," I whispered at the door.

No answer came. I eased the door open, and candlelight poured inside. The room was cold and empty, lurching with the candle's flicker. I stepped in. The bed remained as dusty and untouched as it had been for the last decade.

"Mol?" I asked the darkness.

"Julianna," came a voice from the empty bed. Old Burbage's voice, the way it had sounded as he lay dying, dry and shallow. It was how he sounded as he told Richard, his only son, that I would inherit The Curtain.

Then the old darkness took me, as it had in years long past, and there was nothing.

I awoke the next morning in my own bed, naked and shivering, my legs and back aching. I had been lying upon my arm, and it had gone numb in the night. A flea clung to my flesh just above the wrist. I watched as it latched on and sucked. I meant to flick it away or squeeze it between my fingernails until it burst, but I did nothing. I watched it and hated it. When sensation returned to my arm, it did so with Hell's burning fury.

Theseus and Ariadne wrapped its final performance three weeks later, though I could have let it run for months longer. We were regularly turning away more people than we let in, and the queue of humanity stretched into the street long before the stage candles were lit. There were even rumours that the Queen herself had thought to take in a performance, until the Puritans amassing around her had intervened.

I was anxious to get *David and Bathsheba* on, though. I had finished it alone in the dark of my room, working feverishly. Often I was accosted by dawn's insistent glow as I collapsed into my bed. When it was finished, I presented the script to Mol. Cedric had come to me weeping afterwards, begging to know why he had been cut out of the writing of it.

"Because," I replied, "it was faster that way."

With the very first reading, Mol was Bathsheba up on the stage. There was no boy acting behind her; she had climbed out of my mind and into the playhouse, alive. We made it to the performance in record time, and my Bathsheba poured her story over an unblinking crowd. Their eyes, livestock dim, reflected her like polished copper. On the opening night of *David and Bathsheba*, the candlelight bent and thrust into her. She, in turn, lit the theatre and cast deep shadows, long and black, into the faces of the fevered throng below. When Bathsheba's baby was thrown into the sea because of her husband's actions, the masses gnashed and wept at the injustice, choking on their tears. They came, night after night, until they could pay no longer, then wail outside as someone mortally wounded. Krebs bloodied dozens, leaving them supine in the mud, lowing still.

As spring grew feverish and fell to summer, I became convinced that Mol was my muse. I was compelled to write, labouring for days at a time without sleep. I stopped only when my clawed fingers could hold a quill no longer. As my plays developed, however, I was dismayed to find every character contained a Hell-charred soul. Every creature that dwelt beneath the black surface of my inkwell demanded to be brought to life; to revel in the pain and woe that bled onto my pages from my quill.

I resisted at first, setting out to write only the most kind-hearted and innocent characters in God's Christendom—characters so sickly sweet nobody could like them, but they would invariably twist against one another, and die horribly by each other's hands. I tried to stop writing entirely, but if I failed to pen those devils into existence, they would torture me mercilessly in my dreams. I would be flayed, burnt alive, or flogged. The agony would follow me into the waking after I woke up screaming. On one particularly tormented night, I dreamt of a woman. She wore nothing but her raven tresses as she leaned in close to take a bite from my cheek as one might an apple. The crunch of my flesh between her teeth roused me, and I found my nightshirt soaked in blood. I raced to a mirror and found, to my amazement, no wound. My nightshirt was bloodstained beyond salvage, however, and I disposed of it with fire.

The next night was when people began trying to break in to see Mol. It began with knocking and hollering, then came the shriek of a metal rod prying at The Curtain's chained door. Krebs went out and dealt with them but not before receiving a blow from the heavy iron that would have felled a bear. Krebs did not flinch, though his face was left swollen and purple.

Through it all, Mol became still more beautiful. His skin glistened in the guttering light of the stage candles, and I could swear the boy's slender body swelled in places and narrowed in others as he became Bathsheba. Her wig shone and took on a lustre it didn't have before, even when it was new. Her voice caressed and forced you to listen. Once the curtain had dropped, and she was in darkness, Mol would shift back into the boy's slender frame. That was when the adoration on the other side of the curtain shifted, tilting and toppling into madness. The cheering grew to shouting, and eventually to screams. Krebs silenced the last few who refused to leave. In the aftermath of each performance, a handful of patrons would lay moaning in the dirt or draped over the seats farther back. They were either victims of the crushing audience, the ministrations of Mr. Krebs, or Mol's thrall. Cedric would tend to them all. He would deliver a sip of water and a soothing word before tenderly ushering them out. The play was the talk of London.

Richard Burbage paid a visit sometime around the thirtieth performance. A swampy summer rain had been falling for days when he turned up in my room unannounced; his magnificent mane of hair lay dripping and limp. He had seen the performance that night but had not been one of the lucky few to get a seat beneath the roofed sections. Instead, he had been relegated to the pit, amongst the steaming masses. He stank of them, and it was delicious.

Wandering over to my desk, he picked up two curling pages. He shook his head as he read the first few lines.

"How did you get in here?" I asked, narrowing my eyes.

"Please, this is my home. Lord, it looks exactly as it used to."

I raced over and snatched my pages from him.

"You're as unwelcome now as you have always been." I waved my fist in his face.

"I'm here about our agreement."

"I have all that I owe and twice more again. You will be paid on the date it is due and not a God-forsaken moment sooner."

"I'm not referring to money, Lockerby. I am referring to what is owed. You signed a contract promising me fifty percent of everything acquired from the moment the contract was signed. Tell me, when did you acquire this exquisite Mol?" A damp ringlet twirled on his pinky. "What's more, I have decided to forgive your debt in exchange for a controlling interest in Mol's performances. He will be performing at my Rose Theatre beginning tomorrow."

His face twisted into a malicious grin. It was his *I've already won* grin.

"I agreed to no such thing," I said, sputtering.

"Then how is it I can have a dozen well-respected men swear you did? Who can you muster?"

An ache of dread bulged in my throat.

"No."

"Oh yes, and you know me, Thomas. I am a man who just trembles to see every letter of the law followed."

He eased down onto my bed, and the lumpy straw mattress reached up to embrace him.

"Come now, my Julianna, it needn't be acrimonious."

A stillness came over me. I suddenly knew how our conversation was going to end. I looked down at Richard, who did not.

"Richard. I forgive you. I forgive everything." Burbage's grin sagged with confusion. "Yes. I wanted The Curtain from your father, and I got it. I earned it. And you will die having never had it."

"Tell me what, exactly, you did to earn this place from the Old Man?"

A stage sword was in my hand and thrust into his mouth before I could form a thought. The dulled tip caught in the back of Burbage's throat, and I heaved against it. I was upon him, pushing as hard as I could on top of his struggles. He attempted a scream but only managed gurgling whimpers.

His thrashing gave way to straining, then to stillness. I held him for a long time until I could look down.

Blood, black as the midnight Thames, boiled up over his lips.

I threw him over my shoulder with the sword still jutting from his mouth and carried him up the stairs. They squealed beneath our combined weight. I took Richard Burbage up to his old room. His father's room. Mol's room. I dropped the limp weight of him onto the floor in front of the door, feeling like a cat delivering a mouse to its master. I was breathing hard when I knocked. Once again, no answer came. I opened the door and entered with Burbage in tow.

I removed my clothes until I wore only Richard's blood. There were drying smears across my chest and arms, and my shoulders and back were slick. Just as I had before, I fell asleep on my feet, standing naked in Mol's room. I woke up in my own bed again, cold as death. The blood that had soaked into my skin the night before was gone. I dressed in a daze and raced back to Mol's room. It was lit by a sickly morning light. The bed had not been slept in, and Mol was not there. The blood that had poured from Burbage like oil onto the floor was gone. Everything looked exactly as it had when I dragged his corpse through the threshold the night before. The only difference was the smell. It reeked of the plague dead in that room.

As I choked amid the stench, an image came to me. It was Mol, bestial on all fours, stalking the fogged alleyways and deep shadows of London, consuming the dead. His jaw would unhinge grotesquely, popping and cracking as his mouth gaped and swallowed. The moment I thought of it, I knew it to be true. I was certain, *certain* of it. I was feeding my patrons to him and profiting from it, enjoying it even. I waited for this realization to produce a sickening weight of guilt, but there was nothing. Cedric found me dazed in Mol's room. Days later, there was another Puritan in front of The Curtain. This one was young and pleading, begging upon his knees. I had thought, at first, that it was Cedric. This boy had the same youth, the same innocence. He looked at me with Cedric's swimming eyes, only there hadn't been tears in Cedric's eyes for weeks.

"Please," the Puritan boy wept, "don't you see? Don't you see what it's doing? It came in through the plague. The death and the misery lured it here, and you put it on a stage."

Where is Krebs when I need him?

Eventually, the periods between Mol's performances slipped below the surface of my mind. Mol's voice was the only thing that carried any resonance, any clarity. I seemed hardly to exist unless he was on stage, breathing life into me and into Bathsheba. The frantic and sweaty nocturnal writing, the overwhelming influx of money, Krebs' casual violence. Cedric. All of it seemed like some sort of fabled monster, appearing in glimpses like half-believed folktales.

Only once did anything break through the fog. Cedric came into my room one evening to demand my attention. I was busy frantically penning another wretched character to life.

"How could you finish the play without me?" Cedric said, startling me. I imagine he had been waiting for me to notice him standing there for some time. He stood leaning against the doorway to my room. I did nothing to keep the annoyance out of my voice.

"We discussed this. It was faster."

As he spoke, Cedric's voice built with emotion until it cracked.

"We did not discuss it. You dismissed me as though I was one of the patrons Krebs turns away with his fists! Have you seen what it is like out there?"

I looked up at him then, and his desperation pulled me out of myself. Cedric looked terrible, pale and exhausted. His ear was swollen and yellowed with an aging bruise. Courtesy of Krebs, I'm sure; the man was growing increasingly volatile.

"Bathsheba was mine. First, I don't get to play her, and then you! You promised that everything would be alright. You promised that you would make Krebs leave me alone."

"Everything is alright, Cedric."

"You took me from my family, Thomas. You fed me lies about making me an actor, then you cast me aside when you were finished with me. I wish I had never brought Mol to you. I wish I had let the theatre fall to your ruin. I wish the plague had taken you!"

Cedric fled my room, his face contorted with fury. I snorted before bending back to my scrawling.

The confrontation left me unsettled and brooding, but Cedric surprised me the next day with a suggestion to expand Bathsheba's role. He had rewritten many of her scenes, bulking up her lines and filling out the part even further. He thought of a new, better title as well: *The Tragedy of Bathsheba*. The additions he wrote brilliantly exhibited the extraordinary talent I had all but forgotten about. It would require a couple daytime rehearsals, but it would be well worth it. More Bathsheba. More Mol. My teeth clenched as I thought about it. I could not help but picture the faces in the audience at the end of each performance, distant and pus yellow. They hadn't come in that way. A lurch of remorse threatened to choke me, but I forced it down. It gave quickly under the combined weight of Bathsheba, Mol, and the coin I had needed so desperately a few short months before.

Then came the first rehearsal with Cedric's new lines, the last rehearsal The Curtain would ever see. Mol stood as Bathsheba, reaching to the heavens, burning with despair. Krebs, alone in the pit below, wept and burnt along with her. The brute had stopped allowing anyone else into the pit during rehearsals, giving a warning growl if anyone came near. While his bulk remained impressive, his flesh had begun to sag. The skin around his eyes, at the corners of his mouth, his earlobes, had loosened and grown bruised as the rest of his face faded to ghostly white. He was the first to notice Cedric step out from behind the curtains.

The big man's confused grunt made me aware that something was amiss. Cedric laboured under the weight of a deep jug of oil. He must have drained dozens of lamps to gather that much. In an instant, I realized what he meant to do. Rather than the fear I would have expected, I felt a tight knot of heartbreak. The set of Cedric's face was crushing. There was no anger or fear, only determination. He had been pushed to his limit. Everything had been taken from him, and I had been the one to do it. It all came crashing down upon me; I had heard Cedric's pleas, but they never registered. I had been drowning. At the core of my heartbreak, however, was a sickening and selfish relief. I had known it would come to this. As Cedric hoisted the jug over his head, quivering, I was relieved it was Cedric, the young prodigy with a lifetime of potential, who would die doing what needed to be done and not I.

Cedric charged at Mol.

Krebs, murder in his eyes, leapt onto the stage and took two broad steps toward the boys. Too late. He was too late.

The oil spilt with a thick splash over the tallow candle footlights, and there was a grunt of ignition. Flames quickly obscured the trio at centre stage. I felt the heat blushing my cheeks from across the theatre as the plume burnt from yellow, to orange, to roasting blood before the smoke began to choke me. Through the Hellish inferno, I could make out immolated limbs flailing, Krebs' thick arms and Cedric's slender ones. Mol stood still, reaching a single hand out and speaking as Bathsheba still. As the wig Mol wore burnt away, she continued crying for her lost baby. The flames did not touch her, for there was no fire in Bathsheba's world, only grief. Then darkness took everything. Smoke filled The Curtain, and I was forced to turn and flee. Every breath raked my throat.

Before long, flames licked the sky above the thatched roof. The smoke raced upwards, pale and hot, carrying my theatre away. When only the blackened bones of The Curtain were left, we found the charred remains of Cedric and Krebs reaching out toward each other. There was no sign of Mol.

She walks the streets of London still, my Bathsheba, drawing the eye of every person the Fates bring across her path. Perhaps the Puritans had the right of it all along. I tried to join them, those morose faithful, after I sobered from my grief long enough to form a thought. But they would not have me. I considered taking my own life then, though my cowardice would not allow it. I believe, of all those burnt, murdered, and tormented, I have suffered the worst fate, for I am left with the weight of it all. The guilt—for the blame rests on me alone. I had been warned, and I was too greedy, too narrow. The only way to alleviate the hollow pain of it is to stop him, for I am certain Mol lurks in the dark places of London even now. Wherever there is death and avarice, I search for her—a spider without a web, Mol of the plague. God save us. He must never be allowed to tread the boards again.

Thomas Lockerby, 1593.

***

About the Author

mwirving.ca

Mike is a writer and teacher from Victoria, British Columbia. When he's not enjoying the wilder places of the island, he's doing his best to convince his students that there's magic in words. His work has been previously featured in The Lyre, Flash Fiction Magazine, and the Emerge 2021 Anthology.

Other Works From This Author Links

"Worm on a Hook"
"The Farewell Generation"

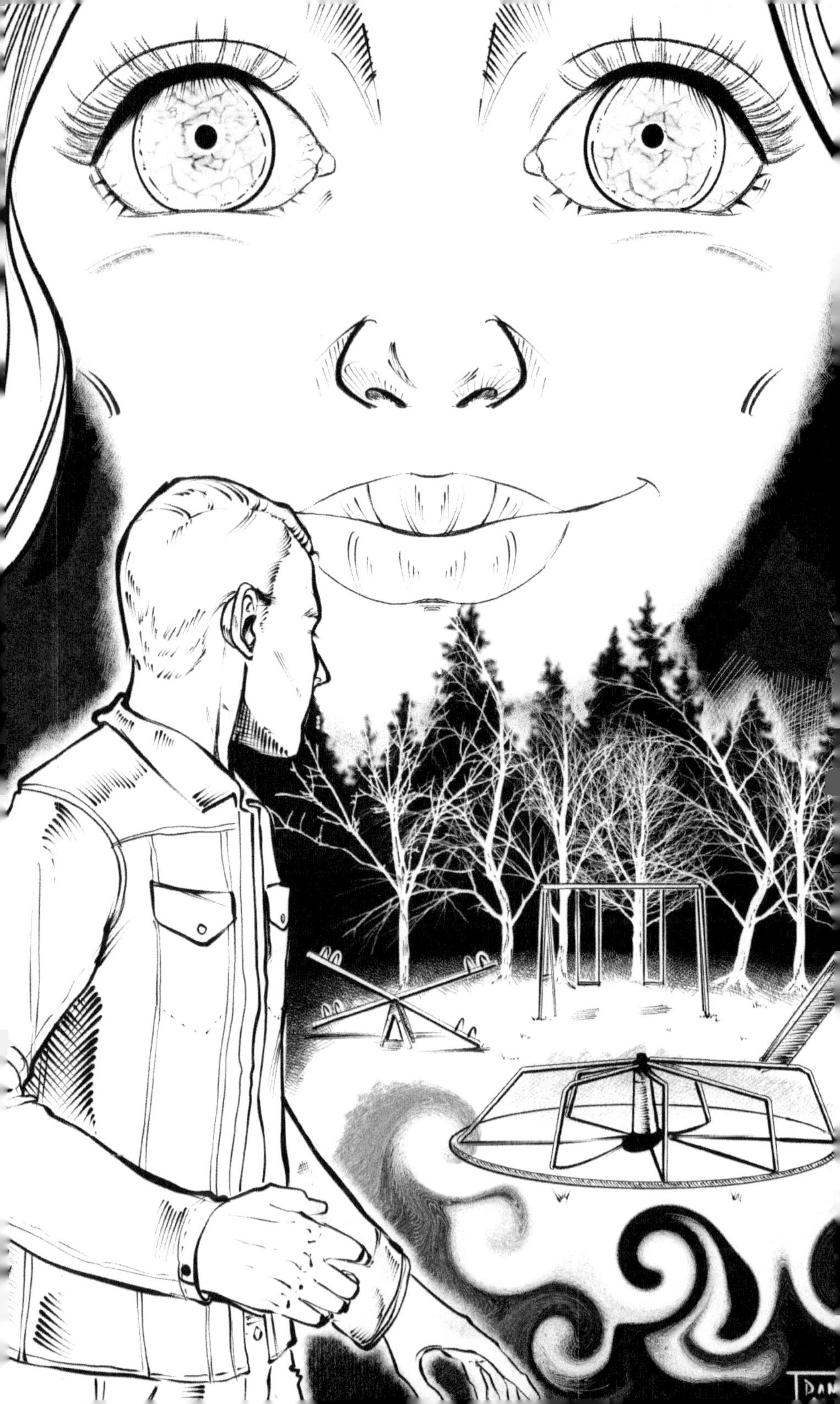

A Little Game of Hide-n'-go-seek

by Thomas Stewart

I stood, absolutely confused. The little girl was just standing there on the playground, smiling sweetly at me. "Hey there, mister." she squeaked.

"Uh, hey… " I looked around. She just stood still.

"You wanna play Hide-and-go-seek, mister?" I looked back at her. She wore a cheeky, adorable, dimply grin. I just looked at the other children, doing my best to keep an eye out for my daughter, Hannah. I couldn't see her, but I figured as much, given how crowded the jungle gym was.

The little girl still stood, smiling at me. As adorable as she was, I was a bit uncomfortable with this. "Um, n-no, no, thank you" I replied.

I'd hoped she would've taken this hint and run off to play. She didn't, though. Instead, she started pouting. "Please," she whined, "I'm lonely and don't got no one to play with."

"What about the other kids?" I asked absently, trying to look for Hannah. She spoke again, this time sounding cold, petrified almost.

"There are no other kids here, mister." I looked back at her.

"Huh? What do you mean? What about all the—" I stopped. I couldn't hear the squealing and laughter of raucous playing anymore. The playground was dead silent.

"What the... Where'd all the children go?"

"There aren't any others anymore, mister." I got up from the bench I was sitting on and ran over to the jungle gym. Frantically, I started searching through every nook and cranny of the jungle gym, inside and out, looking for Hannah or ANY of the other kids that were there just two seconds ago.

"Hannah?!" I called out. "Hannah, where are you, sweetie?! HANNAH?!"

"Who's Hannah?" the little girl asked.

"She's my daughter. Have you seen her?" I called out her name into one of the tube slides. No answer.

"There's no one else here, mister. There never has been." She started tugging on my pant leg, whimpering, "It's so lonely here. Please play hide-and-seek with me?" I ignored her.

"Hannah, come on, it's time to go home!" Still, no answer. I heard the little girl giggling.

"Ready or not, here I come." I heard, coming from somewhere on the far side of the jungle gym. I looked around, though, and I couldn't see her anywhere. I was standing alone.

"Hello?!" I called out. Nothing. "Hannah?! Anybody?!" My heart started pounding. I couldn't find my daughter, the children somehow just vanished into thin air, I was being taunted by a little girl I didn't know, I was all alone, and it was *dead fucking silent!*

Then, before I even realized it, the playground wasn't even there anymore. Now there was just a big empty sawdust pit where it used to be. Still, though, I could hear the little girl giggling.

"I'm gonna find you, hehe." I started swinging my head in every direction. Before I knew it, everything else began disappearing as well. Everything was vanishing into thin air, leaving nothing but a blank space of black nothingness in its place.

Alarmed, I started to run for the park exit, only to find that it, too, was gone. The gate, the cars, the entire damn parking lot, all *gone!*

What the... Where's the parking lot?! Where's everything going? Why is everything disappearing?!

"Gonna get you, mister." This time, the voice didn't even sound like the little girl anymore. Hell, it *barely* sounded human! It was raspy, almost like she needed an oxygen mask. I couldn't see her anywhere.

"Who are you?!" I called out, now starting to shake in panic.

"You better run, mister, before I get you." I looked around again. There was nowhere to go. Everything, all around me, was gone, just a blank, black empty space. I was surrounded by a pit of darkness.

She started giggling again. It was echoing all around me, growing closer and closer. Still, I couldn't see her. She was everywhere.

I froze. I couldn't move. The giggling grew higher and higher in pitch the closer it got. I was surrounded, trapped.

"Leave me alone!" I shouted. My head was spinning, physically and psychologically, with my heart going at least several million beats a minute. "Who are you? What do you want?!"

Suddenly, something that felt like dry ice touched the back of my right leg. My heart jumped, and I whirled around. Then my heart stopped completely.

There, standing and grinning like before, was the little girl. But she didn't at all look like a little girl anymore. Her skin, which *was* a natural sort of olive tan, was now gray and clammy, desiccated. She stood as a living corpse, barely held together with taut, decayed flesh.

I wanted to scream but couldn't even suck in enough air to do so. Her mouth slowly opened, looking like it was an absolute strain for her to do so, and I heard her raspingly whisper, "I... foouunnd yooouu... "

Then everything went dark. Almost immediately, I snapped upright in my bed, sweating bullets and screaming. Once I realized I was in my room, in my bed with my wife next to me, my body started to slowly relax. I was breathing heavily.

My wife stirred and groaned. "Tim, what's going on? What's wrong?" I didn't answer. I sat there, panting and sweating. "Tim, babydoll, what happened?"

I looked at her. She looked normal. The room was normal. *Everything looked normal.*

"N-nothin'." She looked unconvinced. "It's fine, Edna, really. It was just a bad dream, that's all. Go back to sleep."

"This is the third night in a row. Baby, seriously, what's going on?"

"I... I don't... " I rubbed my face and got up from the bed. Sunshine started bleeding through the window. The clock read 7:45 a.m. "Look, everything's fine, okay? I'm gonna wash up and go out for a bit, clear my head."

I took a long shower, ending up running up all the hot water. Edna was asleep again when I came back out. Good thing, too. She'd have been pissed if she knew I used all the hot water. God knew I needed it, though.

After that, I threw on a T-shirt and jeans before going out for a walk. The air was light; brisk, yet not chilly enough for me to feel like I needed to go back for a jacket. Not too windy, either. Just right.

The walk was quiet for the most part. Since it was still early, most people were still in their homes, likely still asleep, trying to get as much of it as possible before they had to work. And because it was the beginning of the new school year, kids weren't out and about like they might be if it were spring or summer break, when it's hot and bright outside.

So I *figured*, anyway. But imagine my shock then when, having walked just a block or two away from my house, I looked in the distance, and what did I see but a small child, standing by the gates of the park. I stopped and squinted, trying to get a better look at her.

I couldn't see her face or any of her features. What I could see, however, was that her skin appeared lighter than it should've been, even from the distance I was at. She was waving at me.

What the hell? I wondered, continuing to watch her wave at me. She quickly turned and ran into the park. Curiosity overcame me, and I went up to the gate but couldn't see her anywhere anymore.

For a moment, I looked around. Nothing but an empty playground. She was gone, having apparently vanished into thin air. I gripped the bars of the gate, debating on whether or not to go in. I started wondering if I'd *actually* seen her. Maybe there really *wasn't* anyone there, you know? I figured maybe my nightmare had just been getting to me, and I was just hallucinating a little girl waving at me from the park.

I rubbed my face. *Come on, Tim, get a grip. You're fine just keep walking.* Taking a deep breath, I continued past the rest of the park and down the street.

About thirty to forty-five minutes later, I made it all the way to the end of the block when I decided to turn around and head back home. When I turned around, though, there she was again. The little girl, standing in the distance, waving at me. I froze.

I tried squinting to see if I could get a better look at her this time. She turned and started running away. I didn't want to lose her, so this time, I took off after her. I managed to catch up with her just a few feet away from the gate to the park.

"Hey!" I called out. I heard her giggling as she tried to keep running into the park. I caught up the rest of the way to her and put my hand, as gently as I could, on her shoulder, stopping her. "Hey kid, what're you doin' out here?"

She turned around, giving me that familiar dimple cheeked smile from my nightmare. My face began to go white as a shiver slowly inched its way down my back. "You caught me, mister!" She giggled.

"Caught you? What? Listen, where are you from do your parents know where you are?"

Still grinning and giggling, she replied, "My mommy and daddy aren't 'round no more." I was confused. More than that, I was starting to get nervous.

"Wh-what do you mean, sweetheart?" She giggled again and looked at the park. "You wanna play a little game of Hide-n'-go-seek?"

"Come on," I said, grabbing for her hand, "let's get you back home to your—wait!" Just before I could take her by the hand, she ran off giggling toward the park gate.

I took off after her. "Wait, come back!" She kept on running through the park gate. I ran up to it and stopped. "Kid!" I shouted. "Where are you?! Come out!"

I looked around. Nothing. The playground was empty. I tried shouting for her again but still got nothing. The sun was starting to climb higher and higher in the sky, yet everything still seemed quiet. No one was coming out like normal to start their day or go to work or anything.

The entire neighborhood was dead silent. A shiver started prickling down my back. *Something's not right here? Why is it so quiet—*

"I'm counting to ten. You better hide!" the little girl proclaimed cheerfully. This broke me from my stupor, and I began swinging my head in every direction to see where she was shouting from. I couldn't see anything, though.

"Ten, nine, eight…"

My heart was racing furiously. *Where the hell is she?! What the hell is going on?!*

"Seven, six, five…"

I looked back toward the gate, ready to make a break for it, when I realized it wasn't there anymore. My eyes widened, and my jaw dropped. What the fuck was going on? Where was the gate?

"Two, one, zero! Ready or not, here I come!"

Panicking now, I saw that the rest of the park was gone, too, replaced with a black wall of nothing. The only area still there was the playground. I heard the little girl's giggling all around me again.

I started to run for where the gate used to be. When I got there, though, I couldn't go any further. I almost fell, finding that the ground cut off abruptly from where the gate was before. The giggling got closer.

Closer.

"Gonna get you, mister..."

It sounded only a foot or so away from me now. "I'm gonna get you, and then I'll win, and you'll be here forever!" My blood froze.

"What?!" I almost shouted.

"You're the only one left, and we'll never stop playing. The only way to stop is to win. The only way to win now is to hide."

The darkness crept closer, inching me toward the playground. "None of the others made it out. You're the only one that's left now. Soon, I'll be the champ of Hide-n'-go-seek."

Seeing nowhere else I could go, I ran to the playground. I headed straight for the jungle gym and began frantically searching for the tightest, most cutoff section to try and hide in. I could hear her giggling again.

"Come out, come out, wherever you are..." she teased in a sing-song voice. I closed my eyes and started holding my breath. Her giggling was right on top of me, all around me.

Please go away! God, PLEASE go away!

The giggling seemed to linger, settling in the air like dirt in the bottom of a drinking glass. She was keying in on me. Testing me, trying to see how long before I'd come out.

"We're gonna have SO much fun, mister. Oh, we'll be best pals! We'll never stop playing. You'll never leave me!" Like the last time, her voice started changing, devolving into that raspy hiss from my nightmare as she spoke. My body was shaking, curled up in a ball like a baby from deep inside one of the tube slides, feeling tears of panic starting to burn my eyes.

Closer.

"Where are you, mister?"

Closer.

"I'm gonna find you..."

Closer.

"Come out, wherever you are..."

Then, for just a moment, everything went silent. My eyes opened, and I looked around. I still held my breath. *I-is she gone?*

I inched my neck out to see. There wasn't anyone there. The wall of darkness, however, was much closer now. I was about to climb out of the slide when I felt something tightly grasping my ankle. My heart jolted into another immediate frenzy. I looked back and screamed.

There she was, staring at me again with that corpse-looking face from my nightmare. Her clammy, withered lips were stretched into the widest and most demented grin I'd ever seen. "I found you!" she rasped. "You lose!"

I tried to yank my foot free, but it was no use. Her fingers were like the teeth on a bear trap around my leg. She began crawling up to me, forcing me to lock eyes with the dead, milky white, lifeless spheres in her head. "Better luck next time, mister… " Then, once again, everything became completely dark.

I snapped awake. I bolted upright, panting breathlessly. I looked around. I was in my bedroom, my wife sleeping next to me.

She stirred and groaned, "Tim, what's going on? What's wrong?" I didn't answer, being completely out of breath. Eventually, my breathing slowed, and I looked at her.

"N-nothin'," I groaned, rubbing my face. "It's fine, Edna, really. It was just a bad…" I stopped.

"What?" she asked. I didn't answer. "What, Tim?"

I stayed silent, lost in thought. Something felt off when I said that. It felt familiar. Repetitive, in a way…

Like I'd done it before!

"Tim!" Edna snapped, waking me from a trance. I looked at her. She was the perfect mix of worried and confused.

"Look, uh… Just go back to sleep, okay? I'm sorry I woke you." She continued to look at me like I was a nut. I got up.

"Hey, babe, I'm gonna go take a—" I stopped again. Again, something wasn't right. I was about to say that I was gonna take a shower, but… Didn't I do that already?

What was I gonna do afterward? Go out. Go for a walk. I'd walk the block, all the way past the park where…

The park. I was gonna walk past the park. I wouldn't go in, of course. No reason to, not like anybody would even be…

There…

My heart thumped loudly in my chest. I realized I'd done that before, too. I'd gone to the park before, and nobody was there, either. Nobody, except for that little girl.

I could hear it in the back of my head, "*You're the only one left, mister.*" What was that supposed to mean, though?

The only one? What does that mean? How am I the only one? There're other people here, in this city. What about them?

I tried to concentrate on the playground, on the little girl's words to see if she may have given any kind of hint at what she was saying. For whatever reason, though, it was like something was blocking it. Like I couldn't remember anything real clearly past just waking up.

"Babe?"

I was snapped out of my thoughts again and looked at my now frightened wife.

"What's going on?"

I sighed and rubbed my face.

"I told you, hon, it's nothing. I just... Didn't sleep well, is all. Nothing major."

"Baby, that's the third night—"

"In a row," I said, finishing the sentence. My tongue went dry. *How'd I know she was gonna say that?*

"Y-Yeah... " she replied, appearing equally as disturbed. She sat up in bed. "Baby, come on, please tell me what's going on."

"I... I... " I trailed off. I didn't know what to say. I didn't know what was going on. All I knew was something wasn't right. "I don't know, Edie. I guess I feel like things are too much the same."

"What do you mean?" she asked.

"Well, you know, like how you feel like everything's just happening the exact same way, over and over again?" She stared blankly at me. I honestly couldn't tell if she'd even heard me. "I guess what I'm trying to say is I'm just tired of the same old thing happening. I know that sounds stupid."

"No, honey," she said sympathetically. "You're just bored, that's all. Here." She began getting up from the bed. She started toward the dresser and pulled out and put on a T-shirt and a pair of jeans. "Come on, why don't we have a day out, the three of us. Hannah doesn't have school today. She'll love it!"

I looked confused for a second. "What're you wanting to do, exactly?"

"Why don't we have a picnic at the park?" My face drained of color. "What? You said we needed a change of pace, and plus, we haven't done anything together in a while." I continued staring at her, petrified. "Come on, it'll be fun."

I wanted to protest. I didn't, though. What was I supposed to say? I honestly wasn't sure what the problem was, myself. That said, though, I still just couldn't help but have the feeling something was wrong. Wrong with the park, wrong with that girl. Just... *wrong*...

The two of us got dressed and got Hannah up before piling into the car. We stopped at the cafè just across the street from the park and ordered two of their family-sized food platters for the picnic before walking over.

We left the car parked at the cafè. Easier than trying to find a single empty parking space in the crowded-as-hell park area. I didn't mind. I figured, should anything take a turn to the left, me and the girls could just run like hell to the cafè, especially since we were the only ones parked there, making it easy enough to keep up with.

As well as this, seeing other people there DID help ease my nerves a bit. Just a bit. I still couldn't help, though, but wonder what that meant; me being "the only one left."

There were other people. Then and now.

Weren't there?

I mean, sure, like I said, the mornings were usually pretty quiet.

Weren't they?

Something started stirring in my head. I'd been here before; at the park. I'd been here. Hannah had been here. *She'd been here.*

Edna said that we hadn't gone together to the park in forever, except... except we *had!* Edna told me twice in a row that I'd had night terrors for three nights straight. Why were the same things happening over and over?

Why do I keep coming here?

We sat down in a clear patch of grass, the only spot where there weren't people covering every inch of the ground. As we dug into the food, I kept looking nervously around. I darted my eyes left and right, in front of and behind me, wondering if, at any moment, I was going to see the little girl and have to snatch my family up and book it the hell out of there.

I didn't see her. I saw millions of people, all mixing or mingling together. But no little girl (well, at least, not THE little girl). Still, my guard stayed up. I knew she was out there. I couldn't see her, but I knew she was there. Almost like I could actually *feel* her there, you know?

"Daddy, daddy," Hannah squealed. I turned to see her running off into the playground area. "Try to catch me!"

I hesitated. I didn't want to move. Didn't want to go to the playground. Even worse, I didn't want Hannah to go into the playground. *Hadn't this also happened before?*

I looked at Edna. "Well, go on," she urged, chuckling. I looked back to the playground. I could just barely see Hannah. I made my way to my feet and started speed-walking toward the playground.

I focused on trying to keep sight of Hannah. As long as I could see her, see her and everybody else, things would be fine. They were still there.

I wouldn't be the only one left.

I waded through the crowds of people. All around me, people were laughing, screaming, and just generally carrying on. It was chaotic. Still, I just kept my eyes forward, my focus solely on keeping track of Hannah.

I could hear her giggling as she ran. She sped past each and every person in her way. She was so far ahead now. People were clustering more and more in front of me. Thousands of people, thousands of bodies, grouping together, cutting me off from her.

"Hannah!" I called out. I was shoving my way furiously past the crowd. I couldn't see her anymore. She vanished completely into the crowd. "Hannah!"

I could still hear her giggling. It seemed to drown out most of the noise around me. I couldn't hear the crowd anymore. Everything became a sort of droning hum around me, with her giggling being the only thing distinguishable from anything else. "Hannah!"

The giggling was louder now. I couldn't even hear the droning of other people anymore. I was surrounded, everybody bumping and knocking me around, cutting me off from the jungle gym. *From Hannah.*

I closed my eyes and started aggressively shoving everybody around me aside. All I could hear was giggling. I pushed and shoved until I couldn't feel anything around me to push or shove away.

Until there was nobody left...

I opened my eyes again. There wasn't anybody around anymore. I could still hear giggling, though. "Hannah?"

No answer, no Hannah. Only giggling.

"Hannah! Where are you, sweetie?" I looked all around.

No answer, no Hannah. Only giggling.

"Alright, y-you got me punkin'. Y-you win, okay, time to come out."

No answer, no Hannah. Only giggling.

"Hannah, come on, sweetie, this isn't funny. Daddy's getting scared!"

No answer...

My heart jackhammered in my chest. Color drained from my face. My body felt cold. I started walking to the jungle gym. I couldn't see her.

No Hannah...

I looked around. The playground was empty. There was no one there.

No one left...

I was alone. It was quiet. Still. The only thing I could hear... was giggling.

"Wanna play a game of Hide-n'-go-seek?" I spun around. There she was, that goddamned little girl, standing a foot away from me, waving with her little dimple-cheeked grin.

She giggled again. I started shaking, my knees feeling like boiled spaghetti.

"Where is she?" I asked, feeling anxiety shooting up through my chest, threatening to burst out at any second, sending me into a heart attack.

"Who, mister?" she squeaked, still grinning.

"My daughter, everybody else, where are they?!" I could feel the desperation in my voice, turning it abrasive. I was caught between the instinct to run up and choke the life out of this little girl until she showed me where Hannah was and just wanting to crumple into a ball and cry, right there on the playground.

"What do you mean, mister? There is nobody else." She giggled again and said, "You're the only one left."

"What're you talking about? There were people here, *just now*! What happened to them? Where'd they go?" She just stood, grinning sweetly at me, like she was asking to help someone cross the street. I looked around, desperately trying to spot my daughter or *anybody* else.

"There's no one else 'round to play with me anymore, mister. You're the only one."

"What is going on? Who are you, and why are you doing this to me?!" Her smile fell. Now she looked shy, like she'd gotten caught doing something she wasn't supposed to.

"I just wanna play," she said pitifully. "There's no one else to play with me anymore."

"What do you mean? There were *thousands* of people here, most of them kids, too. What happened to them?"

"They never won the game. They couldn't find me." Her eyes started to glisten as her skin started to turn a ghoulish, sickly pale. "No one could find me."

Her cheeks started to shrink, growing smaller and smaller until I started to see her bones pushing out against them. She opened her mouth and hissed at me in the raspy voice from before, "But I would find them. They would never win, and now, they'll never leave."

My heart stopped. "W-Where are they?" I stammered, shuddering. She looked at the ground and back at me. I looked down.

"They're gone now. I kept finding them until their time ran out."

"What do you mean 'time ran out?' Look, what do you want from me?"

"I want you to play with me. I want you to find me, unlike them." She looked back at the ground. "They all gave up. Now they'll never leave."

"Leave where? Where did they g—" My throat tightened when I saw walls of darkness around us again. The girl looked up at me again.

"They're in the dark now. They didn't wanna play no more, so they left. I wanted to keep playing, but the others left me behind. They told me I was too good. I'd always find them, but they couldn't find me. They never could, so they quit and left me behind."

"What... What are you talking about? Why am I the only one?" Her skin then started further decaying, falling apart until she was just a child-sized skeleton standing in front of me. Her eyes were the only things to remain, looking stark set in her empty sockets. My throat tightened again.

Her mandible lowered, and she rasped, "They left me here till it was dark, and they never came back for me. They always leave because they can't find me, but I'd always find them. Now, you're the only one who hasn't left yet."

The darkness got closer. I was frozen. Her withered, bony arms raised up and covered her naked eyes. "Now," she hissed, "I'm gonna count to ten. You better hide." I opened my mouth, wanting to protest, wanting to press her to tell me where my daughter was, but nothing came out.

"Ten, nine, eight..."

Time felt like it had slowed. My legs were stiff, rooted to the ground. Every thought raced through my mind.

"Seven, six, five, four..."

Finally, I broke from entropy and took off into the jungle gym. I frantically looked for any place that'd serve as a secluded enough hiding spot. I wanted to go for the tube slide, curl up into a ball and wait there, except...

Except I'd done that before!

I thought about trying to run out of the park, booking it on foot back home, even without my wife and daughter. But the problem was, I'd tried that, too, hadn't I? I thought about standing still, just letting the little brat have me, but I'd done that, too.

All of these things, they'd happened before. They'd happened before, and there I was, trapped again, forced to repeat this, whatever this was. I had to do something different.

I had to win.

"Ready or not, here I come."

I crouched down, ducking underneath one of the step ways leading up to the top of the jungle gym. From where I was, I could just faintly see her as she started toward the jungle gym. She looked around the swing sets first before moving on to the little play domes in the kiddie area that the smaller children would crawl and play around in without getting trampled like they would in the regular jungle gym.

When she came out of there, she moved to the tube slides. "I know you're somewhere around here," she hissed. I watched her circle around it, tapping on the sides of it. Then, she crawled up and into it. The one she crawled in through led to the area directly above me.

I quickly and quietly began scooting my way away from where I was. I started heading for the splash area, where I'd be able to hide at the top of the giant slip n' slide that led to the small kiddie pool with the sprinkler field. From there, I figured I'd also be able to keep an eye out for her. I made it there, trying to run as hastily as possible without making too much noise, and climbed to the top and waited.

I thought the best way to be able to beat her was to keep an eye out for her. I knew I couldn't just hide in one secluded place and wait her out. Whoever she was, and whatever she was doing, I realized she had a home-field advantage. She said no one could find her, while she always knew where *they* were. In other words, she knew all the hiding spots.

So instead, I had to keep moving while also keeping my focus on watching her, turning this little cat-and-mouse game around on her. For a while, everything stayed quiet. I didn't see her, still in the jungle gym about four feet from the splash area. I remained alert, ready to move.

"Gee…" I heard her say hoarsely. "This sure is tricky." I saw her coming out of the jungle gym. I ducked down, still just barely peeking out. "You in here, mister?"

She waded into the kiddie pool. "I wonder if you're hiding under here like a fish." I heard her let out what I could only guess was supposed to be her trademark giggle, only a wheezing parody of it, before adding, "I like fish." Then she ducked under the water. I took this as the opportunity to move again. I scrambled back down the steps and took off towards the soccer field/picnic area.

I looked back over my shoulder once as I ran. She hadn't come up yet. Admittedly, a small part of me hoped maybe she wouldn't come back up, like maybe she'd drown or something. I wasn't gonna put chips on that number, though. I had to keep going.

I made it to one of the picnic pavilions. Looking around, I wasn't sure what to do. There weren't really any places I could hide. Worse, the walls of darkness I saw were now closer. They were closing me in, trying to shut me out from running anywhere else.

I started to panic, swinging my head in every direction until I landed on one thing. One place I could possibly hide where she might not find me. A trash can at the far end of the pavilion.

I looked back one more time. She still hadn't come out of the splash area. I bolted to the trash can and stuffed myself inside, keeping the lid cracked open just enough to see out. Like before, some time went by with no sight of her.

What I did see, however, frightened me just as much. The walls were now all around the pavilion. The pavilion and the stretch of distance leading to the splash area were all that was left. This was it. Nowhere else to run or hide.

Finally, here she came, making a beeline for the picnic area. My body seized up. I could feel sweat forming in bullets on my forehead. "Where are ya, mister? I can't find ya."

I could see her eyes, wide and twitching excitedly. Her skeletal body was shaking. "Where are you?!" she shrieked. I watched her somehow, despite being only a little girl, supernatural or not, rip the picnic table from the cement and hold it up to look underneath. "You under here?!"

Seeing this caused me to shrink lower into the trash can. She stayed like this for a moment before slamming it back down, causing it to snap in half. I was shaking now, trying to hold myself still to not give my position away.

She started doing the same to the other picnic tables, ripping them up and even tossing them to the side like wrapping paper from a Christmas present. She started shrieking and howling.

She's getting desperate...

Soon, she turned her attention to the trash can. Like the picnic tables, she picked up the can and hurled it through the air. The can landed hard on its side, and I ended up cracking my head against the side, knocking me dizzy. My head felt so light yet so heavy at the same time, and everything felt like it was twisting and spinning.

Both my hearing and vision were blurred. I could just barely hear the little girl as she shrieked again, "WHERE ARE YOU!" I stayed put, being mostly too dazed to move anyway. Her shrieking and howling grew louder and louder, becoming damn near deafening.

The walls of darkness inched nearer. Nearer. Slowly, they began swallowing the pavilion. The little girl picked up one of the picnic tables again and hurled it again at one of them.

The wall closest to me began to eat the ground around the trash can as I began to slip from consciousness.

Faintly, I heard the deranged shrieking devolve into pitiful sobbing. Soon, the ground around me was gone, and the sobbing got fainter and fainter. Then... blackout.

I woke up in my bed. This time, I wasn't panicking. I wasn't sweating or out of breath. I wasn't ready to run screaming either. It was quiet. Calm.

I was in my bed. Edna was beside me, snuggled against my chest. I stroked her hair.

Everything felt calm, soothing. Everything had felt like a bad dream. Just a dream. Though, everything was alright now. Right?

I sat up and looked out. Outside, people were walking about, mingling like usual. Everything was normal, as it always had been.

Hadn't it?

Edna stirred awake. "Tim, what's going on? What's wrong?" I looked at her. She looked confused and groggy.

She did before, too.

I was going to open my mouth to speak, telling her "nothing" when I stopped. I'd said that to her before. Just like last time and the time before that. She had asked me the exact same question at the exact same time, and I'd replied the exact same way.

It's all happened before.

That's when I also realized, that this sequence always somehow, in one way or another, led to going to the park. That would then, inevitably lead to the little girl. To playing another little game of Hide-n'-go-seek."

I looked out of the window again. I decided, like how I made it out of the game, I would have to change my tactics here, starting with this very conversation.

"I thought I heard sirens outside. I hope no one got hurt."

"What kind of sirens?" she asked.

"Police sirens, I think."

"Oh, God. Maybe you should skip your morning jog, at least till the smoke blows over." I looked at her and grinned.

"Yeah, I think you're right. We'll stay in today. Wanna watch a movie?"

"Ooh," she squealed excitedly. "Hell yeah! We haven't done that together in a while, and Hannah's home from daycare today. She'd love it."

"Yeah," I sighed. "That'd be a nice change of pace."

***

About the Author

PsychoToxin Press

Thomas Stewart is 21 years old with a fascination with the art of terror and the macabre. When he's not watching horror movies, or reading horror novels or stories, he's always crafting his own chilling gospels of horror to terrify and eternally rob you of a peaceful slumber.

Other Works From This Author Links

Damned Whispers
The Other Side
Masks of Death

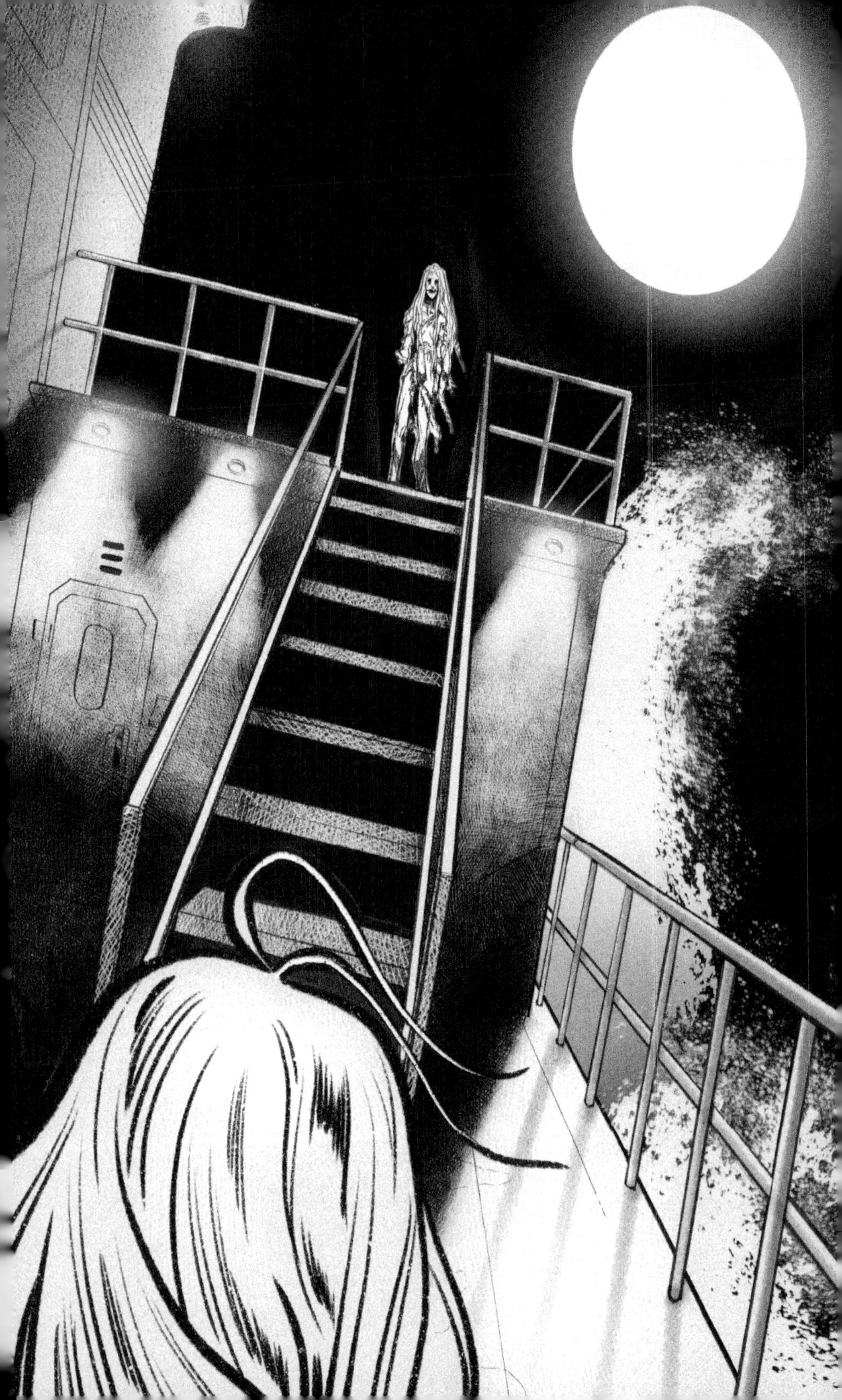

Hark, Now I Hear Them

by Brandon Ebinger

*F**ull fathom five thy father lies;*
Of his bones are coral made;
Those are pearls that were his eyes:
Nothing of him that doth fade,
But doth suffer a sea-change
Into something rich and strange.
Sea-nymphs hourly ring his knell:
Ding-dong.
Hark! now I hear them—Ding-dong, bell.
William Shakespeare *The Tempest*

It is estimated that 2,000 men and women lose their lives to the sea every year, many of which, are never found.

1

It was in the home stretch that *The Gemma* ran into trouble. Normally, it was a routine five to ten days from the Port of New York and New Jersey to the Port of Piraeus in Athens, and another five to ten back. Nothing that Kathy hadn't done many, many times before. However, it seemed that this time, fate had other plans.

"The whole thing's fucked," Leon, the navigating officer, said, turning away from his equipment to face Kathy, a forced smile on his face. She and Leon had served together many times and had bonded over a mutual interest in video games and Magic: The Gathering, interests that seemed all too rare among the working-class people that normally chose to make their living hauling crates from ship to port (and vice versa). Even when she was a newbie, mocked and derided for being a woman, Leon had been friendly to her, and now that she had proven herself to most of the old-timers (a task which she accomplished by doing twice the work for half the acclaim) he remained her best friend off-land.

"Define 'fucked,'" Kathy said, returning his smile.

"It's like I said," Leon responded. "All messed up, totally *pilattu.*"

Leon had carefully crafted an accent that was so neutral that it still surprised Kathy when he slipped into his native Finnish, even after all these years.

"What are they picking up?" she asked.

"To put it simply, my dear, they aren't."

2

Kathy sighed, staring blankly out into the endlessness that seemed to surround her. There were many psychological perils to life at sea, from depression to homesickness to a creeping sense of agoraphobia that moved in here like nowhere else on planet Earth. To Kathy, however, the worst was the boredom, the endless days of pure *nothing* that stretched on and on until they became bleak soldiers, marching slowly but surely on her psyche until all she wanted to do was scream at the top of her lungs until the poison was drained. No matter how many times she went out, how many years she served on merchant vessels, the boredom always found her eventually.

And now she was going to be out here even longer.

They had reported the problems to Captain Pierce, a quiet, stoic man that appeared every bit the stereotypical salty sea dog, from his leathery skin to his salt-and-pepper beard. He had responded by asking, as calmly as if he were speaking about the results of a recent sports event, how many days it would add to the trip. Leon had assured him that he would be able, if all went well from here on, to get them back to port in an additional day or two using manual calculations.

"That quickly?" Pierce had said, his fluffy eyebrows raising. "Even with no computer data?"

Leon had nodded. "It's a game I play anyway, trying to chart courses using just my head and a paper map, seeing how close I get to what the computer comes up with. I like to think it makes my ancestors proud." Leon came from a long line of fishermen and sailors, and he never seemed to tire of joking about it with the other seamen.

So now, two days of crippling boredom (that no amount of movies, music, or fantasy card games could quite alleviate) instead had become three or four.

Kathy sighed again. She sometimes wondered why she put herself, again and again, in this situation, but realized that, even with her almost psychotic aversion to boredom, she loved the sea life. Even in her wildest fantasies, she couldn't imagine doing anything else.

"I can do this," she said, her words carried out to sea by the gentle winds. "I can do this."

3

That night Kathy heard the noise for the first time. Returning from her watch shift (11:00-2:00 GMT), she fell almost instantly into a sleep so deep that the noise didn't wake her, weaving itself instead into the tapestry of her dreams.

Kathy was eight years old again, sitting at the end of a long table, surrounded by her family and favorite people from school. She had just cut into her favorite cake (black velvet, with just the right level of creamy goodness) and was about to take a bite when she first noticed the sound.

It started out subtle, mixed almost subconsciously with the din of party sounds and "real world" sounds of the night sea and the ship that was floating upon it. The sound slowly grew louder, however, and before long, became a mournful wail, an utter ululation that threatened to overcome everything around her.

"What's going on?" she asked her guests, who sat frozen, their grins rictus, having not been told that the pleasant dream-script had been changed.

Kathy stood up, her now small legs carrying her through her childhood home, past the familiar bookcases and overstuffed chairs and shiny bright kitchen utensils, searching for the origin of the sound, which seemed to emanate from the walls themselves. Though her logical, conscious mind told her that this new development should be disturbing, her dream-thoughts found it calming, welcoming. Somehow, she just knew that whoever was singing (she found herself no longer thinking of the interruption as a noise, but a song) was the same being who gave her the wonderful dream-memory to begin with.

She had begun to climb the stairs to what had once been her bedroom when she saw another figure, taller than her child-form but still small, standing at the top of the stairs, mouth open wide, one hand extended to Kathy in friendship...

Someone was pounding on the door to her sleeping berth.

"Wha?" she muttered, pushing away the dream cobwebs as she spoke.

"Hey, it's me," a familiar voice called from behind the door.

"Leon?" Kathy asked, pulling herself into a sitting position. "What's up?"

"We can't find Trace. He's gone missing."

4

Ryan "Trace" Tracy was one of the good ones. Undaunted by his small stature and high, melodic voice, he quickly got past the jeers and insults of his fellow sailors when they realized that not only could he make the tasteless food that they were often forced to subsist off of delicious, but he could also outfight men twice his size. Not that he was a violent man, far from it, but when faced with danger, there was nobody you'd rather have on your side.

He was also, to put it quite simply, likable, and this quickly got past the seemingly inborn biases of the others. Kathy (who as one of the only women in her line of work and therefore also a veteran of the derision wars) respected him a great deal.

And now he was missing.

They searched the ship, stem to stern, three times, finding not a single trace of the cook. Finally, they were forced to conclude that, for whatever bizarre reason, he was no longer aboard.

"This sucks," Leon muttered, kicking a wall.

"It really does," Kathy agreed.

"Where the hell could he have even *gone*?"

Kathy shrugged, unconsciously looking out to the endless waves. She was reminded of an old saying, repeated again and again by her shipmates until it became a part of her personal subconscious as well, "*Everything aboard a ship sucks but the vacuum cleaners.*"

"You didn't see anything, right?" Leon asked. "You were on watch before he disappeared, right?"

"Maybe," she said. "It was either me or Carlos, who replaced me 'bout an hour and a half before you woke me up."

"Carlos said he didn't see anything."

Kathy nodded. "I didn't see anything either."

They fell into silence once more. Leon stopped kicking walls and sat down, pulling his deck of Magic cards from a pocket of his cargo pants and absently shuffling them.

"Wanna play?" he asked.

"I'll have to get my cards, but yeah."

"This sucks," Leon repeated.

"Unlike our vacuums," Kathy responded by rote.

5

On the second night, sleep did not come easy.

Kathy tossed and turned, twisting violently this way and that, desperately seeking the magical position that would allow her (temporary) escape from the waking world and its myriad worries. Finally, pillow folded in half beneath her head, she succumbed to her tiredness.

Now she was nineteen years old, gloriously free from her parents' rule and loving every minute of it. Standing now in the grimy nightclub bathroom, she smiled into the cracked mirror. She had always been fascinated with places like this, where one could get lost in the flashing lights and throbbing music, but having overbearingly conservative (but well-meaning! Her mind insisted) parents meant that it had remained a fancy.

But now she had her own place, a little studio apartment with cracked walls in the city, just like in her childhood fantasies, and no one could tell her what she could (and could not) do.

Outside of the bathroom, the music suddenly changed. The simple 4/4 beats becoming something altogether slower, more mournful. This new song filled Kathy with a deep longing that she couldn't quite explain, and she made her way, like a somnambulist, to the bathroom door, which swung open before her.

A small figure stood on the other side, her pale hand reaching out, imploring Kathy to take it...

It was the coldness of the metal stairs against Kathy's bare feet that woke her. She was still dressed in her sleeping clothes (an old Alice in Chains shirt and black shorts) and had, somehow, found her way out of the berth and into the stairwell leading above deck. She noticed that her arm was extended, as if reaching for something, and quickly lowered it.

"What the hell?" Kathy said aloud. Who knows where she would have ended up if she hadn't been startled awake when she did. Aboard *The Gemma*, the possibilities were as varied as they were deadly.

"That you, Kathy?" a ragged voice called from below her, from the bottom of the stairs.

"Yeah," she responded, blinking to shake off the sleep and turning to face the voice.

"What in God's glory are you doing lurking around at this time of night, kiddo?" The voice belonged to Xavier, an OS that Kathy had served with several times before.

"Just out for a walk," she responded. For some reason, Kathy didn't feel comfortable telling this man the whole story. "So, what are *you* doing?"

"Oh." Xavier chuckled. "Just looking for my errant bunkmate. Kid is off wandering somewhere. Must be the night for it or somethin.'"

"Yeah. Must be," Kathy said.

Later on, they would find out that Xavier's bunkmate, a kid who looked like he was barely old enough to shave, had also gone missing.

6

Captain Pierce was furious. "How, in the holy Hell, do we lose two people on a tiny boat like this, in the middle of nowhere?" He snarled at the remaining crew, who had all gathered in the mess after the second fruitless search in so many days.

Nobody had a good answer, so they remained silent.

"Did they even know each other?" Pierce wondered aloud. "Is this some sort of crazy suicide pact thing or something? Did they jump overboard hand in hand or some craziness?"

The assembled crew remained silent.

Pierce clenched a fist and pulled it back, but instead of punching the wall (which he really wanted to do) he took a deep breath, relaxing his hand. "Do any of you have any good news for a change?"

"I just might," Leon said.

Pierce raised an eyebrow.

"Well, not about the missing people, I got nothing on that front. But... even with our equipment all frazzled, I was able to get us back on track."

Pierce made a *go on, keep talking* gesture.

"And... if my calculations are correct, and I think they are, we should be back in New York tomorrow."

Pierce's facial expression remained unchanged as he stood up.

"Well, that is good news. Just keep your eyes peeled for Xavier and Trace. I don't want to explain to their families why we came back without them."

Kathy and Leon sat together on Kathy's bunk, drinking the remnants of their dinner coffee. As usual, it was pretty bad but strong enough to peel paint.

It was exactly what they needed.

"So..." Kathy said, taking a sip of the coffee, managing to only wince a little at its bitterness. "What's up?"

"It's about the disappearances," Leon said, staring into his cup instead of at Kathy.

"I figured," she replied.

"I wanted to ask you..." Leon trailed off.

"Yes?"

"Well... the past two nights... I've sorta been having... well..."

"Weird dreams?"

Leon's eyes grew wide. "How did you know?"

"I've been having them too."

"Really? Like really good dreams, about..."

"Good times in your life?"

"Yes."

"Like, I dreamed I was out hunting with my dad last night. I never liked hunting, never could quite get myself to kill anything, but just being there, smelling his aftershave and everything. It was one of my favorite times as a kid."

Kathy nodded, and they sat in silence for a moment.

"I guess what I'm saying is that I don't wanna sleep tonight." In that moment, Leon looked younger than his years, a little boy clutching a teddy bear. Kathy wasn't sure why he had come to her with this, where she ranked in his mind to allow this vulnerability, but she decided to not question it much. After all, she was happy for the company.

"Me neither," she replied. "I don't even want to close my eyes until we're back on shore."

"Mind if I sit with you, *ystävä?*" Leon asked.

"Nope," she replied.

They sipped their coffee and waited, both of them exerting their will to stay awake.

Kathy's eyes fluttered.

She forced them open.

She blinked.

Five minutes passed.

Then ten.

Fifteen.

Kathy was aboard another ship, younger and with more spring in her step. A routine bit of maintenance (deemed unimportant and forgotten to her dream-mind) had kept her a few moments, and she was a bit late to meal call. She paused at the door to the mess, imagining the jeers and jokes that the guys would fill the air with, blaming her lateness on "girl problems" or "emotional instability" or some other foolishness. And on this day of all days...

She pushed the door open.

"Surprise!" the other crewmen shouted in unison, as a dozen balloons floated to the ceiling.

She stood, agog.

"You made it five years!" Leon said, slapping her on the shoulder. "Congrats!"

She smiled, wanting to cry in joy but not wanting to give the men the satisfaction. She knew that this was a sign that they had accepted her, finally saw her as a valid member of the crew, a hand that could be not only relied on but befriended. She was no longer "the girl." She had become "one of the guys."

Except, she wasn't the only girl in the room.

That's not right. I was the only woman on board that day, as usual.

Even though Kathy couldn't see the woman, she knew (through the magic of dreams) that she was there. The other crewmen froze in place, grinning widely like something from a surreal painting, as the sound (song) began once more.

She saw the figure moving in the crowd. It reached out its hand to Kathy...

"No!" Kathy shouted, propelling herself from sleep.

"I'm awake, I'm awake!" she said, looking to her right, where Leon had sat what seemed like seconds before.

He was nowhere in sight.

7

"Leon?" Kathy called out as she made her way out of the berth and down the narrow hallway leading to the stairwell. She somehow knew that if her friend was anywhere on the ship, she would find him here, where she had found herself the night before.

There was no reply.

Though it could never be said to be *quiet* on a ship, the air held an eerie stillness that made Kathy doubt, just for a moment, her wakefulness.

She made her way up the stairs, now and again calling out for her friend, loud enough to be heard by those still awake but quiet enough (she hoped) as to not to startle her fellow crewmen from their sleep. Finally, she was at the top of the stairs, at the large steel door that led above decks.

Kathy knew that there was a lot of ship that she was leaving unsearched, but, trusting her gut over her mind, she quietly opened the door and ascended to the deck.

Cold sea-wind smacked her across the face, causing her hair to fly in every which direction and shattering, one and for all, the illusion that she could still be dreaming. She hunched her head and shoulders against the wind and continued her search. It did not take long, even in the less-than-ideal conditions, to find what she was looking for.

A girl stood on the railing of the ship, somehow balancing herself and bracing against the wind, a feat that Kathy would have said was impossible, especially when you took into account the girl's small size. Hell, Kathy doubted that she would be able to accomplish this feat, and she was twice this kid's size.

Kathy took a few more steps, and the girl began to take form, details rising toward Kathy through the wet air.

The girl looked young, early twenties at the oldest, and slender, her slim body wrapped in a sea-faded gauze shift, which waved and snapped in the wind. Her skin was the pale white of a fish's belly, and her long blonde hair had a greenish tint and hung in a tangled mess to her slim waist. Even from a distance, Kathy could smell the girl, briny and damp. She had no doubt that this girl was the "figure" from her dreams.

Kathy took another step forward and saw that the girl held another figure in her arms, a larger form that Kathy recognized at once as Leon. He lay limp in her arms, unmoving.

The girl bent at the shoulders, in a contortion that should have been impossible, and brought her face to Leon's. At first glance, Kathy thought the girl was kissing him but realized that her mouth was positioned not on Leon's lips but against one of his closed eyelids.

With a sickening sucking sound, the girl pulled her head back. Something red and wet connected Leon's head to the girl for a moment, then she twisted her head violently, and the crimson cord snapped and fell against Leon's cheek, leaving a trail of red down his sunburned face.

"Hey!" Kathy shouted, struck stupid by what she had just witnessed.

I know that that girl didn't just suck out Leon's eye. That's impossible! I must still be dreaming, wind be damned!

The girl smiled, and between her red teeth (small and pointed, like those of a river pike) sat a gooey globe, just the right size and shape to be, no matter how much Kathy tried to deny it, Leon's eye. Then the girl closed her mouth suddenly, to the accompaniment of a popping sound that Kathy could somehow hear over the howling wind. The girl began to chew with a playful smile.

Kathy, freed from her shock-paralysis, rushed toward the girl, only to stop suddenly once more.

It was a feeling that stopped her from rushing the girl, from giving in to her primal instincts and protecting her (quite probably dead) friend. It was a feeling of immense power and age, the sort of feeling that Kathy imagined came from witnessing something beyond the threshold of what one had seen before, the feeling an astronaut may get while gazing out a spaceship window, perhaps, or the feeling a child from a landlocked land may feel, deep in their bones, when gazing upon the ocean for the first time.

She knew that if she were to look overboard (a feat that she found quite impossible in her state) she would see the water rippling and splashing, disturbed by whatever immense being was causing all of these feelings. She also knew that to do such a thing, to actually witness the being itself, would cause her to start screaming and never stop, at least until a host of white-masked doctors filled her full of happy juice and left her a vegetable.

The thrashing in the water grew louder, more frantic. Kathy could now hear the disturbed waves splashing against the steel of the ship's side. In that moment, she understood the people in endless films and books, who, when faced with something beyond their ken, dropped to their knees in terror or fainted dead away. She realized, for the first time in her life, that there were indeed things that the human mind couldn't wrap around.

There are more things in Heaven and Earth...
And that didn't even call into account the sea...

The girl yelled then, her high-pitched voice (the same one from the dreams, Kathy was sure of it!) cutting through the sounds of the water and wind, machine and sleeping men. The scream was in no language known to Kathy, but she recognized it at once as not only a word, but a name, said with utter reverence. Whatever was in the water, Kathy realized with horror, was akin to a god to this strange, eye-eating girl. Then the girl straightened up in a graceful wave and, with seemingly no effort, lifted Leon's body with one delicate hand.

His body dangled there, for just a second, and then the girl let him go, again yelling the eldritch name as she did so. When Leon hit the water, the thrashing became more violent for a moment and then grew still.

The girl turned and looked at Kathy, again smiling her needle-tooth smile. She brought one slender finger to her lips and pressed it there, hissing a soft, "Ssssh."

"Go back to bed, dear poppet," the girl said, and then, with the grace of an Olympic diver, was over the side of the ship and gone into the darkness.

Kathy's eyes fluttered, and then closed. Slowly and ploddingly, she made her way back down the stairs and to her bunk. She slid under the rough sheets and, like a child, tired from a day of festivities, she slept soundly until *The Gemma* found its way, safe and sound, into port.

8

Kathy's memories of the trip were spotty, at best. She vaguely remembered snippets of memories (was there some sort of party onboard? Some sort of cake?) and a strange sense of loss, though what, or who she had lost, was a mystery.

She would never eat grapes again. Something about the shape and texture filled her with revulsion now. "I'm allergic," she would say, though she had no allergies that she was aware of.

She continued to go out to sea. In fact, she took on even more jobs, feeling especially drawn to those bringing her into the waters of the Ionian sea, bringing her close to Greece. During these voyages, she would sometimes feel restless and spent many nights staring out into the vast ocean, like a widow from an old movie, waiting for her lover to return from the war.

***

About the Author

Twitter | Faceboook

Brandon Ebinger is a horror/dark fantasy writer that lives in Western New York with his fiance and cat. He likes video games, Gothic Rock music and all things Halloween. He holds a BA in creative writing and works as a haunt actor when the season is right.

Other Works From This Author Links
Broken Night
"Faze" and "Blood Sisters"
"On Jensen's Farm"
"First Night Out"

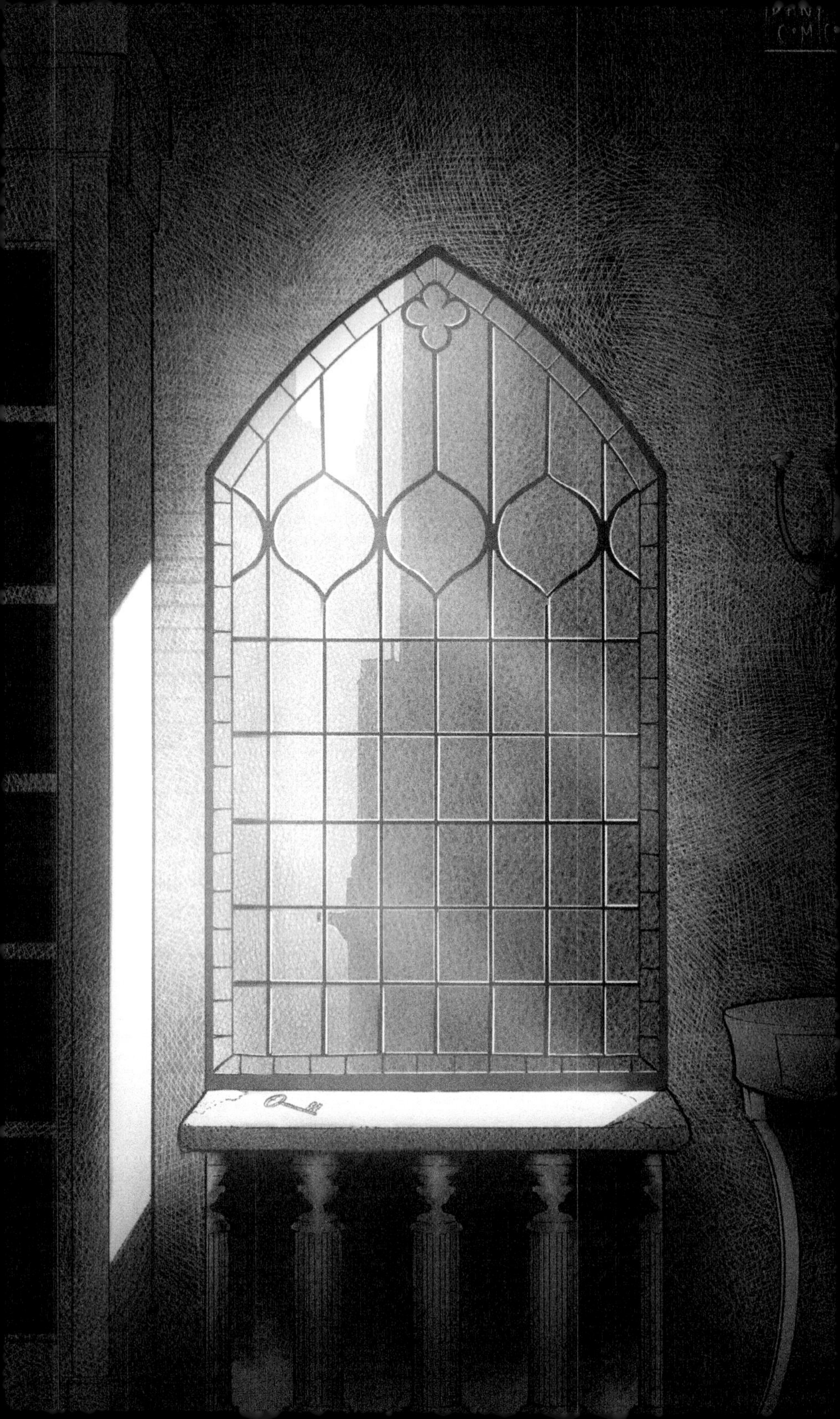

A Nook Obscure

by Thomas Bales

Sober scholars will tell you that there is no staircase J in the second court of St John's College. These same scholars will explain that this is because the Latin alphabet leaps straight from I to K, and any self-respecting college of Cambridge University will have Latin at its heart.

While it's not for me to comment on how self-respecting colleges think, I can tell you that in the case at hand, the scholars are mistaken. There is a staircase J in the second court of St John's College, but centuries ago, tragedy began to befall all who set foot upon it. Fortunately, the occultist John Dee was an alumnus of the college. So quiet words were had over wine, then quiet words were chanted beneath a blood moon, and staircase J was hidden from the eyes of all but adepts in the mystical arts.

Unfortunately for me, I have some small talent in those arts.

I first noticed staircase J on my sister's birthday.

It was also the day of my admission to college as a research fellow in philosophy. To answer your questions: yes, philosophers do still exist in the 21st century; and no, my parents were not impressed by my choice of career.

The admission ceremony took place in the wood-panelled splendour of the combination room, where the fellows had gathered along one wall to watch. Across from them, drizzle-speckled windows looked out over Second Court to red-brick walls twined in mist. Thinking back, it would be tempting to imagine that I felt foreboding on witnessing the mist's spectral writhings. Yet I believe in speaking the truth, and the truth is that in the warmth of the combination room, I barely noticed the world beyond the windows.

I was dressed in a suit and academic gown, and when my name was called, I swore an oath beneath fickle candlelight. Sober scholars will be pleased to know that the master of the college recited his response in Latin, and so I was admitted.

This ceremony was to be followed by a Domus evening, a dinner to give the fellows a chance to mingle. But "Domus" means family, and on this day of all days, I felt disquiet when I thought of this word.

Family.

It seemed to me that on that night, my thoughts should be on my sister and not on the celebration. So I declined the invitation to dinner and opened the door to Second Court. The cold hit me, and I almost changed my mind, glancing back as the last of the fellows stepped into the medieval hall. Then the door swung closed behind them, and suddenly it felt too late to reconsider, even though doors once closed can be reopened.

I stepped out into Second Court. It was as I hurried across the cobbles, that staircase J caught my eyes through the mists, though I couldn't tell you why it drew my attention. It looked no different to the other staircases: a doorway with no door and, beyond this, the stairs.

Above the doorway, the windows were dark, but for one at the top of the building, which was illuminated by the flickerings of a candle. A figure was framed in this light—a student, I assumed at the time, though there was something familiar in the way they stood as they stared down into the court.

Then the figure stepped away from the window, the candle was extinguished, and I thought no more of it as I continued to my room.

I liked living in college. Each day, I'd eat lunch at fellows' table, and I was made to feel welcome for all that I was new, and the others were old friends (or occasionally, old and quiescent enemies). On warm days I would walk the paths along the river and watch people fall into the water from their punts. I even enjoyed the sounds of students partying; in those times, I wore my loneliness heavily, and there was serenity in realising others were finding joy.

Yet living in college could also be hard. I should confess that I'm prone to spells of anxiety, and when such spells strike, I find it agonising to be noticed—agonising to be looked at or spoken to or to find myself on the same planet as other humans. In college, I could never escape those who knew me. If I missed lunch, people would comment.

If I sought serenity in a riverside stroll, I would run into someone who wanted to talk.

It was on one of those anxious days, as I walked through Second Court, that I saw the friendliest of the fellows walking towards me. In moments of anxiety, nothing is more terrifying than friendliness, so I took the only sane option available. I adopted a look of panicked rush and, trying to make it seem like this had always been my destination, I stepped through a nearby doorway and onto the staircase beyond.

I stepped onto staircase J.

I ascended the steps, which formed a tight spiral of foot-worn wood, and the climb was almost hypnotic. With a straight staircase, landings break the pattern of your tread, but with a spiral, the rhythm of your footsteps need never be broken. Perhaps that's what lulled me into continuing upwards even once I could no longer be seen from the court.

At the top of the stairs was a landing. At the end of the landing was a door. The door stood open.

The small room beyond was coated in dust. There was dust on the floorboards, dust on the chair and the heavy oak desk by the window, dust on the mantle above the fire and on the tarnished silver candlesticks that sat upon it. No one had set foot here for some time.

This raised a question: if the room had long been unoccupied, then who had I seen on the Domus evening standing in this very window?

Still, on noticing this puzzle, I dismissed it, thinking that perhaps I was confused about where I'd glanced. Knowing what I know now, all I can say in defence of my foolishness is that, at the time, I had no reason to think the occult was in play. Even one adept in the mystical arts doesn't assume magic when mundane incompetence suffices as an explanation. So I thought no more of it.

I stepped into the room.

My feet kicked up flurries of dust as I walked to the desk, and I had to wipe the chair clean before sitting. From here, I could look out over Second Court, which was deserted despite Lent Term having started a week before.

Beyond the desk, on the windowsill, there was a key. I picked it up. It was heavy and old, and I walked the few paces needed to confirm that it fitted in the heavy, old lock of the door. Then, because I am an upright type, I returned the key to the windowsill, placing it just as I'd found it. In so doing, I saved myself from a great deal of suffering.

Or, at least, I delayed it.

The next day, I asked about the room at the top of staircase J.

I'd arrived early to lunch, and my only companion was an elderly fellow who'd long since retired but still lived in college. His forehead crinkled.

"Perhaps you mean I staircase," he suggested. "There is no J. It's to do with Latin, you see?"

I will not bore you by recounting the lecture he proceeded to give on the intricacies of the Latin alphabet. Sober scholars will tell you that there is no staircase J in Second Court; they will go on to explain why in tiresome detail.

By the lecture's end, I remained perplexed. I certainly did *not* mean staircase I, but I couldn't explain why the room would be unfamiliar to someone who'd been here so long that he'd voted for the admission of women (though that day was not quite as long ago as we might wish).

Still, whatever confusion remained, I left lunch sure that the room was not in use.

This thought led to another. In my own rooms, it was eleven paces from bed to desk. Setting aside lunch and my daily walk, these were the bounds of my world. Constricted into this space, the lines between work and rest had blurred, and I'd often found myself working late before stumbling those eleven paces to bed. But what if I could split apart the domains of work and rest? What if there was a room elsewhere in college I could use as an office?

The next day, I took my laptop to the dusty room at the top of staircase J. The day after, I returned with cleaning supplies and bustled around until the room was dusty no more. There was, for reasons I did not understand, no electricity, and so I brought across a camping stove, a kettle, and a cafetiere. I polished the candlesticks and placed candles within. When it was cloudy, I would light them, letting the wax mark the silver.

I said before that on anxious days, I find it hard to be noticed. The truth is that on such days, speaking to others makes me despise myself. I question my every action, wondering whether I'm speaking too much or saying the wrong things. On difficult days, every person I meet is a dark mirror, reflecting back my worst thoughts about myself. Alone, in the room at the top of staircase J, there were no mirrors, and so this became a place of solace. I took to calling it my nook.

Eventually, the room began to feel like it was truly mine, so I took the heavy key from the windowsill and claimed it as my own. I began to wear it on a chain around my neck so that a part of my nook could be with me whenever I faced the world.

By now, you're probably wondering when I first got a hint that something strange was afoot. I suppose that to tell you that story, I must explain what happened to my sister.

One night, when she was fourteen and I was a little older, a fire broke out in our house. I got out. My parents got out. My sister did not. The investigators said it was the smoke that killed her, not the flames, and I've never been sure whether that was a kindness—I didn't dare to ask.

I don't remember the fire well. Sometimes, when the smell of smoke catches me unaware, it's like I'm back amidst the heat and the flames, but it's more a feeling than a memory: a few fleeting images against the backdrop of a racing heart. I cannot remember how close the flames came, how I escaped the house, or when I realised we hadn't all got out.

What I can remember are the final words I'd spoken to my sister the evening before. "Go away," I'd said. "I'm busy."

I know, it's not as if I said I hated her or wanted her to die, but words don't need to be dramatic before you regret them.

I think of those words all the time. I think of her all the time. Sometimes I catch sight of her out in the world, flashing past on a bicycle or lining up in the supermarket, only it's not her, of course.

Normally, my confusion lasts only an instant. On the night when I realised there was strangeness afoot in the nook, the confusion was not so quick to fade.

I was working late, and the court below was dimly lit by sulphur-yellow lamps and light leaking from windows. I glanced up from my laptop, and my gaze was caught by a figure pacing back and forth across the lawn. You may already know that only fellows are permitted to walk on the grass, but perhaps you're not aware that even fellows rarely do so. This figure was an oddity.

At first, I assumed they were a student who lacked respect for the lawn-related rules enshrined in part 9.12.18 of the college's handbook, but as I continued watching, my heart began to hammer. The way the figure walked was familiar.

They walked like my sister.

I drew in a shaky breath. I tried not to think of words once spoken.

It was dark. That's what I told myself. It was dark, and I could barely see the figure, and my sister was on my mind, as she often was.

But it wasn't just the way the figure walked. It was the way she paused and stared into the sky. It was the way she raised her hand to brush her hair back. It was—

The chair toppled as I stood. I took the stairs at speed, stumbled halfway down but caught myself, didn't slow, reached the bottom, burst out the doorway...

The figure was gone.

In the second court of St John's College, I heaved in a ragged breath, and I wept.

I returned to my nook the next day. Of course, I did. All I'd seen was someone who—from a distance on a dark night—looked a little like my sister.

So I returned to my nook, and on that day, no oddities occurred. Later, I wondered why I'd been given that moment of peace. Was it a kindness? Or perhaps whatever force inhabits the staircase simply felt no need for haste?

I suppose it doesn't matter. Whatever the reason, that was my last peaceful day in the nook.

The next day, a pigeon fell down the chimney and died, splayed feathers black with soot and suffused with the smell of fires past. I buried it in the corner of the Fellows' Garden, but thereafter the scent of smoke permeated the nook.

Another day, the candles refused to light, and then on the third try, they flared impossibly high, and I could feel the heat. I was back in that house, and by the time I'd calmed, the candles had burned to stubs.

Every day, the nook was frigid. This was in the season when the world revels in cold, damp, and dark, but the nook was colder than it should have been, and damper, and darker. It... well, I suspect you'll now question my sanity, but I became quite certain that the nook wanted me to light a fire to drive out the cold. Of course, I did no such thing.

It may surprise you that I kept returning amidst these oddities. Here, I must place the blame on six words uttered to me by a counsellor some years prior.

After the fire, I felt guilty, you see, and not just for the words I'd spoken. My sister had changed in her final months, her mood ever swinging between furious and melancholic. Afterwards, I tried to remember the good times, but it felt like they were buried beneath the memories of this turbulent creature. That's how deeply I failed my sister; I couldn't even remember her properly.

When I was still struggling months later, my parents sent me to a counsellor, a balding man who was unduly enamoured with the word "frank."

"I'll be frank with you," he said towards the end of our first session. "I don't think this guilt is productive."

It's funny, we recognise that lawyers can focus so much on their clients' interests that they defend immorality, but we fail to realise the same is true of counsellors. When we do something wrong, it's right that we feel guilt.

I told the counsellor this, and he frowned, and then our time was over.

He tried a different tack the second time we met. "The latest research suggests," he said, "that rather than considering whether destructive beliefs are true or false, it's better to change how we relate to them. If I can be frank, I think you would benefit from this approach."

Can you imagine that: being told by someone who hadn't even known your sister to dismiss the question of whether you'd wronged her? Suffice it to say that session, too, ended with a frown.

The final time we met, the counsellor's composure cracked. Frustration tinged his voice as he spoke six words. "You're letting your guilt haunt you."

When the oddities occurred—when the pigeon died, and the candles flared, and the nook turned arctic—I remembered these six words, and I imagined that all I was doing was haunting myself once more, only somewhat more literally this time. I'd seen someone that looked like my sister, and now I was seeing patterns where there were none. If I avoided staircase J, I imagined I would give power to that haunting. So each day, I returned.

Until the incident on the stairs.

That day, I'd been so caught up in work that lunch had passed me by. By the time I packed my things away, I was tired and hungry, and when I blew out the candles, the room dropped into darkness.

A flutter of dizziness struck as I picked my way across the room. On the landing, I paused, leaning against the wall to rest, before locking the door by feel. The darkness was a deeper thing without even the thin light from the window, and I considered illuminating the way with my phone, but I was too tired to bother. I crossed the landing by memory and by the feel of my hand against the wall.

A gust of cold air brushed against me, and the sound of my breath was heavy in my ears. Another wave of dizziness struck as I reached the stairs and lifted a foot to descend.

Something grabbed my ankle.

I tripped, stumbled the first steps, and half-caught myself before my knee gave out. I fell. A tumble of motion. Pain in one hip, an arm, my head. I came to a stop, sprawled against the wall.

My body protesting, I scrambled to my feet. There was no sign of whatever had grabbed my ankle. It was dark. I hurt. I staggered down the stairs, encased in pain and the hollow echo of my feet on the wood. I could hear breathing behind me. No footsteps; just inhale and exhale, always a step behind.

As I flew through the door, out into Second Court, I collapsed to the ground. Through the pain, I realised that I could hear my own breathing and no other. In the lights of the court, no pursuer could be seen.

Later, I thought that perhaps I was haunting myself once again, finding fear in a moment of clumsiness. Then I remembered the feel of those fingers on my ankle, and I swore that I would never return to staircase J.

The first time I woke clutching the nook's key, I was standing at the foot of my bed. The key was hot in my hand, and it clattered on the floor when I dropped it in shock. I found myself thinking of fingers grasping my ankle and of a pigeon splayed in death. I slept fitfully when I returned to bed.

The second time I woke clutching the nook's key, I was standing at the edge of Second Court, and I knew at once where I was heading. I wrapped my arms around myself and whimpered. Then, because I knew well the power of symbols, I hurried to the Fellows' Gardens and buried the key beside the pigeon. Perhaps there it could be laid to rest. That night, it took me so long to return to sleep that my alarm woke me almost at once.

The third time I woke clutching the nook's key, my hands were dirty, and I was a step from staircase J. I didn't sleep again that night. I walked the paths of the Scholars' Garden over and over, not daring to stop lest tiredness take me. I considered throwing the key in the river, hoping to cleanse it. Then I imagined waking with water filling my lungs. I slipped the key back around my neck. Another solution would need to be found.

The next morning, in search of such a solution, I climbed the spiral, wrought-iron steps to the college's old library. At the top, a cast of Wordsworth's face was displayed, and here I paused, thinking it might be a sensible time to treat the dead with particular respect. I bowed and proclaimed, "Mr Wordsworth, your portrait in the hall is magnificent. Indeed, how could it not be given the incomparable brilliance of its subject."

Feeling pleased with my diplomatic nous, I turned to survey the library. Sunlight filtered through the stained glass behind me, dappling colours across the closest of the oak bookcases. There were forty-two of these, running the length of the room and arranged to create niches off to either side of a central nave.

Forty-two, I said, but staircases are not the only thing that can be hidden from view.

There were forty-four bookcases. At the room's far end was an extra case on either side, hidden from the sight of ordinary eyes. I'd noticed them on a previous visit and soon realised they could be seen only by adepts and by librarians, who had their own form of magic when it came to books.

The rest of the room was bathed in light, but these final cases stood amidst darkness, so as I approached, I fumbled for my phone and its torch. Beneath its beam, I peered at the books crammed on the shelves. Some were grand tomes, hardbound in muted greens and blues and reds, their gold-leaf lettering peeling with age. Others were tattered notebooks, bindings worn away almost to nothing. One such item belonged to Newton himself, and I happen to know that it was stolen from Trinity College in a moment of uncharacteristically-ungentlemanly behaviour from a fellow of St John's.

It was this notebook that I reached some hours later, and therein I read about the disturbance of harmony. When malevolence slumbers, it can be awoken by the smallest change, and the most dangerous of changes is confiscation: the taking of something. A treasure pilfered. A drink consumed.

A key placed on a chain around your neck.

I could feel it resting against my chest. I imagined it warmed a little as I read the words in the notebook. Was that burning feeling real? I did not know. All I knew was that I'd sworn never to return to the nook at the top of staircase J. All I knew was that if I was to restore the key to its rightful place, I would need to break my oath and climb those stairs one final time.

Newton's notebook stated two principles. First, the malicious force would resist harmony's return. Second, harmony would be restored only once the confiscation had been undone and the intruder had escaped the haunted place.

As I climbed staircase J, these principles echoed over my thoughts, each reduced to a single word.

Resist. Escape.

I climbed the stairs in a stilted rush, eager to be done and yet fearful of another fall. The ascent stretched to an eternity. The walls crowded closer than I'd remembered. My ankles tingled, the memory of fingers brushing against them.

The wood of the landing creaked as I crossed it, and my hands shook as I took the key from around my neck and slipped it into the lock. I could feel the latch resisting—rust and weight and age fighting to keep the door closed—but eventually, the key turned, and I swung the door open.

Beyond, the nook looked as it ever did. The desk. The chair. The candles on the mantle. I drew in a deep breath as I stepped into the room. Nothing happened, and after a pause, I let out that breath and hurried to the desk. My gaze caught on the lawn where the figure had paced, but I kept moving, placing the key on the windowsill in just the place it had rested when I'd first seen it.

Still, nothing happened. As I turned from the desk, Newton's first principle echoed in my head.

Resist.

Resist.

I was halfway across the room, when wind roared down the chimney, hurtled from the fireplace, and slammed the door shut. I froze as eddies played around my legs. The air stilled, and I forced myself to continue to the door. I grasped the handle.

The door would not move.

It was locked.

I twisted the handle forcefully. I hauled at the door. It did not budge.

From the fireplace, there came a sound that at first seemed to be wind, but that grew in volume to become the crackle of flames. I caught the whiff of smoke, and a second later, it was billowing from the fireplace and into the room.

I couldn't move. I could think only of my sister.

The smoke grew thicker, heat stroking my skin. I began to cough, and this pushed me to motion. I heaved at the door, but it didn't open. I clawed around my neck for the key before remembering I'd returned it to the windowsill. I staggered across the room, struggling for breath, trying to stay low where the smoke was less dense. The key was hot when my hands closed around it, and I dropped it, and scrambled on the floor to pick it up.

I crawled towards the door, dizziness striking. I almost collapsed but pushed myself onwards. Smoke obscured the lock, so I found it by feel, trembling hands missing the first time I tried to push the key inside. The second time I succeeded, turned the key, and hauled the door open, the handle burning my hand.

The air was clearer on the landing, but I was too weak to stand, so I crawled to the stairs. As I began to slide down in a barely controlled descent, I looked back. The smoke was gone. The nook was empty.

Then another breeze blew up, and within it were whispered words. "Go away. I'm busy."

The sound that tore from my throat was like nothing I'd ever heard, an animalistic cry of sorrow and fear and pain. I half fell, half slid down the stairs, accompanied by my whimpers. I crawled from the staircase and coughed and cried until I felt that I could breathe once more.

It was only then that I realised I was still clutching the key in my hand.

I almost gave in to despair. Perhaps I would have, but for the fact that, after the first counsellor—the frank counsellor—there'd been a second.

This one had listened when I spoke about my sister. When I was done, she thought for a time. Then she suggested that while I was perhaps right that we should feel guilt when we wrong another, such guilt can weigh us down until we have no energy left to redeem ourselves through action. Redemption, she suggested, is guilt constrained.

And then she gave me the mantra that carried me through the months that followed:

Take one more step.

Sometimes, your legs feel so heavy that they seem impossible to lift.

Take one more step.

Sometimes, all you want to do is curl up on the bathroom floor.

Take one more step.

Sometimes you can't take even a single step, and you don't, but then the next day or the day after that or whenever you can... **Take one more step.**

So when I realised I was clutching the key in my hand, I took one more step, and another, and another, until these steps carried me to the library once more, in search of an answer in the hidden shelves and their hidden wisdom.

For the next week, I returned each day. I read books in Latin, Persian, Dutch, Igbo. I read passages that revealed themselves only beneath the light of a thrice-blessed candle and others written in letters that seemed themselves to burn. I read, and I tried to focus on the words on the pages and not the words that had been hissed at me as I fled the nook.

At night, I no longer woke mid-stroll, but now I barely slept. I couldn't relax, couldn't stop the thoughts, couldn't... just couldn't. I found myself gripping my arms so hard that the marks were still there when morning came. I worried. Had I locked the door? What was that noise? Why was I so warm? I shouldn't be warm. It was wrong. My body was wrong.

In desperation, I bought sleeping tablets, and they sat beside my bed. I needed to sleep. Just one good night so that I could make it all make sense. Each night, I would hold a tablet in the palm of my hand, fill a glass with water... but no, that's what the nook wanted. I could tell.

It was all about my sister.

The investigators said that she might have lit the fire herself. They said that she stole sleeping tablets from our father and took some. They said that perhaps on the edge of sleep, she'd lit the fire and crawled into bed.

That's what they said, but she would never have done that.

Still, that was the story I couldn't forget, and I knew that was the story the nook would haunt me with. It wanted me to take the pills. It wanted me to lie on the bed. It wanted me to sleep so deeply that I did not wake when my legs carried me to it. By the time I stirred, the smoke would be too thick to escape.

Each night I would hold a pill in my hand, and then with a start, I would hurl it across the room to clatter to the floor alongside the rest. I was always punished for this. Lying in bed, voices would hiss at me, telling me I was pathetic, a loser. Hands would grasp at me in the darkness, and the next morning my skin would be marred by finger-shaped bruises.

It became harder and harder to hurl the pills away—harder to take the next step. My body was mottled with bruises. I was so fucking tired.

Then I found the *Illustrium Maioris Britanniae Scriptorum*.

This book wasn't on the hidden shelves, for it was no great work of arcane knowledge. It was merely an old catalogue of British writers. Yet this version of the *Illustrium Maioris* had been owned by John Dee, whose scribbled annotations filled the margins.

To most, these notes would seem banal, but I could see the occult hidden within the ordinary. Obscured by code, Dee outlined the ritual that had once lulled staircase J into slumber and that could do the same again. A ritual that must be performed in the nook.

And the nook would resist.

When people think of magic, they think of chanting and candles and polished sticks of yew. Yet while such things play a role, much of magic is simply recognising when ordinary actions are given power by circumstance: recognising when taking a key is just taking a key and when it will awaken something best left to slumber; recognising just the right way to set a key upon a windowsill and walk back down a staircase.

Still, the rituals matter. So when I reached the nook, I drew a knife across my palm and drew a circle in chalk and blood on the floor. I incanted words in a dozen languages and gestured with fingers that danced and flowed, tearing the world apart and stitching it together again.

Then the real work began.

To this point, the nook had been quiet. Dee's notes had described it as a Place of Slow Terror, saying it would act with haste only once the intruder returned that which had been taken.

Careful to keep my feet within the circle, I placed the key on the windowsill.

From the fireplace came the howl of wind. It raged into the room and tore at my clothes and skin. It hurled the door shut.

The smoke followed, each wisp writhing from the fireplace, caressing my heels before drifting to the ceiling. My heart hammered. I did not flee.

This was the secret. To quiet the haunting, you must quiet yourself. You must stand in stillness amid terror, and you must accept the turmoil of your being. Not overcome it; just accept it. Once. Twice. Thrice. And the nook would sleep.

So as the smoke grew thicker, I spoke a truth that I'd never before spoken aloud. "I lit the fire that killed my sister." The flow of smoke slowed a touch as I continued. "I was just playing with the lighter, burning bits of paper. It wasn't meant to get out of control. I didn't know my sister's insomnia had got so bad she was taking sleeping tablets."

I drew in a ragged breath and made my final confession. "The investigators knew that someone lit the fire, but when they asked, I swore I hadn't done it. I don't think they believed me, but my parents did, and they came to think that my sister had made a choice. So I killed her, and I made a lie of her final moments."

I spoke my truths, and in so doing, I accepted my turmoil once.

As if in response, the smoke billowed forth faster than ever. I drew it in with my breath, coughed, and could feel heat searing my lungs. Terror struck me, so potent that my mind ceased to be my own, and I stumbled one step towards the door and another and—

With a shudder, I stopped. Dee had written of how the nook would fight to drive the spellcaster from the circle. I looked down. My foot remained within the line of chalk and blood. Just.

My voice was hoarse as I spoke again, this time addressing my sister, though I did not know whether she was there or ever had been.

"I'm sorry," I said. "I'm sorry for the fire, and for my last words to you, and for the lies I told." My next words were broken by sobs. "I'm sorry, and I love you."

I spoke my apology, and in so doing, I accepted my turmoil twice.

The smoke roiled, so thick I could barely see. I crouched down where the air was cleaner but still coughed, choked, and struggled to pull in each breath.

I forced myself to rasp, "I don't forgive myself." I tried to picture a boy, sixteen and broken by the loss of his sister. What would I think of that boy if he hadn't been me? What would I say to him? "I don't forgive myself, but—"

There was movement in the smoke: a shape, a figure, stalking towards me. There was the crackling of flames, and in that crackling, there were words.

Go away.

I fell to my knees. My vision blurred. I could barely breathe.

"I don't forgive myself," I whispered, "but sometimes I think that you would forgive me if you could."

I imagined forgiveness, and in so doing, I accepted my turmoil thrice.

I looked up at the shape in the smoke and reached a hand towards it. I closed my eyes.

Darkness claimed me.

When I woke, the smoke was gone. The door was unlocked. The stairs were quiet.

As I staggered out to Second Court, I collapsed on the cobbles, where a student found me. He stayed with me until the ambulance came, speaking soothing words while I sobbed. In the hospital, they treated me for smoke inhalation, and they asked me questions, and when I answered, they looked worried.

They sent me to you.

You asked me to write down my story, and I've done as you asked. I know you won't believe me, but that's okay.

Here's what matters: I hope one day to return to the shell of my childhood home and stand at the bottom of the crumbling stone staircase that led to my sister's room. I hope to picture that sixteen-year-old boy, broken with loss.

I hope to forgive him.

And even if I cannot bring myself to do so, the nook is sealed once more, and sober scholars will continue to say that there is no staircase J in the second court of St John's College.

***

About the Author

Thomas Bales Website

Perhaps Thomas is a spacetime worm or perhaps he is the temporal part of such a worm. Either way, he is a being who hates writing bios and so prefers to retreat into abstraction.

Other Works From This Author Links

Coming Soon

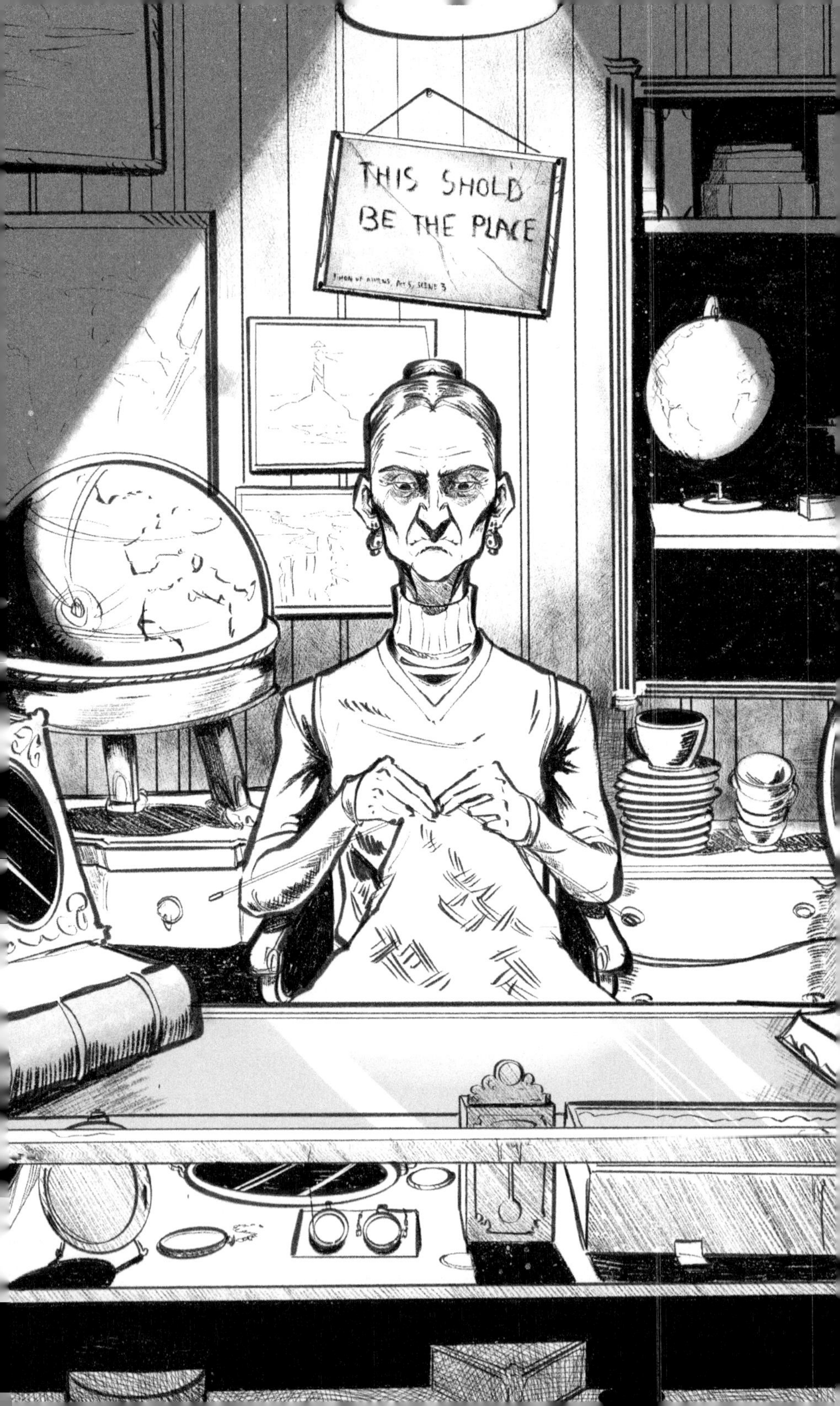
THIS SHOLD
BE THE PLACE

THIS SHOULD BE THE PLACE

by Stuart Freyer

The day did not suggest deceit. In fact, being a typical Massachusetts fall day, it was quite beautiful. The reds were just at that edge which is both translucent orange and scarlet. The yellows were peaking, bright as from a child's crayon. And the greens—oh the greens—due to the sufficient rains, were straight from an Irishman's dream. That is the way it looked to Norman Rhine as he exited I-90 in his Mercedes station wagon and headed east. Periodically, and always after making sharp turns, he swung his head to check the safety of the carefully bubble-wrapped package in the flatbed behind him.

He was at the house in fifteen minutes. Formerly the estate of a famous composer, it had gone into decline. Norman convinced the family that after his purchase, he would revive it. He did, and now it had doubled in value: typical Rhine. The painters were just finishing the nook where the O'Keefe would go.

Norman left the selling of old Masters, De Koonings, and Schnabels to others. He had found a niche: the primitives. Masks, dogans, memorials, a century old at the latest. As a youth, he loved trekking the then-dangerous parts of Africa and Asia. By chance—more likely due to his cordial performance—Norman won the friendship of an old trader who took him under his wing. *Take out a local Peace Corps worker, find out where the missionaries are, then go downriver to the village just past them as they will still be friendly to the white man.* In a few trips, he had absorbed a jungle master's degree dealing with native peoples, recognizing fine works of ivory, ebony, and the like. He learned also how to work around exportation nets, who to pay off, and what shipping containers attracted the least interest. In time, when he was away exploring for new prizes, he left excellent managers at his rapidly growing galleries in New York and San Diego.

He saw a magnificent lemonwood altar in a dusty rural Bolivian church and was the man to convince the local priest to part with it. Small money for Norman, but large enough to prop up the tiny congregation for a generation. Few others knew how to disassemble and export the two-story treasure. It sits today in a major city, housed in a circular museum at a price that was only a slight strain on its budget. Hence the country house, the West Coast house, the salaried cleaner/maids, and the cook on retainer when he was in town.

He did his homework. He knew what textiles Saudi sheiks liked, what certain cocaine cartel dons put in their chapels, and what statuary hedge fund managers collected. Some called him the Steve Jobs of primitive. His intimates quipped that Jobs was the Rhine of computers. They meant, of course, that if Norman Rhine showed you something, you wanted it.

And who were Norman's intimates? Several highly placed professionals, some recognizable by name, others in the art business. He was divorced from a handsome Jamaican woman, and had a son and grandson who visited infrequently at the California house. As to romance, many women called on the dapper bachelor who was inclined to bright shirts and colorful sneakers. There were also a few men, so that the staff cleaning the rumpled king-sized beds in the main or visiting bedrooms could not tell you who had slept where or with whom with any accuracy. For the most part, they suspected he slept alone.

The techniques that worked in the bush came in handy. In the past two decades, some valuable pieces were traded up to those DeKoonings and Schnabels for his personal collection. Now the O'Keefe, in exchange for a mint Porsche which had been swapped for four pristine nineteenth-century Cote d'Ivoire war masks, sat in the back of his car heading for its latest home.

"The wall's dry for hangin' tomorrow. That OK?"

"Fine. Thank you, Chip. It's in my car. Careful."

Norman remembered the name of every workman, maid, and driver, as he did foreign chieftains. It was good business.

"Oh, and Joe left you somethin'. It's in your office."

So it was done.

In the office adjacent to his bedroom, he unwrapped a heavy article, removed two signs and placed them side by side on the couch. Joe had used the same flooring nails to frame the edging. The paint was weathered. That woman, Rita, would not be able to tell the difference. He turned them over. The panels on the backs matched, even to the knots. As agreed, Joe had cut a small divot on the upper border of the counterfeit. Except for that, they were all but identical. Perfect.

Primitives, like antique furniture, were often created by unknowns. The ability to fake age led to abuse. The pieces Norman sold, however, had impeccable provenance. In a field rife with fraud and counterfeits, he had a reputation for honesty and dependability. His clientele relied on that, and they were never proven wrong. This facsimile, however, would be his little secret and was *never* to be sold or bartered.

A personal joke, really.

No harm done.

Several years ago, he discovered a poker game. He was in the neighborhood country store, the kind that sells fishing lures and orange hunting caps as well as tolerable wines and the *New York Times*. Norman liked to walk there from the house, purchase a few items, chat with the clerks, and meet some of the locals, a habit of ingratiating himself in hamlets around the world. He retained, though, a sense of examining them from above. Perhaps it was his upbringing. His Irish mother, a poor widow since his infancy, was fundamentally reticent. But she hid it behind an attitude. Whereas other children might be told they were as good as the next, he was assured he was better; unique. He understood it to be false but never could shake himself from acting on the pretense. So while he sought community, he viewed it as through a microscope; he on both sides of the eyepiece. And when acting among the other bacteria, he watched himself playing the part well.

Someone next to him had taken a pack of cards from the shelf and added it to a cart filled with groceries. "Poker?" Norman asked with an open smile. The gentle-faced man had a cheery glint in his eyes. They exchanged first names. Max was a local dentist, and yes, there was a weekly game. An informal group, Wednesday nights in various homes. Besides Max, there was an eye doctor, a dairy farmer, a fireman, and a teacher. Norman was invited to join when he was in town.

He played in college. Although not gifted, he liked its social aspect, how one could discover things seamlessly. He made use of games in his travels. Every tribe had one. Whether you scooped stones out of holes in the dirt, cast sticks, or moved checkers on a crude Parcheesi board, it was the same. Whoever was winning felt relaxed and was prone to disclose information. Norman didn't try to lose at poker. But he did not mind. Losing had its merits.

Wednesdays after his dinner at home—Nina, a sweet retired woman, cooked for him—Norman drove the wagon to a cape on a quiet dead-end street or a farm on the outskirts of town. He carried a six-pack and, for Sam, the eye doctor, a beefy fellow who considered himself something of an oenophile, a decent merlot. There would be pretzels in the center of a card table and soda for the asking.

The others were already in the simple living room. They knew his reputation: the multiple houses, the help, had seen the famous art during rotations at his place. Due to Norman's personality, they had become comfortable but not completely chummy. Sam might be kidded about whether he had a two-for-one price on cataracts; the fireman queried whether he had a light or, sniffing the air, allusions made as to whether Rick, the dairy farmer, was spreading manure that day. But no one poked fun at Norman. It would be a bit like kidding the president. He represented something of the exotic, the sophisticated world outside the small county they knew.

"What are you working on now? Raise," Norman asked Joe that particular evening.

"Barn up on Oden Hollow. The trees around it are real nice. See you," said Joe.

Joe Baker, the fireman, fascinated Norman. A self-taught painter, he had a local reputation. Norman, who had two of his works, might frequent the local stores, but he would not buy art unless it had merit. Joe couldn't know it, but the fact that Norman admired his work said that, in time, he could well be recognized by a surprising number of people. The future value of his board landscapes would surprise him even more.

"There'll be more paint on your painting than on that old barn," said Max folding.

Rick called.

"That's why I like it. And I like this too," Joe said, winning the hand.

Sam asked Rick when he was going to grow something "like grapes, for instance, to feed humans instead of cows." Max said to be careful of methane production. The dentist was the winner for the evening: twenty dollars. Norman broke even.

It was at one of those card nights that Norman had thought about what Joe could do.

Recently, on a Saturday morning, Nina had arrived somewhat late and apologetic due to a sick grandchild but made up for it with a fine breakfast of Belgian waffles. It was a lovely day. Norman decided to drive through the hills west of town to the neighboring one that bordered the river.

Western Massachusetts has a flavor like Vermont and the rest of New England. One might think the citizens either fear the town dump or have a strong streak of sentimentality. They hate to see old things wasted; the number of second-hand shops and lawn sales is striking. He cruised into the valley where houses sported the usual white paint and sometimes alternated with a 7-Eleven or a small farm. Finally, beyond a trailer park and a logging mill stood a gray shingled building he had noticed on previous trips.

The name *Ernie's Topside* attracted him. There was a black anchor affixed over the entrance. There were three car widths in the gravel parking area, and he pulled into one. The shop occupied the ground floor. Apparently the owner lived upstairs, since he could see the bright window curtains. He swung open the screen door, peeked in, and entered. A thin woman in a blue sweater sat knitting behind a glass counter filled with old watches. She paid him no attention. The rest of the space held wicker chairs, old snowshoes, rusty scythes, and scratched bureaus. Only rarely did a set of buttons with an anchor motif or an ancient toy wooden boat justify the name outside. He finished his tour at the counter where the woman sat. Behind her, above the window, looking out on the parking area, hung a sign.

THIS SHOULD BE THE PLACE.

On the right lower border, he saw in smaller lettering: *Timon of Athens*, Act 5, Scene 3.

How to explain the magic of certain phrases? This group of words, a catchline for two old burlesque comedians of a heyday that peaked before he was born, had made him happy since he first heard them. What was it—a TV show, black and white, when they were no more than revues, watched excitedly with his mother? Yes. The comedians would be introduced, and then the curtains separated to titters of laughter, and there they were. Two fools in baggy pants and sloppy hats. The backdrop, he remembered, was a nondescript street corner. The buffoons would commence yelling at each other,

"Dis should be da plaiz."

"Are you sure dis is da plaiz?"

"Der is no udder plaiz but dis, so dis should be da plaiz."

Utter nonsense but infectious. Now to discover that the lines were from a lesser-known Shakespeare play. A coincidence? Had Wayne and Shuster—that was the name!—realized? Were they making a sly reference expecting no one in the audience would know?

The words invariably shunted him to the past. How strange associations were! When hiking, he always remembered an ancient aunt who, when he was a child, sat in a large straight chair. He had never seen her outside of her kitsch-filled living room, never seen her walk or stand. A woman in a polka-dot dress brought his ebony ex-wife to mind, perhaps because polka-dot was one thing she said she would *never* wear. And when he entered a simple settlement anywhere in the world, *This Should Be The Place* ran through his head, even with that mock German accent, and synonymous to him with anticipation of adventure.

"Husband a Navy man?" he inquired.

She looked up from her knitting. "Ayup. Twenty-five years."

"Then you located here?"

"From here, came back."

"Travel much?"

"We did. Pacific, Germany."

Norman kept himself from diving in.

"I stayed on base, raised my boy." She was warming up. No doubt remembering spotless apartments, a nearby PX, and other straw widows. She looked beyond him, perhaps at the past.

"Husband out looking for treasures?"

Her face became stolid. "We weren't back five years. Reroofing. Fell off the shed. Blood clot in the brain. Gone in two days. Just me and the boy now." Norman offered his condolences. She minded the store, and the *boy* here did the buying. He had come down the back stairs and stood next to his mother, a pale man, balding, with a handlebar mustache. He did not look the type to be reroofing a shed as Ernie had done. Norman offered his hand for a shake.

"Tom," the man said.

"Norman," he replied. "Nice sign. How much is it?"

Tom opened his mouth to speak.

"Not for sale," she said, reviewing her knitting.

"Sentimental?"

"Oh, I don't know really. Just had it from the beginning. I think Ernie found it in the attic. They say it's from Shakespeare. Never read Shakespeare. Lot of big words. I prefer my romances. Not sure he even liked it so much after a while. But it jus' stayed there."

Tom touched his mustache. "How much would you offer?" he said.

"A hundred dollars."

She looked up.

"That's a nice number, mister, but it's not for sale."

Tom twisted to face her and turned up his hands.

"You never said this before."

"I know, but no one has ever wanted to buy it and—oh, I don't know."

Norman gave his most winning look. "It's always been a special slogan for me."

Her head angled slightly toward her shoulder.

"And my mother."

"Oh?"

"Reminds me of sitting with her in the evenings when I was a kid. Will you think about it? I'd go two hundred."

"Sure. But I don't think so."

He bought the set of anchor buttons. They exchanged names again. Norman. Rita. Maybe Rita would respond to the part about his mother. Her face had opened for some seconds, then settled back to no. He wanted the sign. His mother, long dead, got her attention. And the sign. It wasn't art, really. On the other hand, it was. Symbols covering space that evoked a response. In his case, a very strong one. Yes. It was primitive art.

On a return visit, he was refused again, the last offer five hundred. By now, Rita must have found out it had no great intrinsic value. It was as if his increased interest accentuated the importance of the sign to her. Obstinate woman.

He supervised the delivery of a very early set of Yoruba Shango dance staffs and several Chokwe masks to a client in California, spent a month in the San Diego house, settled a large purchase in Peru, and then returned to New York. He thought about the sign; pictured it over the lintel of his office door in the Berkshire house as if it had always been there.

He went back on a Sunday in a suit and tie. There was a little post-it on the sign now: *Not for Sale*. Rita saw him looking at it. Her eyes said, "It's over, don't ask." He made a tour around the shop, chatted about the weather, bought a nutcracker in the shape of a bulldog whose jaws did the work, and left.

He returned the next day.

"This is hard for me. Remember, Rita, I told you about my mother?"

Rita's lips tensed as if for battle. But her eyes were soft.

"Well, she doesn't have much more to go. Cancer. The sign would brighten her last days. I really understand your connection with it—but—how about this idea."

She squinted and leaned her ear forward.

There was always a hook. He had told the Maasai that their ancient mask or spear would live in the hut of a great chieftain. A hedge fund manager is a kind of chieftain, no?

"Could I borrow or rent it—for her—for her last few months. I know it would mean so much. Then I'll return it."

Rita slumped in her chair, a dreamy look coming over her face. Then, as if he were a sick child and she was going to carry him to bed, she said, "Of course."

Tom was puttering nearby but alert.

"I'd be glad to pay rent on it too."

"Wouldn't think of it. You just take it and get along now and give your mother my best. Bring it back whenever.

He had called Joe that night.

"I have something I would like a copy of for another house. Can you do that? It's old, but not that old."

"Shouldn't be a problem," Joe said when he saw it. "Gray barn paint, old lath behind, flooring nails."

"You can duplicate it exactly?"

"Sure. How many do you want?"

Norman chuckled at the idea.

"One."

Now it hung across from his desk over his office door. In the corner, still stuck the post-it, *Not for Sale*. The twin in the closet waited on his mother's "death" for its return. It was important to keep the original.

Two months later, the first light snowfall seemed like a fitting time to complete the switch. A shallow white blanket covered the true earth.

He had looked up the line in a biography of the playwright. *A soldier seeking Timon finds a rude tomb and declares, "By all description this should be the place." Unable to read if it is Timon's, brings a rubbing of the inscription to his general.* The symbols mysterious to one are obvious to the other. The play was rife with questions of honesty and hidden agendas.

One night Norman dreamt he confused the fake with the real, had taken the plaque back to Rita and then was not sure which was which, the two having become identical. Another time he imagined that if he chipped the original by mistake, both would have the same identifying gouge on their border. But they were inventions of his mind. Today though, was authentic. Today was the last step.

When she saw him with the board, Rita greeted him like an old friend, even coming from her perch behind the counter.

"I guess..." She touched his arm softly.

"Yes," he said. "But, she was comfortable to the end."

That much was true. His mother passed away peacefully ten years ago.

"And here it is. I can't thank you enough."

"No problem. Glad to help."

She held the panel and smiled down at the lettering. "Actually, I was surprised at the people who noticed it was gone. Become a bit of a conversation piece between me and Tom—the story, your borrowing it and all. I still wouldn't sell it, of course."

Tom replaced the wood plank on the protruding nail behind Rita. Norman felt a fluttering sensation he tried to erase by mentally retracing his steps that morning: to the closet, take out the copy, unwrap the copy, check the gouge, and place the copy in his car.

Rita again refused any money and walked out with him to wave goodbye.

There was a barn he was fond of a mile off the return route. It was set back and to the side of a neat white cape. A slanted roof of cedar shingle, the vertical plank boards burnished by time, it was, in a way, a large version of the village artifacts he was drawn to. They were a vernacular that spoke from their time and people. He felt a kinship with barn movers who took those gorgeous heirlooms apart to re-erect and preserve at a new site. He turned at the lonely road to spend a few moments gazing at it.

As he approached, something was different, perhaps the interposition of the buildings. Stopping to fix his vision better, he felt a jolt. He saw the barn's rectangular shape, then didn't, as if he was seeing it and yet through it. A ghost. No. It was gone. The building had burned down, perhaps last night. The base was a still steaming pile of blackened timbers harsh against the white of the snow, here and there a memory of a board or shingle. But driving slowly in those last seconds before realizing he had seen the barn as it had been, as it *was*. He rubbed his eyes and stared for a long time.

That evening he felt odd. Nina prepared roasted game hen with garden vegetables. They were bland. Perhaps she had left out salt or some herb. He did some work in his office and slept uncomfortably.

The next morning was bright. Snow, having returned in the night, bounced the sun back in a way that seemed to wash everything clean. The dining room furniture was pale. Even the breakfast eggs were lighter.

"Did we get these eggs recently?"

"Farm fresh," Nina said.

They did not taste like fresh eggs. They didn't even taste yellow.

In his office to check over deals for the coming weeks, he noticed a brown smear on his settee. What could that be? No one else was here. And the seat was narrower than he remembered. He sat in it and couldn't be sure. He looked at the sign and laughed at his strange thoughts.

He walked through the living room. The couch was altered. It was moved slightly, perhaps misplaced by the cleaning women. And the books. He checked several rows of bindings and could not find any discrepancies. If one or two were missing, he couldn't identify any. But the ones that were there might not be the same ones he knew. Even the scattered used ones. It was as if they had been made for today and were not the same ones here yesterday.

Nina, too, looked changed at breakfast. He had read that if men merely parted their hair on the opposite side, they looked different, almost like another person. Car mirrors have a small sign warning that things are closer than they appear. Funhouse mirrors. How can you tell what things are? People? You can't be sure by appearances or the roles they play.

Norman returned to the kitchen. It was well designed and refurbished with the latest in refrigeration, cooking range, and oven, identical to the kitchen in a house purchased from the estate of a famous composer. A house he had bought at one time. He peered out through the wide-mullioned windows. They were making new snow outside. Tiny wisps of white fabric were falling. Trees almost looked real in the distance.

He turned to ask again about the eggs.

"Farm fresh," answered the strange woman who said her name was Nina.

***

About the Author

Stuart Freyer is a Pushcart Prize nominee and his stories have appeared in American Fiction Volume 14: The Best Unpublished Stories by New and Emerging Writers, Glassworks, december, Timber Creek Review, and Zahir: A Journal of Speculative Fiction, among others. He has been an otolaryngologist, acupuncturist and standup comic. He lives in Williamstown MA on a dirt road.

Other Works From This Author Links
MOMMA'S FAMOUS SOMEWHERE
"The Jacket"
"Fascination Hall"

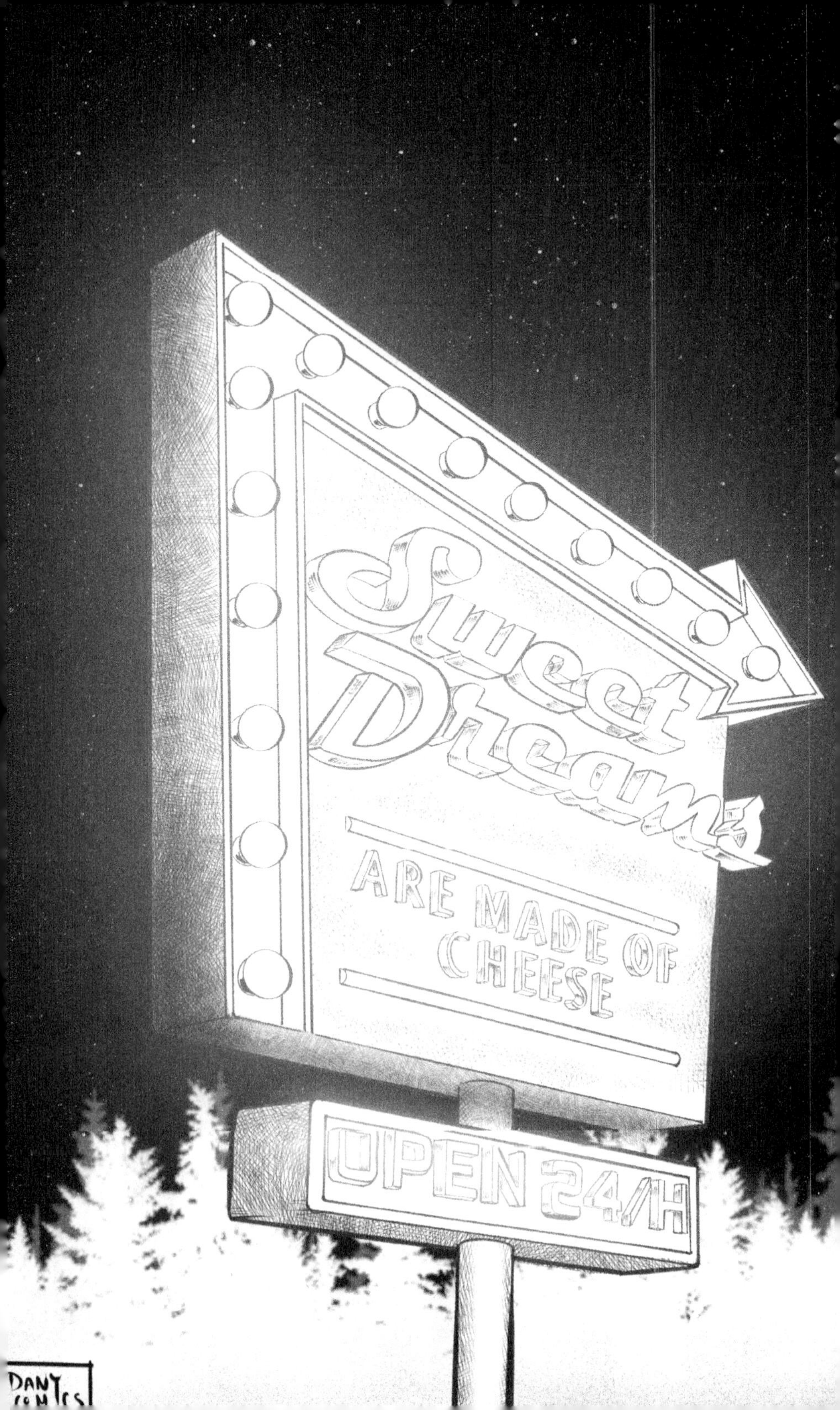
Sweet Dreams
ARE MADE OF CHEESE
OPEN 24/H
DANY COMICS

House of Reverie

by Susan L. Lin

Thirty-six hours into her interminable journey east, Lucia Vail hasn't yet decided what she's running from. The list of possibilities is as long as the deserted twelve-lane interstate that stretches before her, but it's stowed out of sight, along with her other belongings, in the cardboard boxes locked inside her trunk. She's not at all equipped to unpack any of it now.

The clock on the dash reads half past midnight. She's bleary-eyed and sleep-deprived by the time one of the pole pylons rising above the freeway bridge nearly brakes her in her tire tracks. sweet dreams, the mammoth sign declares in a luminous retro script. An addendum on the narrow panel directly underneath: (are made of cheese). Pulsing pink-and-yellow neon tubing creates the illusion of movement. Maybe the lack of rest is garbling her mind, but as the bright lights migrate from her side window to the sedan's rearview mirror, Lucia finds it difficult to imagine what sort of business lies below. A mattress store? A delicatessen? Some unearthly combination of the two?

Before she even realizes what she's doing, she's on the exit ramp, ready to make a U-turn under the overpass and double back on the access road. Whatever this place is, she hopes they sell energy drinks because she badly needs a caffeine boost. The aluminum can in her center console cup holder is yet again nearly empty. Plagued by recurring nightmares and disturbing visions of an apocalyptic future, she hasn't had a good night's sleep in she doesn't know how long. If her eyes shutter for even a moment, the horrific images threaten to bleed into her waking life, too. No hour, day or night, is safe. Especially not since some of the more distressing dreams started coming true.

Once Lucia pulls into the parking lot, she can plainly see that the building in question houses an '80s-era diner, though the furnishings inside look too shiny and new to truly be decades old. Yet another establishment looking to capitalize on the recent nostalgia craze. She can't exactly blame the owners for their sound business acumen, but she struggles, as usual, to understand the world's collective obsession with the past. Sure, the fate of the planet is looking more and more dire with every passing day, but taking solace in cozy reminders of bygone eras doesn't seem like the most fruitful answer. In any event, she's too tired to care anymore. Maybe that's how the whole globe feels.

Her presence at the front door triggers an electronic bell, which cheerfully sounds the opening instrumental bars of the Eurythmics' familiar synth-pop tune. As soon as Lucia steps inside, an older woman in a cotton-candy pink uniform calls out to her from behind a glass counter, which houses a tantalizing display of mouthwatering cheesecakes and buttery danishes. "Welcome to Sweet Dreams! Take a seat, any seat! I'll bring our menu right over."

Lucia looks around at the kitschy decor. The booth seats are a striking teal vinyl, but the vintage Bubbler jukebox in the corner, a glowing arch of rainbow gradients, is still the most eye-catching piece in the room. Nondescript new wave music emanates from an unseen speaker system inside the walls. The rest of the restaurant is empty, but considering the time of night, that isn't unusual. Hardly anyone eats out anymore anyway. The smog and smoke have made it nearly impossible to breathe safely without protective equipment. Why would humans risk their health when inescapable drones could now deliver almost anything straight to their doorsteps?

The older woman's name is Ginny, at least according to the name tag pinned to her breast pocket. "As you might have suspected from the name of our humble enterprise, we're obsessed with cheese here at Sweet Dreams," she announces once Lucia has settled in at a corner table. "Every single item on our menu uses some variety of cheese as a key ingredient. And please don't worry if you're vegan or lactose intolerant! Our dairy-free substitutes are just as popular as their inspirations. Take a look for yourself and holler when you're ready to order."

Lucia blinks at the laminated menu she suddenly holds in her hands. The periphery of her vision warps in waves, and she feels like a character in an old movie, transitioning from reality into a murky flashback or daydream. For a moment, she has difficulty focusing on the words in front of her. But then the foreign feeling leaves her body as quickly as it arrived. Paneer naan! Aligot! Cacio e pepe! Poutine! Fried mozzarella sticks! Cheesy dishes from every corner of the world cover the front page. Her eyes zero in on the House Special, a chicken-fried steak smothered in country gravy with a serving of "downright dreamy" queso on the side.

Lucia has never felt homesick for unfamiliar places, but she sometimes experiences intense cravings for foods she's never even tasted before. This is one of those times.

"An excellent choice!" Ginny exclaims, before disappearing into the kitchen with a wink. "You won't regret it."

Time seems to pass in slow motion as Lucia waits for her food. She gazes out the window at the headlights on the interstate, but they're few and far between now. The dark night is barely visible past the glare of her own reflection. Lucia hasn't looked in a mirror since she got behind the wheel and started driving, avoiding the sight of her face in gas station bathrooms, afraid of the hard truths she might find there. Her make-up and wet wipes haphazardly abandoned in the trunk with all her other baggage. With creeping unease, she realizes she already looks half-dead.

"The House Special." The return of Ginny's mellifluous voice and the welcome appearance of an oval plate loaded with hot comfort food work in tandem to shake Lucia out of her reverie.

"White gravy," she blurts out at the sight of it, poking tentatively with the tines of her silver fork. "I've never seen that before."

Ginny laughs, though not unkindly. "You're not from around here, are you?"

"No, I guess I'm not." Lucia doesn't elaborate. Instead, she busies herself by sawing off a slice of the main course before dipping it in creamy melted cheese. She pauses, savoring the perfect marriage of their rich, complex flavors. "Wow, this is incredible!" She quickly cuts another bite-sized piece, then samples the ramekin of chili mac and the loaded potato skins. They all taste exquisite.

But Ginny's obvious pride is masked with visible concern. "Look, this may be none of my business, but it's real late. You must be exhausted. You got a place to lay your head tonight?"

Lucia stalls. She gulps from her ceramic mug of Scandinavian coffee, where cubes of sweet cheese float to the top like floes of ice. As with everything else she's tasted here so far, it's heavenly.

"Again, maybe this isn't such a surprise, given our name and all, but here at Sweet Dreams, we aren't solely in the diner business."

Lucia sets the warm mug back on the table. "You're not?"

"No, here at Sweet Dreams, we're actually in the hotel business as well."

Lucia wonders at first if Ginny is joking. Though the mere idea of a hotel is more than tempting, she hadn't noticed any other buildings in the vicinity when she pulled up. If this place is what it claims to be, where are the rooms? Besides, how would she pay for an overnight stay? The crumpled twenty-dollar bill in her back pocket barely covers this meal.

"There's no extra charge," Ginny reassures her. "Our homey rooms are complimentary with any order of our House Special between midnight and four a.m."

Until now, Lucia hasn't spoken to anyone since she skipped town, always ordering food and drinks from vending machines at roadside automats. The sensor-activated faucets at rest stops have barely acknowledged her freezing hands. If she stopped at a convenience mart after leaving this diner, the sliding doors would probably fail to part for her body. With each passing second, she feels less and less like a real person, less and less like a living human being.

An overwhelming weariness overtakes her so suddenly that she can barely keep her eyes open any longer. Somewhere in the back of her mind, she hears a faraway voice (*her* voice) acquiescing to Ginny's outrageous offer without asking any of the critical questions that run laps around the crevices of her brain. Before long, she's following Ginny through a swinging door behind the counter. She'd assumed that it led to the kitchen: After all, her steaming plate of food had just emerged from it earlier that night. Instead, the narrow corridor leads to a stairwell. She can't help but feel like the clueless protagonist in a bloody slasher film, on the verge of meeting her inevitable death in a killer's underground lair. It's her fault for stopping here to rest her tired feet. She should've kept running until she could no longer move another limb. Ginny has been nothing but hospitable, of course, but first impressions can be deceiving.

Lucia's eyes widen in disbelief, however, as soon as they descend the steps and turn the corner. The cramped space immediately opens up into the lobby of a grand hotel. The vast place looks expensive and luxurious.

"Did you know that studies have shown late-night cheese consumption can alter the depths of our slumber and invite vivid dreams into our subconscious?" Ginny ducks behind the reception desk and strokes the old-fashioned keys that dangle from numbered hooks. Her southern drawl seems to have evaporated with the change in elevation. "Scientists have been studying this phenomenon for decades. Much of the early evidence was anecdotal at best, but that's why we created this place."

Lucia looks on in a daze. The swaying miniature mousetrap key chains are mesmerizing. She's not sure she understands Ginny's continued use of the first-person plural. So far, she hasn't seen another soul on the property.

"We currently offer beds in twenty-four rooms," Ginny continues, pointing down the long hallway at a plethora of closed doors. "Each room corresponds to a different cheese. For example, in Room One, you'll be served a midnight snack of sharp cheddar before bed. In Room Two, a block of marbled blue cheese awaits your parted lips. In Room Three, a modest feast of crumbled feta. And so on. Have a gander at our full list of offerings here on this screen." She taps the large display on the counter with a manicured fingernail. "We hope to expand to many more varieties in the coming years. Now, here's the most important part: A guest book has been placed in each room. In the morning, when you return to the corporeal world, the first thing you must do is write down everything you remember about your dreams. No detail is too small. The blank journal is stored in a drawer that won't open up until your wake-up call. This way, suggestible minds can't be swayed by previously reported experiences."

Lucia has heard of laboratories where researchers conduct experiments on individuals during sleep, but as far as she knows, they're usually affiliated with university programs. She wonders if anyone else knows what's happening down here. If the operation is even legal. She desperately wants to pore over the collected data, to satiate her piqued curiosity, but Ginny would probably claim that doing so could compromise the integrity of the experiment. Lucia is fading fast anyway. Consuming dairy products before bed and writing about the ordeal afterward seems harmless enough. A small price to pay for a comfortable place to rest for the night. Maybe the cheese, as ludicrous as it sounds, can even strip away her chronic nightmares. She would welcome a return to the innocuous fantastical phantasmagoria of yesteryear. Those abstract, benign shapes and colors and feelings that she recalls from childhood. Ones that didn't predict a treacherous future. "Is there a ricotta room?" she hears herself asking Ginny. She had always loved lasagna as a kid, but at some point in her life, she'd given up carbs, and she'd given up her favorite foods along with them.

"An excellent choice!" Ginny slides the corresponding key off its hook with one fluid motion. "Room Twenty-Two. And don't you worry about these silly mousetraps. They're purely decorative." She gestures vaguely down the hallway. "Keep on walking 'til you reach the dead end. Please follow the directions you find inside your room. You can set the alarm to wake you at any point between eight and ten in the morning, but you must check out before noon. Come find me upstairs in the diner when you're ready." She swivels to leave.

"Wait, but... " Lucia turns her head to find that Ginny is already gone.

At the end of the hallway, the door to Room Twenty-Two opens easily with a turn of her key. Lucia takes a brief moment to survey the ordinary room. The framed painting on the wall is a solid off-white color. She'd almost say it wasn't a painting at all, except she can clearly see the brush strokes when she examines it up close. The bathroom is stocked with all the necessities. She washes her face and combs her hair. She changes into the soft pajamas she finds hanging in the closet. They're a perfect fit.

A mini fridge beside the bed opens up to reveal a lonely plastic tub with the distinctive Sweet Dreams logo on the front. The use-by date stamped on the bottom is a week away. Lucia peels away the lid and breathes in. The ricotta smells fresh and inviting. Her stomach growls, despite the fact that she just devoured a full meal less than an hour ago. Suddenly, she is ravenous. She swallows one spoonful, then another. She licks the utensil clean when she's finished.

Lucia has been an insomniac since adolescence, right around the time her nightmares began: persistent visions of jagged rifts appearing along faults in the land, the earth quaking with alarming frequency, a deluge of water rushing ashore with every rainstorm, raging flames burning down every last tree in the woods. Then came hallucinations of shadowy figures that visited her late at night, their incomprehensible silhouettes framed by the doorway of her bedroom, their mouths unhinging to snarl at her in a strange language made up of low groans and moans that she could not begin to understand. She grew to dread dozing off, to fear the way that in-between state heightened her senses and opened a portal to a threatening alien landscape.

But the fatigue brought on by the intervening years is what consumes her now, and in this unadorned room, the promise of sleep envelops her with its inviting al dente noodle arms. Just as she's drifting off to dreamland, she thinks of her forsaken car in that vacant parking lot somewhere up above, all her life's possessions still locked away in the trunk. All her reasons for leaving home. She was foolish to haul it all the way here, so much dead weight bringing her down. It's nothing now but an unpleasant reminder that she can't ever go back. She can't ever go back...

Ginny Fowler stares at her blurry, distorted reflection in an aluminum mixing bowl as she scrubs its exterior under a steady stream of water. She's not sure what's wrong with her eyes, or maybe her mind, but everything she sees or thinks or feels lately has seemed hazy and warped in a similar way.

This nagging doubt baffles her. She's always had such a sharp memory. In fact, she still remembers, in blistering detail, her first taste of chicken-fried steak all those years ago. The dish had been on regular rotation in her elementary school cafeteria. She remembers the speckled plastic lunch tray in her hands. She remembers the carrot and celery sticks served on the side. The disposable bowl of canned corn, the carton of fruit juice. The overcooked, paper-thin slab of meat was hardly worth recalling as a main entree, but Ginny didn't care at the time. She rarely had a warm meal to eat at home, so those daily lunches were nothing short of a dream. She remembers happily dunking a dry sliver of breaded steak into a paper soufflé cup of ranch dressing as her friends looked on in horror.

As Ginny dries off all the dishes, she keeps replaying that formative childhood memory in her mind on a loop. There is something wrong with it, she thinks. Once upon a time, it had made her smile to reminisce about her favorite food and the origins of her love for it. But her fond recollections have soured over time. Whenever she revisits the day it happened, she's now troubled by the fact that the memory never changes. Try as she might, she can never make any new connections that branch out to other memories. And now the moving picture is starting to fade, the colors melting into one another like the worn-out ribbon of an obsolete video cassette.

The young woman who'd wandered into the diner tonight looking like a lost child? Something about her primal hunger had reminded Ginny of an earlier iteration of herself. But no matter how deep she dredges, she can't piece together who that was. She can only unearth the same handful of memories from each year of her life before this diner was established. Those mental souvenirs have outstayed their welcome at this point. They're starting to disintegrate.

Ginny stares at her hands after she finishes wiping down the kitchen counters. She stares at the lifelines running across both palms. She distinctly remembers experimenting with chicken-fried steak recipes in her youth, years after that first taste. She distinctly remembers adding and subtracting spices and seasonings until she had created the perfect batch of queso to serve on the side. In her mind's eye, she sees a right fist pounding the slab of meat thin with a tenderizer. She sees the back of two open hands coating the flattened cube steak in a flour mixture. She sees a left hand wrapped around the handle of a whisk as the pale gravy thickens below.

Lately, she's becoming more and more suspicious that the hands in these memories aren't hers. That these memories are not, indeed, hers. Maybe they belong to someone else entirely. Maybe they've somehow been planted in her mind. Maybe they're just unrealized dreams.

Ginny distinctly remembers the day she conceived of Sweet Dreams. She remembers the day the restaurant opened its doors to the public. She even remembers some of the hard days of work in between. The rest of the memories are dimming. Maybe they were never there at all. She takes one last look around the gleaming kitchen before she turns out the light. This space feels like hers, but at the same time, it doesn't feel like hers at all. Those warring emotions transform her mind into a battlefield. What she can't ever seem to remember is that one particular side proves victorious every single time. And then she'll forget all about it. Until the whole cycle starts over on another day.

The next thing she knows, the sun has come up. Its blinding rays are streaming into the diner through the plate-glass windows, casting shadows along the floor as she prepares to open for the morning rush. She doesn't remember going to sleep. She doesn't even remember where she sleeps. Even so, she never feels at all tired.

***

About the Author

susanllin.wordpress.com

Susan L. Lin is a Taiwanese American storyteller who hails from southeast Texas and holds an MFA in Writing from California College of the Arts. Her novella GOODBYE TO THE OCEAN won the 2022 Etchings Press novella prize and is now available to purchase at susanllin.wordpress.com, where you can also find her other published work.

Other Works From This Author Links
Touching the Morning
The Pimento
Dear Pluto
The Cloud Artist
Title Subject to Change

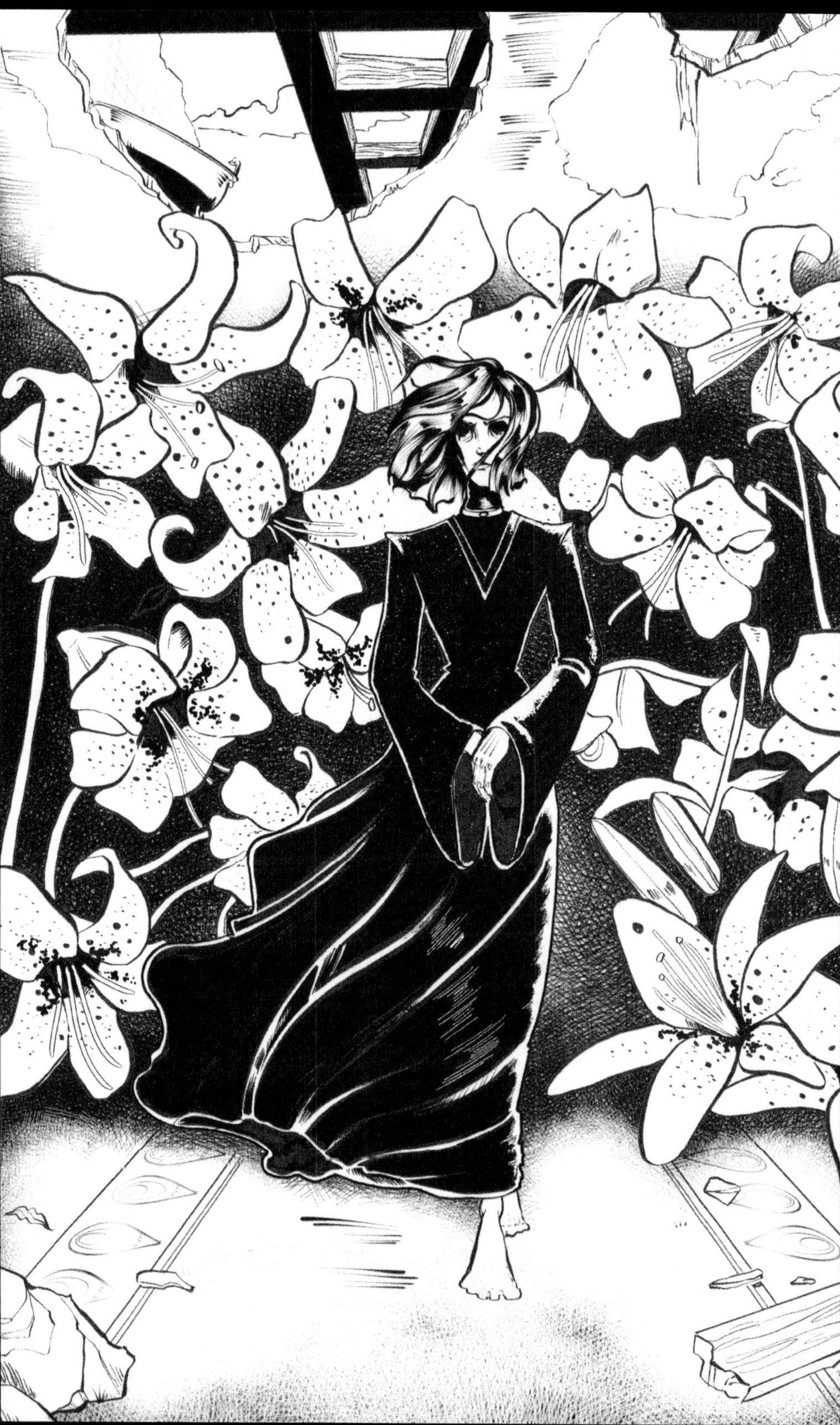

Changeling

by Christopher Yusko

I guess it always was strange, the presence of the Black House in our neighbourhood, but it became a fixture, a place we gravitated to when our parents got fed up with us burning hours in front of the TV, watching cartoons and playing video games, and finally banished us outdoors. Some kids have woods or a ravine to explore. Others amuse themselves at a nearby construction site. For children, these places of vague danger shine with mystery. The crumbling, shuttered manor was ours. I don't think it ever occurred to us how at odds that dark ruin was with its surroundings.

In our defense, I don't remember any adult ever warning us away. We treated the place as a private clubhouse, playing tag or "Monster Hunter" or "What Time Is It, Mr. Wolf?" among the chipped and broken statues out front (I can't call to mind their appearance, even though I remember lying in their long shadows on the scorched lawn, staring at those stone faces as I picked devil's paintbrush). Sometimes we chased one another around the scummy stagnant pond, threatening to fill our Super Soakers with that water, though none of us ever did. No one went inside the house. You didn't *go* inside. The trick was to dare another younger kid to enter, so you could spend the rest of the day mocking them for chickening out.

Thinking back on these times makes my brain hurt. There's so much that doesn't make sense. For one thing, why do I think of Sunnybrook as "our" neighbourhood? Most of the kids I played with were old-stock Anglo types, and we Catholic kids didn't really mix.

I don't remember much of my childhood before the Black House. I don't mean that wistfully, like the memories have faded. I mean that my clearest recollections start when I was nine, maybe ten. Almost all of them revolve around that house, and anything earlier is more like a confused dream. As for my friends, some I remember with near-perfect clarity, others hardly at all. If I ask Mom about those friendships, she'll shut down the conversation like she always does—"Josie, enough is enough! If you don't remember, then I sure don't." Then she'll ask if I've finished all my homework or redirect me to some chore.

I figure this: when we were younger, Mom cleaned houses for wealthy families to bring in a little extra income. She must have dragged me along because I was too young to stay home by myself. But the rich kids accepted the cleaner's daughter? Not just accepted: I remember belonging. Being at the center of things, even. It doesn't seem likely, but... I guess?

No, that's wrong. As I write, it comes to me that I wasn't *always* accepted. It feels like there were two distinct phases with that house: one filled with happiness and belonging, the other bleak and lonely, when it felt like the other children didn't know how to relate to me, and I didn't know how to put them at ease. I remember a period of lashing out, too. Small acts of vandalism and aggression. Being rough with the cat (who, I now cringe to think, had been declawed and couldn't fight back). Cutting a slit in a dress at the mall with an X-Acto knife. Throwing someone's ball through a window of the Black House. Shattering the glass.

These don't seem like things I would do. Something else, too: I had a series of vivid, recurring nightmares around this time. I'd be in a hospital, weak, in pain, and too tired to move. Nothing much seemed to happen in these dreams. Sometimes there were flowers and cards on the windowsill. Once, a blonde woman brought the flowers near, and I turned away from their overpowering fragrance. Sometimes I'd be attached to tubes like they were vines growing over a sleeping girl in a fairy tale.

'Kay Josie, focus. It's the house that matters, not your stupid dreams. At least now I remember how we got in: by breaking that window, I changed the rules. One day I climbed through the shattered pane and convinced the others to follow. The air inside the house was musty but breathable. We stuck to the enormous entrance hall, which was enough adventure for us. Fear kept us from exploring further. A sweeping double-stairway was blocked part-way up by shifting rubble from a collapsed section of the roof. Some of us, the older kids, played a game; swashbuckling with a rusted fireplace poker. Cole sulked and waited outside because I accidentally whacked his knuckles.

There was a huge domed skylight overhead. No matter how bright it was outside, the light fell softly on dusty mirrors and sheet-covered furniture. I'd made myself dizzy staring up at that great high ceiling, spinning in circles with my face raised to the sky, laughing, feeling freer there than I had in my whole life.

Plaster peeled from the walls. There was always broken glass underfoot, even when the older kids tried to clear it out, but I don't remember anyone ever cutting themselves. Ian liked to drape dusty sheets from the furniture over himself and leap out and chase us, but this game stopped after he chipped a tooth, tripping over the faded rust-colored carpet that stretched from the entrance to the stairway. We watched in horror as blood spotted the fabric while he struggled to pull the sheet free.

It wasn't all mischief. Sometimes someone would bring decks of trading cards, and we'd lay down a blanket and play one another. I remember a boy I thought of as a brother. His name won't come to me (another shade flitting on the edges of memory), but I *know* he and I read comics there.

To me, the hall was a hushed space, but not a threatening one. It made me think of cathedrals and incense and being connected to things bigger and older than myself.

I don't know why the others stopped coming. Maybe I was the only one who ever felt at ease. Maybe my dares and taunts eventually lost their power. *Forget them*, I thought. I'd outlasted them, and I'd made the house my own. This period is all jumbled up with those hospital dreams, but it seems to me I spent a lot of time at the Black House. Even when I went out searching for Emily or Abby, I'd find myself in that entrance hall. I must have *told* Mom I was going out to play, then snuck off to binge-read Lemony Snicket or whatever. Soaking in the atmosphere.

Eventually, I started to explore. The whole "left-hand" wing—I'm not sure what to call it—was blocked off by vegetation grown rampant, thick enough that you'd have needed a machete to hack your way through. The hall to the right was flanked by two vases with withered, almost skeletal flowers. That area, along with the rooms I could access through the central doors, offered more than enough to see. I'm tempted to write this off as my child's perspective, but the house seemed far bigger than it should have been. It's not that I wasn't aware of that fact at the time, so much as I wasn't bothered by it.

I'll skip over the minor discoveries that impressed me with mystery—a collapsed door fallen inward on an empty checkered floor, a delicate mouse's skeleton in an old crib, a section of roof fallen in so that you could see into an upstairs bathroom. I've been warming up to it, but this is a ghost story. And it doesn't really begin until I saw The Lady in that impossible garden.

One day, the garden was simply there, a new addition to a passage I'd been through many times before. The structure above had half-collapsed, resulting in a courtyard that was exposed to the elements and filled with white lilies that grew in orderly rows.

I didn't know lilies grew so tall. It felt like I'd been carried away or like I'd drunk the shrinking potion from *Alice in Wonderland*. The sweet, slightly sickly breath of the flowers was heavy in the air. Their massive blossoms sagged under their own weight. I felt vaguely afraid of the petals, which gaped like predatory mouths. Their appearance made me hesitate.

That hesitation probably saved me from being spotted by The Lady sooner, although I don't know if it would have mattered much in the end. In a short story I wrote about the encounter, I named her The Lady of Lilies. A bit grand, maybe, but I like that *Wuthering Heights* sort of stuff.

The woman was veiled in shadow, blonde but insubstantial, a greasy, slightly shimmering smear on the air. Shadows transformed her eyes into pits. The face was otherwise a bland mask. There was an elegance to her long fingers, which blurred to indistinct tips. She drifted among the lilies, disturbing the air as she went so that the flowers nodded and swayed as she passed. When she reached the end of the row, The Lady faded from sight. I backpedaled from the garden, almost tripping over my feet in my hurry to escape the house.

No lie, I was shook. I'd thought the house was for me, but the appearance of The Lady proved otherwise. Was I jealous? Afraid? Let's call it defiant. Because if anything, I became even more determined to make that house my own.

Of course, I saw her again. I'd duck behind some rubble when I spotted her moving down the halls or creep backward if I came upon her crouched with her hands pressed to her face. I'm sure I felt *some* fear, but I figured: The Lady had passed me by without notice. That proved to me that, if she was a ghost, she was a ghost caught up in her own drama. I did go cautiously from that point on. "Rats feet over broken glass" as T.S. Eliot says in my favourite poem. (I call a different type of rodent, though. Hamster? It's my story, and I reserve the right to shift shapes.)

Somehow there was always more house to explore, which was one of the things I loved about it. The Lady wasn't always active. Sometimes the place felt empty of her presence, and at other times I could sense echoes of her reverberating through the corridors, like she was a bat firing off sonar. If that made the house feel unsafe, it also kind of made her easier to avoid. I guess I can't explain it, but I still felt freest in the Black House. Being inside those walls was a *relief*.

(Not sure what I mean by that. The thought was there, but I lost it.)

Anyway, nothing felt truly dangerous until I discovered the Theater. Peeling grey wallpaper, an old recliner, an end table, and a sad, dusty film projector pointed at the wall: it wasn't much, but I don't have words to explain the dread that room inspired. At the time, I loved nothing more than to cozy up in the dark with a good movie, so you'd think I'd be all over a find like that. But no, I felt attacked. From the moment it appeared, it felt like the Theater wanted to swallow me up. Like it would spell the end for me.

I did my best to avoid that room, but it moved along with the rest of the house. More often than not, it seemed as if the Theater would be waiting in ambush down some darkened hallway, its door creaking open as I surged through a familiar corridor toward the entrance.

One change broke in my favor: one of the other kids returned. My memories of her are a reflection cast on choppy water. We called her Bean, I'm sure of that much. That's because her mom always sent her with a bag of jellybeans to share (not the fancy kind).

I tried hard to make things fun for her so she'd stick around. I went easy on her, content to play and hang out in the entrance hall, sharing stories of what I'd found until curiosity set in. I heard her clearly the moment we first went beyond the hall, "They need new cleaners." It set us off in a feedback loop of giggles, each of us losing it again the second the other pulled it together.

    We were like castaways together. Bean loved to play hide and seek among the wreckage, under the spell of being isolated in such a creepy and abandoned place. The game made me nervous at first, but I relaxed when I realized she was afraid to wander too far away from me.

    I don't think she ever did see The Lady, and I'm not sure if she even could. I made a game of it the rare time we did have to take cover. Bean was obsessed with all those creepy legends kids torment each other with, and she flipped when I told her about Slender Man. From that point on, all I had to do was whisper, "Slender Man's coming!" and she'd scurry for whatever room or cover I'd gesture to, sitting red-faced and giggling nervously. When I felt sure The Lady was gone, I'd shout, "He's here!" Then I'd tickle her until, dying of laughter, she'd swat my hands away.

    Everything was better with Bean in tow. Most of the time, our laughter, echoing through the halls of that house, was a counterspell to The Lady's increasingly oppressive presence. This is one of my strongest memories, one where I feel I can almost visualize my friend's face (though if I try to force it, I end up picturing my own features instead). In one of the rooms, we'd found this beautiful mirror stand. The glass had been removed, so the frame was all that remained. Twin boys were carved into either side, each stretching an arm overhead as if they were trying to touch in the middle. Positioned as if we were reflections, Bean and I made a game of copying one another, taking turns trying to make the other crack up. When that got old, we used the frame in our play, leaping through it, imagining it was a doorway to far-off places. I'd always try to get her to stay a little longer when her mom came calling, sometimes wrapping myself around her legs as a joke, as she waited with crossed arms, an expression on her face like, "Seriously?".

We could have spent forever that way, but time intruded into that mysterious house. Bean was gradually "discovered." I'd been safe from the Theater when she was around, but one day it was waiting for us, and Bean darted in before I could react. It seemed to me the room had grown subtly larger. Vases had appeared on the end table, in the corners, and the sight of them filled me with a pure, child's terror, electric, prickling at the back of my neck. Bean was about to touch the projector reel when I grabbed her hand and pulled her violently from the room; she was too shocked to resist. As I exited, I heard a whirring click as if the reel was starting up, and I saw the light on the projector flicker briefly, then dim. Afterward, I told her the room was dangerous and that she should never go in there.

She listened, until she didn't.

The appearances of The Lady also became more frightening. Her face grew elongated, just enough to be disturbing, and there were deep, gaping recesses of shadow where her eyes should be, as if the darkness, like an acid, had eaten deeper into her being. Her mouth was a black and hungry openness, as though she had gorged on shadow, and stained her lips with it. There was a brittle "jaggedness" to her outline, and her movements were more frantic. Disordered. Sometimes she would stop and quiver, like she was being boiled from within.

Why did I keep going there? This is a question I work at often, and I still don't have an answer. It seems to me that I had a knack for *surfacing* at the house. I know I didn't sleep well at the time. The nightmares of being trapped, of pain and suffering, tormented me. It was so bad that I was afraid to sleep, but I would sometimes nap in the entrance hall when Bean wasn't there, because it was the one place The Lady never appeared. Besides, there was such a calm to that setting. It felt like the same motes of dust from when we first entered the house might be suspended in those slow shafts of sunlight, preserved as if in amber.

Sometimes I'd wake, and my whole body would hurt. I shed my fair share of tears. Areas of the house started to feel unsafe, and I encountered ruined and mould-darkened rooms more often. I kept a brave face for Bean's sake, but there's no way I could have fooled her, and she started to avoid the place.

Nothing that happened without my friend mattered. The house, The Lady, myself. We were a trinity entangled, never fully meeting. I sometimes imagined I was the one haunting that place and that Mom would need a Ouija board to call me home. Yet here I am, flesh and blood, eight years later. At the doorstep of the University of Toronto. Not bad for a ghost.

When I came to the Black House on that final night, I could feel a deep change, a glamour unraveling, all protection gone with it. The house was darker, the decay greater, the air heavier, and mould spreading all around. Dust and plaster spilled from cracks in the ceiling. The perfume of the lilies made me gag.

Bean's return was a fever dream I still can't bring myself to believe. Her casual betrayal shouldn't still hurt. It's a sad reality that kids test attachments. Sometimes we draw blood just because we can. Still, the question haunts me: *why* did she run? Bean bolted the second she saw me, whereas I was overjoyed to see her. It was like she didn't recognize me. I should have drilled it into her: the house wasn't safe without me. But I couldn't, because I'd been too afraid to scare her away.

I'm sure I'll be dancing around that final night in therapy for the rest of my life. I have this idea that I'll somehow create something out of these awful memories and, in doing so, force them to mean something.

These days I'm obsessed with film. When I close my eyes I see little movies running through my head. In the scene that plays in my mind, Bean moves in slow motion as she sprints down the hall. The camera dollies in, tracking her with a fish-eye lens. I see myself following, unable to keep up. She's *trying* to lose me. The house falls apart all around us, beams splitting, ceilings caving in. A wall collapses. Not all at once, but the slow demolition of a set piece. Rubble and brick and plaster block avenues of escape. The actors are in no real danger as long as they obey the director's will.

We were led through the garden, where the lilies had been harvested, leaving only stems and empty rows. On through those mazy halls, with no sign of The Lady. Raw hurt hardened to anger as I tried to guess the direction Bean had run. The destination was obvious, but I didn't know *where* I'd find it.

Around a corner, I spotted her standing stiffly at a doorway, light flickering on her damp and frightened face. I was too far away to stop her, and she stepped into the Theater. My legs were boneless. I was sure they were going to give out, but I forced myself to cross to the doorway to confront The Lady.

The whir of the projector filled the room. I was hit once again with the suffocating scent of lilies. Bean stood rapt, watching the vision projected onto the wall. It was only the grainy, jittering image of a set of polished black doors with silver handles, but fear gripped me, and my knees felt weak. I let out a little moan as I traced the beam back to its source.

The Lady waited in the recliner, sitting primly with a vase of lilies at either side. She was terrifying in the projector's unreal light. My friend was oblivious to The Lady's presence. I screamed, "Don't touch her!" as she raised a hand to stroke JB's hair.

The spirit shook in agitation, and the shadowed mouth widened as if to speak, but no sound emerged. I stepped towards them. I didn't know what I was going to do, maybe push Bean out of the way. With that step, something shocking happened. My outstretched hand began to jitter with the same spasms that wracked The Lady, and grew insubstantial. I recoiled, and the disturbance passed, as the surface of a lake calms when the wind dies down. As I cradled the affected arm, The Lady raised a finger towards the doors on the screen, directing me to watch.

All too slowly, the doors swung open.

At first, there was only consuming darkness. For a heartbeat, I saw the hairless head of a child sick in a hospital bed. A sheet was pulled to the chin. From the way it bunched up around the jawline, I couldn't even guess the gender. The kid lay motionless, eyes closed.

A blonde and terrible form materialized and snaked out from within that room. I was rocked by The Lady's scream as she inserted herself between me and that hospital bed. Only, as the scream died away, her aspect became gentler. Tears streaked her face. She reached for me, pleading, not threatening. Radiating grief.

I looked back, and The Lady was gone from the recliner, but the decay that afflicted the house was catching up to us, blistering the room even as I watched. I stepped towards the doors. When I put my foot down, I broke through a section of rotting floorboard.

Only the leg I'd put weight on dangled into the floor below, but I was off-balance, and I landed painfully on my knee. It was like stepping through thin ice and seeing spiderweb cracks spread out all around you.

Somehow I yanked myself free. When you feel sure something's going to grab you from below, it's kind of motivating. In my hurry, I savaged my calf, but it barely slowed me. Adrenaline powered me through as I got to my feet and grabbed Bean's hand.

The image of the doors had become more substantial, more *real*. The Lady was gone, leaving only a gaping darkness. It still felt like whatever waited would be the end of me, but I'd gladly take that fate over being crushed by falling debris. Pulling Bean along, I hobbled to the opening. We went through together. I had a flash of being lifted, pulled from that hospital at great speed, and then... nothing.

I came to in the dust of the entrance hall, dazed and aching. My vision was a soft blur, and it took time for my eyes to adjust. The hall was restored, the ruin undone.

When I turned my head, I nearly screamed. My heart ached for the painfully thin child lying beside me, the one I glimpsed briefly in that room. I didn't recognize this girl. She wasn't Bean, I'm sure of that, but she was probably our age. The hairless head seemed too large for her body to support. The worst thing of all were her large, searching black eyes. They looked so scared, so confused. Tears rolled over the bridge of her nose and down her cheek. I reached for her hand, but she was collected as easily as a kitten, cradled by The Lady, who carried her down the hallway. The girl's terrified eyes locked on me. I was too wrecked to go after them.

The next time I opened my eyes, I was outside, a breeze rustling through the dry yellow grass in the yard. It was evening but still bright. I felt the shadow of a cloud bank pass overhead, relieving the pressure of the summer heat. I felt super guilty—a feeling that's never really left me. I don't know why. About that girl, I guess, but what could I have done? Let's just say when Father Angelo talks about the saving power of grace, it feels like a lifeline.

A woman stood over me and said it was time to go. She insisted she was my mom, and she became livid when I said I didn't know her. Panic came next, once she realized I was serious. Some kids passed by who seemed to know me, and they asked what was wrong. They backed up Mom's story. It helped me trust the situation, at least enough to go with her.

Mom rushed me to the hospital for a marathon of neurological tests. The doctors had no idea what to make of my case. There was nothing physically wrong with me, which suggested that I had developed "selective amnesia in response to trauma." I think going through that door started all my memory trouble.

The following weeks were tough on the family. I didn't know how to behave around the people who were supposed to be closest to me. There was no way I could talk about my memories of the Black House. I knew instinctively that sharing wasn't safe.

I learned to fake memories so that Mom could hope I was improving. She needed that. We all did, but Mom let herself believe in a way I don't think Dad or Luca ever could. Dad... I don't think he ever came to terms. Sometimes I think there's more than one reason he quit the pharmacy to travel the country, pushing pills for Big Pharma. I don't know if it's one of his "old country" superstitions, like he's going to catch amnesia or something, but it's hard not to think that he's *afraid* to be alone with me.

For a while, Mom kept taking me with her to Sunnybrook, hoping it would jog something. I was afraid to go. For one thing, the Black House was simply gone. There's no possible way that I made the place up, but that didn't stop me worrying that I was headed for a psych ward. I kept hoping to run into Bean, but I never did. Maybe I wouldn't have recognized her anyway. After a few embarrassing and uncomfortable run-ins with some neighbourhood kids, we mostly avoided each other. It was a mutual breakup without much drama. Summer was almost over, and we all knew it was for the best.

Besides, I was an afterthought—rightly so—compared to the Irving family's tragedy. Willow, the oldest girl, had been diagnosed with cancer early that summer and suffered a steep decline, passing away early that August. Mom cleaned for the family, but I gather the Irvings were always away: when they weren't at the hospital, Mrs. Irving travelled the globe chasing alternative remedies and "New Age" treatments. I'm not being judgy. If I had children (I won't, but that's beside the point), I'm sure I'd do anything in my power to save them. Kids used to say she messed with "black magic" and other forbidden practices, but knowing how kind Mrs. Irving can be, I never bought that.

Mom was devastated to hear about Willow. Apparently, we played together, and I honestly wish I had some memory of her. Mom thought it might come back to me if we went to the funeral—horrible idea, for the record. I hung off Mom's hand at the door while mourners passed us. I could feel the fury roll off her because I was "making a scene." It turned out to be a closed casket, but I was afraid to see the body.

During the service, I kept my attention on Mrs. Irving, who was pretty, blonde, and elegant. With her devastated husband beside her, and their son, Thomas, clutching her arm, she was the unbowed centre of her family. I don't think she shed a tear. She kept turning back to look at the children in attendance. She seemed a bit dazed, but once she noticed me, she stared as if her life depended on memorizing my features. There weren't a whole lot of kids there, even ones from the neighbourhood. I think our being there touched her.

Mrs. Irving came over as soon as she could. Grief hits everyone differently. I understand that. When she grabbed me, she saw her daughter's friend, and that was as close to Willow as she was going to get. Mrs. Irving crumpled. She dropped to a knee and crushed me to her chest, sobbing.

It was super uncomfortable, I have to admit. Maybe if I had been expecting it. Maybe I'd have turned my head or braced myself or something. Mom eventually pried Mrs. Irving away as gently as she could. I'll never forget the shock on her face as she hissed, "Mrs. Irving!" as quietly and with as much dignity as she could manage. The woman composed herself and told me she was glad I had come, then made me promise we'd talk later.

Mom took me to Sunnybrook a few more times, but Mrs. Irving was always... *intense*. Not creepy in the way you might expect—if anything, she was too nice, almost to the point where she'd go out of her way to talk to me. Even when she wasn't around, it felt to me like she was *trying* not to be around. I don't know if that makes sense. Mom must have picked up on the weirdness because she stopped bringing me. Once that happened, Mrs. Irving didn't have any more work for her.

I swore this time I'd write the whole thing out, full honesty... but I still hesitate to include that. The worst I can say about the woman is she made me uncomfortable one summer when I was a kid. So what? *Grief* is uncomfortable, and Mrs. Irving had been through the worst thing imaginable. Over the years, she's always looked out for me in various ways and has invited the family to dinner more times than I can count. If anything's embarrassing at this point, it's Mom's avoidance. I don't know what she thinks would happen. If she thought Mrs. Irving was going to abduct me or something... well, by now, I think we can relax.

That's why I've never told Mom and Dad about all the "chance" run-ins I've had. There's way too many to be coincidence, and it's more obvious the older I get. "Wow, Mrs. Irving, it's kind of you to sponsor the Catholic Youth Soccer Team I volunteer coach with. Aren't you Presbyterian?" I'm not stupid. She's interested in my life because I'm a link to Willow. That doesn't *have* to be weird. If it helps her. Plus, at least she's nice. At least *one* adult takes an interest in what I do. That's why I don't refuse if she offers to take me to lunch sometimes. She's only stepping into a place Mom and Dad carved out for her.

Maybe this is the real reason I'm finally writing all this down. Mrs. Irving's offer, I mean. It feels like taking advantage. On the other hand: wow, that family's net worth! I think they can spare it. Joking. But is letting Mrs. Irving cut me a tuition cheque any different than her setting up a scholarship for some random student?

I'm not undeserving. My grades are good. I treat people with kindness, and I still volunteer with the Catholic Crusader Athletics Program. I'm a good person and a good teammate. I bike to St. Francis every Sunday, even if Mom and Dad won't go anymore. And I pray for them. I do. There are schools that will offer me scholarships based on my achievements, but is it wrong to want to go to a great one?

Outside my window, the sun is setting. I've been sitting with that last paragraph, watching the sky light up in orange and pink. Downstairs, Luca opens and slams cupboard doors as he looks for something to make himself for dinner.

It's the word "deserving" that's tripping me up. Here I go with the melodrama, but sometimes it feels like there's this sucking pit of quicksand at my core, and all the good I do is a wall raised brick by brick to keep people from seeing inside. And if that's the case, do those good acts count for anything at all?

I think it might help if I could see Bean again. Sometimes I wake with a crushing weight on me, a suffocating guilt that I left her behind. I've worked through this a million times. I did everything I could. Chased her down, pulled her into that hospital room, the same way I escaped the house's collapse. More than once, I've plunked myself down at a library computer to go through a summer's worth of news, day by day. I never find anything. There's nothing to find. If a little girl went missing from Sunnybrook, the whole country would have known about it.

I tell myself these are intrusive thoughts, not much different from, "Did I turn the oven off", or "Are the doors locked?" But when do they go away? It's not like I can even do anything about it. I've been that idiot, taken transit down to Sunnybrook, walked around hoping to find her. Even if she still lives there, it's a city of millions. With my wormy memory, I'd never even recognize her.

I think guilt can be corrosive. Like I wrote about The Lady: a darkness eating into your very being. I've lived that way, with a shame at even existing. Hard *not* to feel it, when your own parents treat you like some cockroach they're forced to care for.

But you know what? I'm over self-pity. All I can do is toughen up.

When I have this entry exactly right, I'll print these pages and burn them, like I've done with past failed attempts. Someday maybe I'll even destroy the USB I keep hidden in my Monokuma plushie. I want U of T to mark a new chapter in my life. I want to put even more distance between me and that mysterious Black House, and let a cascade of new memories, comforting or painful, joyful or sad, fill my heart and seep into the cracks and push that summer when I was ten ever further from my core until it's only a molecule of me. Then I'll make art from it. Purify it. I feel like directing is maybe something I could do. There's nothing to feel guilty about. Dreaming a thing doesn't make it true. I'm in a good place. God has given me many blessings, and if Mrs. Irving is one more that He has put in my way, then what's the harm in accepting the help? Is it a sin to accept a gift? Maybe the sin would be in wasting it.

I am Josie Adorno, 18 years old. The future is open. I'm so ready to drink my fill.

***

About the Author

Christopher's Author Page

Christopher works as a librarian somewhere in the frozen wastes of Canada, where he lives with his wife, his two daughters, and a cat named Dave Waller. His short fiction has appeared in Speculative City, and in the Christmas anthology Of Silver Bells and Chilling Tales.

Other Works From This Author Links

"The Drifting Bodega"
"My War on Christmas"

00:00

Dr. Marcus

by Terence Waeland

Tomorrow, I will see Dr Marcus, and I know exactly what I'm going to say.

There was a hint of moisture in the air that night, but nobody seemed bothered that the celebrations might be rained on. Regent Street was becoming livelier as midnight approached, and I knew that this was nothing compared to what we would be facing imminently. Rob and Baz were already in a party mood and yet, somehow, despite having had as many drinks as them, I was feeling a little detached from all the proceedings, philosophical even. I don't know why; I was looking forward to the fireworks display as much as anyone.

We reached Piccadilly Circus where many people were milling about, like a backwater from the main stream flowing towards the Embankment. "There's no point hanging around here," shouted Baz from behind me. "If we don't get a move on, we won't be near enough to see anything."

At that same moment, I stopped still as I noticed a pair of eyes watching me. Baz overtook and joined Rob ahead. "Come on!" he called back to me. "What are you doing?"

"It's all right. You go on. I'll catch you up," I replied.

"You'll never find us. And we're not waiting."

"Fine. Don't worry about me. If I don't see you two again before midnight, well, Happy New Year!" With a frown, Baz shrugged his shoulders and walked off with Rob, along with the crowd.

She was still looking at me when I turned towards her, but shyly turned her face away when I began to approach. Clutching a large bottle of champagne, she was standing with her arm around a lamp post.

"Hello," I said. "You on your own?"

She cocked her head towards the growing crowd and laughed. "Are you blind, or what?"

"You're not saying you're with everyone here, surely?" My smile was as wide as I could make it.

"What I mean is, you don't seem to be with any group. Or any particular person." Someone near me was shouting as I spoke these last words.

"What did you say?" she asked me. "I didn't hear that."

Now I was starting to feel embarrassed. "I said, are you here with anyone in particular tonight?"

"Oh. No, my friends have left me behind. They've gone to see the fireworks," she shouted. "I've been abandoned."

"Do you mind if I get a bit closer? It's hard to hear you above this noise."

"Sure. I mean, I don't mind." She swung out slightly from the lamp post in a gesture of acceptance, but still clung to it. "I'm not budging from here, though."

I moved in and held the lamp post, too. "Looks as good a place as any, I suppose," I said. "I've been abandoned, as well."

"It didn't look like that to me; I thought it was you that let your friends go on ahead."

"So you *were* watching me!" I grinned. Now it was her turn to be embarrassed. "Anyway, why did you not go with yours?"

"Because they're idiots," she replied. "You need tickets to see the fireworks. I told them that, but they wouldn't listen."

"They sound like my mates," I said. "They reckon they'll be able to sneak in."

"No chance." She took a swig from her champagne bottle. "Want some?"

"Really? Are you sure?"

"I wouldn't ask you otherwise." She almost looked cross, but I could tell she wasn't.

"Go on, then." I grabbed the bottle and drank a bit too much in one go—the bubbles exploded in my mouth, and a white froth dribbled down my chin. She screamed with laughter. Once I had regained my composure, I managed to say, "No flutes?"

"I don't think you'd hear them above this racket," she replied, a little perplexed.

"No, no! I mean champagne flutes. You know, glasses..."

She smiled as she took the bottle from me for another hearty slug. "Far too posh." A few minutes later, she suddenly slid down the lamp post and sat on the ground. She looked up at me. "I'm just having a break—I've been standing here for ages."

"I'll come and join you, if that's all right." I nestled down beside her.

"If that's all right? You don't need my permission!"

"Sorry. Just being polite."

"Maybe you are a bit posh, after all. And now look at you: huddled next to a stranger who's sitting on the pavement like a tramp!"

"I've seen worse-looking tramps."

She raised an eyebrow and handed over her bottle again. "Well, at least it's not Special Brew…"

"I guess I can slum it, in that case, flutes or no flutes."

"My name's Melanie, by the way," she said, stretching out her hand.

I shook it. "John," I responded. "Just plain old John. You've definitely got the posher name."

"Yeah, well. What's in a name, though?"

I paused only briefly. "Quite a lot, actually."

"Actually!" she teased. "Mr Posh!"

"OK. Tell me this. What's the name of that statue over there?"

"You mean Eros? Come on, you can't pretend you don't know that!"

"Ah, but I do know. And his name's not Eros."

"What do you mean? Everyone knows it's Eros!"

"Then everyone's wrong." I looked at her slyly. "OK, not everyone. But probably the majority."

"All right, then, Mr Clever-Posh-Pants," she said in a mock huff. "You tell me what his name is."

"It's Anteros."

"Anteros? Never heard of it."

"And he's not the god of love, either."

"So, what is he? The god of anteaters?"

I couldn't help but laugh. "No, he's the god of *requited* love. Like Eros, he hung around Aphrodite, the goddess of love, but he was not exactly the same."

"I see." I was hoping she was impressed.

"And, what's more, he's also the punisher of those who scorn advances of love..."

Melanie seemed lost in thought for a moment. Slowly, she turned to me and looked me straight in the eye. "That, John, sounds to me like the introduction to the poshest chat-up line ever! Here," she said, passing me the bottle. "I think you need another drink."

"But there's not much left. Don't you want to save some of it for after midnight?"

"Why wait? Live for the moment, that's what I say!"

We both polished off the bottle and stayed for a little while longer, sitting on the ground. As twelve o'clock approached, the crowd pressed around us, and it began to drizzle with rain. "Come on," I said to Melanie. "We should at least stand for the countdown, otherwise we'll look like the world's biggest party poopers."

She nodded in agreement, and I gave her a hand up.

From our lamp post, we had a clear view of the giant illuminated screen, which displayed in bright numerals the remaining seconds of the final minute to midnight. Once it reached ten, the boisterous crowd began to chant the numbers down to zero, and finally raised a massive cheer. At that very moment, I pulled Melanie towards me and kissed her deeply and passionately.

Everyone around us was still celebrating and yelling "Happy New Year" to each other when we finally stopped.

Melanie looked at me with her eyes wide in disbelief. I was the first to speak. "One second into the New Year," I shouted. "Now I'll never forget the exact moment I first kissed you."

The next morning I awoke to the smell and sound of sizzling bacon. Still half-asleep, I wasn't sure where I was, and then I remembered: I had offered to walk Melanie home. The night buses had either been too full or had simply not turned up, and so we had trudged through the rain for nearly two hours before we reached her flat. After inviting me in to dry myself off, she'd opened a bottle of wine and hadn't had the heart to send me on my way when we were finally ready to go to sleep. Now I was sprawled out on her sofa.

Melanie walked in from the kitchen. "Morning, John. Would you like some coffee? I'm doing some bacon sandwiches if you'd like some."

"It smells amazing. Yes, please."

"So, how was your night?"

"A bit of a squeeze on here, but after all the wine last night, I could have slept anywhere."

"You didn't need to sleep on the sofa..." She looked at me coyly.

"I think the floor would have been less comfortable."

"You know that's not what I mean!"

There was an awkward pause. "Oh, I see!" I said. "No, no way. I couldn't sleep in a tent in the garden at this time of year. Far too cold!"

Melanie laughed out loud as she came over to the sofa and planted an affectionate kiss on my forehead. "Come on," she said. "Get your breakfast!" I followed her into the kitchen, and we ate together at the small pine table that took up most of the room. "It's a little bit cramped in here, I'm afraid. The rest of the flat I'm quite happy with but, for some reason, they decided to build this area like a tiny cell. They probably thought it was a good idea to have everything within arm's reach. As if it would be awful to have to use our legs and walk across a room."

"It's cosy..." I said as I sipped my coffee.

"Not enough wall space, though. I want to put some big photos up. What I'd really like is a dramatic fireworks shot."

"Taken by you?"

"Why not? I like taking pictures. I fancy having a go with the New Year fireworks, especially after the way we missed them last night. But we need to book well in advance next time."

We. I was hoping she meant me.

Another time, another coffee. It was Valentine's Day, and we were just finishing our meal in *La Pergola*, an Italian restaurant a short walk away from Mel's flat. The waiter brought over our drinks: Mel had ordered an espresso and, before starting on it, she leaned across the table and inspected my coffee.

"Cappuccino, eh?"

"Yeah, what's wrong with that?" I said.

"Nothing." Her mouth twitched a little, and she looked a little tipsy from the wine.

"Go on. Tell me."

"Well... OK. If I was drinking one of those, I'd have the impression that I was snogging a monkey."

"What?! How on earth do you get an idea like that?"

"The coffee's named after the monkeys, n'est-ce pas? Capuchin monkeys."

"No, it's not!"

"It is! See, you don't know everything, Clever-Posh-Pants." That had become her pet name for me: *Clever-Posh-Pants*. "Capuchins are fluffy, coffee-coloured, and they have a dark bit at the top of their heads that look like they've had chocolate sprinkled on them. That's why the drink is named after them."

"It's not. You've got it all wrong. They're named after the Capuchin monks who happened to wear brown habits."

"Says you!" I noticed her nostrils were flaring. "Anyway, the monkeys have been around far longer than your monks!"

"My monks! Obviously, the monkeys came first, but you've got it the wrong way round, because the monkeys are named after the monks, just like the coffee. And, for your information, the monks were called Capuchins from *cappuccio*, the Latin for 'hood.'"

"You're always so bloody clever, John. You never let me have the last word, do you?"

I kept my mouth shut and fixed my gaze on her. We both refused to speak, and the tension grew. Eventually, it became unbearable, and I was the first to crack: "I'm sorry."

"There you go. You're doing it again: having the last word!"

"But—" At that moment, the waiter sidled up to our table and, without warning, snatched away my coffee. "Wait, I haven't finished with it yet..." My voice trailed off as I realised my protest had fallen on deaf ears.

"I think he's trying to tell us something," whispered Melanie.

"Stop shouting," I replied in an even quieter whisper.

Melanie smiled and suddenly looked away from me towards the waiter, who was approaching again.

"Signor, I bring you a fresh cappuccino," he said, placing it in front of me and hastily retiring.

We both looked at the cup: on top of the froth, sprinkled in chocolate, was the perfectly-formed shape of a heart.

"Well," I said, "at least it's better than snogging a monkey!"

"Or a monk!" said Melanie.

We both began to giggle uncontrollably.

I moved into Mel's flat at the end of March. She watched me from the doorway as I emptied the waiting taxi of the various cardboard boxes I had packed.

"This is only a one-bedroom flat, you know," she said as I shut the front door behind me. "Where's all this going to go?"

"We'll sort it out. By the time I've found a place for everything, you'll hardly notice any difference. And don't worry, I've only brought the essentials."

"Essentials? What's this box here?" she asked, opening it to get a better look. "These look like old LPs."

"It's a passion of mine—I collect vinyl. The sound's so much better—"

"But I haven't got a record player!"

"Ah. OK. Nor have I at the moment," I said. "I tell you what—I'll buy you one for your birthday. When is it, by the way?"

"Two weeks ago."

"Haha, very funny. Seriously, when is it?"

"Seriously, two weeks ago."

"You're kidding! Why didn't you tell me?"

"I don't know. Maybe I just like to keep a few surprises up my sleeve."

"Like the fact that you're weird," I said, shaking my head. "Anyway, let's start shifting all of this stuff, shall we?"

A couple of weeks later, we were sitting in *La Pergola*, which had become our favourite eating place since our little scene on Valentine's Day.

"Happy?" I asked.

"Very. Why?"

"I thought I'd try and make you happier still."

"Oh, yes?"

"I've got you this." I handed Melanie an envelope.

"What is it?"

"Why do people always ask that? It's in your hand, and you immediately ask me what it is. It's an envelope!"

"I know that!"

"Actually..." I was waiting for another *Mr Clever-Posh-Pants* comment. "Actually, it's your overdue birthday present." Mel held it in her hand without moving. "Well, go on, then—open it!" I was expecting a shriek of delight when she saw the contents—two airline tickets to Rome—but she couldn't speak, and tears welled up in her eyes. "You see," I continued, "I can do surprises, as well."

"Have you got any coins?" asked Mel.

"Why?"

"Because I'm not going to throw a ten euro note into the water."

"Fair enough," I said. "I suppose you'll want three."

"One'll do."

"But you're supposed to throw three into the fountain, aren't you?"

"That's only if you plan to get married."

"Really?"

"See! You *don't* know it all, Clever-Posh-Pants! It's one to return here, two for a new romance and three to get married." I gave her one coin. "At least you didn't give me two," she said with a smirk.

"Exactly. You don't need a new romance. And..."

"Yes?"

"... I could do with the money."

"You little sod!" she yelped, punching me on the arm.

"Come on. Chuck it in."

"You don't just 'chuck it in.' You've got to throw it with your right hand over your left shoulder." She stood by the edge of the fountain and hesitated.

"I'm waiting," I said.

"No. I'm not doing it."

"Why ever not?"

Mel gave a little shrug. "I guess I just know I'm going to come back here one day. I can feel it." She turned away from the fountains. "So there's no need to waste the coin."

We walked off towards the Pantheon, the next port of call on our sightseeing itinerary, and Mel seemed lost in thought.

"Hang on a minute," I said. "I've just realised you didn't give me back my coin. That was pretty sneaky."

Mel laughed. "You caught me out! I tell you what, though. Why don't I keep it, and I promise I'll throw it in the next time we're back in Rome?"

"OK, darling. I'll keep you to that."

It was the night before we were due to fly home to England. Our romantic final dinner had been simply perfect and, when we got back to our apartment, we hadn't been able to keep our hands off each other. Melanie fell asleep at first with her head rested on my chest, and I had never felt so completely satisfied in my whole life. I woke up while it was still dark and checked the time: nearly three o'clock in the morning. Rolling over to the other side of the bed, I stretched out to caress Mel's hair. With a start, I realised she was not there.

I sat up and switched on the bedside lamp. Presumably, she had gone to the bathroom, and so I waited. After a while, I climbed out of bed to check: the room was empty. Guessing she must be on the balcony, I wandered over, but that was empty, too. A cold panic seized me. Why on earth would she not be here? There was no reason for her to have left the apartment. I sat on the edge of the bed and tried to reason this out. Maybe she went back to the restaurant because we'd left something there. Her bag? I looked across the room and saw it on the floor by the chair. I went back to the balcony and scanned the streets below but could see no sign of her. Where could she be? At first, I paced around the room, but I couldn't bear to do nothing, so I threw on my clothes and headed downstairs. Should I call the police? Would they take any notice of me, I asked myself, when she'd only been missing for a couple of hours at most?

I opened the front door and felt a wave of relief as I saw her walking towards me, her silhouette unmistakable beneath the amber light of the street lamps. "Melanie!" I cried. "What are you doing? Where have you been?"

She waited until she reached me and put her hand gently on my face. "I'm so sorry, John. I didn't want to wake you. Let's go back up."

We both got undressed in silence and slipped into bed. "Well? What's going on?" I asked.

Melanie sighed. "I just needed a little time to myself."

"So, what did you do? In the middle of the night?"

"I decided to walk over to the Castel Sant'Angelo again. John, it was amazing, floodlit against the black sky. So atmospheric."

"I could have come with you. I wouldn't have minded if you'd woken me up."

"I'm sure you wouldn't, but I needed to think."

"About what? If you don't mind me asking."

"That's OK. It's just that..." She started to cry. "It's just that I wanted to take all this in. I never thought I'd be here, like this, with someone like you. I'm sorry," she sniffed.

"Don't be. There's nothing to be sorry about."

"You see, most of my friends are younger than me, and they've all found someone by now. I was starting to think it would never happen to me. And then I became afraid that this might not last."

"I'll never leave you."

Melanie threw herself around me and hugged me so tight I thought she was going to break my arms.

We were back in *La Pergola*, trying to recapture the flavour of our Roman trip. Once the waiter had brought us our pasta dishes, I leant across the table to pour Mel some wine but, before I could do so, she put her hand over her glass.

"I won't today, John."

"Fair enough—more for me, then!" I said with a grin. "But it's not like you; you were happy enough to glug it down on holiday."

"I know. I'm just being careful."

"Careful? But we're not driving..."

"John, I'm pregnant."

"Yeah, right!" Mel said nothing. "You're not serious, are you?" She began to look worried. "What? I mean... But that's fantastic!"

I reached out to hold her hand. Mel's expression immediately relaxed. "Really? Are you sure, John? I was worried that you'd be upset or something."

"No! Not at all. I just... I can't believe it." I noticed a tear glisten in her eye. "But this is great news! You're happy about this, aren't you?"

"Of course!" she replied, laughing.

"Good!" I took a glug of wine just to calm myself down. "Shouldn't you be making special arrangements now, though? You know, take it easy and all that?"

"I'm not even two months yet!" she protested.

"Sorry. It's just that I've never had one before."

"Nor have I!"

"True. OK, so when did you find out?"

"To be honest, I knew the night it happened. I'm sure of it. You remember when I went for a walk on my own to the Castel Sant'Angelo?"

"I certainly do. I was really worried about you."

"Well, I wanted to savour the moment, to share it with my unborn child. I suppose that sounds silly."

"It sounds wonderful." I raised my glass. "Here's to our new baby!" Melanie smiled a little shyly and took a sip of water.

"When are we going to tell your parents?" I asked. "You can't hide it now, can you?" Mel had still not introduced me to her parents—which was not that surprising, considering they lived in Liverpool—but I was looking forward to meeting them.

"Actually..." she said, sarcastically imitating my *Mr Clever-Posh-Pants* expression. "I've had an idea. Ready for this? I was thinking of not telling them."

"You can't do that!"

"I don't mean not tell them ever. I just thought, wouldn't it be great to turn up unannounced, married and with a baby. The look on their faces!"

"They'll probably have a heart attack!"

"Oh, I don't think so. They know what I'm like: a bit unpredictable."

"A bit! Hang on: you said 'married.'"

"That was my other idea. Why don't we get hitched in Gretna Green? You know, elope? It'd be so romantic!"

"You mean, not tell anyone at all?"

"Exactly!"

"Does this mean you're proposing to me?"

"Exactly!"

I stood at the anvil in Gretna Green's Old Blacksmith's Shop, waiting for Melanie to arrive. The recorded music started, and I knew she had entered the room. As she came up beside me, I turned to her. She looked stunning, but I noticed a quizzical look on her face.

We made our wedding vows before two witnesses and afterwards stepped outside into the bright August sunshine.

"Happy?" I asked.

"You always ask me that. Yes, very."

"It's just that you seemed a bit perplexed when you arrived."

"Did I? Oh, yeah, that's right. I just thought the music was unusual, that's all. Nice, but a bit gloomy. Did you choose it?"

"I did. I wanted something fitting, so I went for the introduction to Act Three of *Tosca*. It's set in the Castel Sant'Angelo."

"Ah, I see. Now I get it—what a nice idea. It's still a little moody, though."

"That's not surprising. The hero's about to be executed at dawn."

"Oh, great! Appropriate, don't you think!"

"Well, it is... actually." She raised an eyebrow. "He's a poet, and he sings about his true love. You should hear the aria. I'll play it for you when we get home. I've got the classic de Sabata recording on vinyl."

"Oh, yes? And what do you think you're going to play it on?"

"The new hi-fi system I just ordered. It's my little wedding present to you. And when baby arrives, you'll be able to play nursery rhymes on it, too."

I sat Melanie down on the sofa. "Right. Now put your feet up and listen to this." I walked over to the new turntable and placed the stylus on the record. "This has to be the first thing we play. Remember this?" I joined her back on the sofa.

"Our wedding music! Still a bit moody, though..."

"Just wait for the tenor to start. It's glorious." We listened initially to the shepherd singing offstage, and soon the jailer approached the poet Cavaradossi. "Right," I whispered to Melanie. "I'm not going to translate all of the Italian, but what's happening now is he's being told that he's got one hour to go before he faces the firing squad, and Cavaradossi offers the jailer his ring to be allowed to write one last time to his lover, Tosca." I put my arm around Melanie, and she rested her head on my shoulder. "Here we go. This is it." The singing began, and I felt myself melting into the music. Halfway through the song, there was a loud click, and the recording jumped back, and the same line was repeated, over and over again. I leapt up in annoyance and immediately turned the record player off. "I don't believe it. I don't know how that's happened; this LP used to be fine. I'm really sorry."

"Don't worry. It's not really my sort of music, anyway." As a consolation, she added, "I'm sure I'll get used to it, though."

"Cheers," I said, raising my glass of wine to Melanie. "I'm feeling a little guilty, though. It's not me who's six months pregnant, and all you're doing to celebrate is having a glass of water."

"Don't worry. If I can give up smoking, I can easily go without wine for nine months."

"I didn't know you smoked."

"Not anymore. I stopped last year. Did it with hypnosis."

"Really?"

"Yeah. I was treated by Dr Marcus. He's a friend of the family, sort of; he was often round our house. When I was young, I used to call him Uncle. Anyway, he'd been doing research into combining psychoactive drugs with hypnosis. Very leading edge, apparently. And he offered to carry out one of his experiments on me for free. He joked that I was one of his guinea pigs."

"Sounds a bit dangerous."

"Well, it worked! In any case, I trusted him completely; we'd known him for years, after all." Melanie went over to the kitchen drawer and pulled it open. "Hang on a minute, I've got his card somewhere... Here we are... Take it, John. You never know when it might come in handy." She handed me the dog-eared business card.

"His name's down as just Dr Marcus," I said. "Marcus is his surname, then?"

"Maybe. To be honest, I'm not sure. It might even be his first name. I've just always known him as Dr Marcus. At any rate, I recommend him highly—he can work miracles."

A few fireworks were being set off when we went to bed. "Why can't they wait for Guy Fawkes Night tomorrow?" I muttered. "People are always so impatient nowadays."

"John, you sound like a grumpy old man. Get to sleep."

I slept fitfully that night, bothered by thoughts that wouldn't quite crystallise into anything specific. After such a shallow sleep, I woke up before the alarm went off and decided not to fight it and to go to the office early. Despite doing my utmost not to wake Melanie, she rolled over in bed just as I was leaving the bedroom. "Hmmm?" she mumbled sleepily.

"Don't worry, darling. I'm just off to catch the 7:38. I've got a pile of paperwork waiting for me."

"Don't I get a goodbye kiss, then?"

"No time, sweetheart. I'll blow you a kiss, instead. Must go."

I shut the door quietly behind me and ran all the way to the station.

It was late in the afternoon and already dark when I got the phone call at the office from the hospital. The nurse sounded worried, despite doing her best to stay calm and professional. "Yes, she's in the emergency room right now, and the doctors are doing everything they can... No, I don't have any more details at the moment... Yes, I think you should get here as soon as possible."

After two long and frustrating train journeys, I finally made it to the hospital. My heart sank when they told me they were still operating on her.

There was nothing I could do but wait. My stomach rumbled with hunger, but there was no way I could eat anything. Eventually, one of the team, a senior-looking consultant, came out to see me and I could see it was going to be bad news.

"Is the baby all right?" I asked, more in hope than expectation.

The doctor shook his head. "We couldn't save the baby—"

"But Melanie. She's OK, isn't she?"

"I'm really sorry to have to tell you, but we lost both of them."

"What? How? It can't be—" I couldn't come out with the right words.

"There was too much loss of blood, I'm afraid. We couldn't stop the haemorrhaging. The whole team was fighting for her but, in the end, she had no more strength to carry on."

My throat constricted, and now I couldn't speak at all. A nurse gently ushered me over to a seat, where I sat motionless for a very long time. Somebody brought me a cup of tea, but I didn't touch it.

Once I had regained a little composure, I stood up and walked over to the window. In the distance, the sky was lit with fireworks, silent bursts of colour through the double-glazing. Despite myself, the thought that kept forcing its way into my mind was not my grief, nor how her family would react… No, I couldn't help but stupidly brood over the fact that Melanie had missed the fireworks again.

Remarkably, I managed to fall asleep when I finally went home in the early hours of the morning. Once I woke up, reality hit me once more, and I felt at a complete loss. After wandering around aimlessly in the flat, I had an idea. Digging out the card from my wallet, I made a phone call. "Hello, is this the right number for Dr Marcus?… Yes, may I speak to him? …Well, it's very urgent. It's a personal matter. Could you tell him it's about Melanie?" For a moment, I forgot her maiden name. "Erm, Melanie Sullivan. Please, it's very urgent…"

A man's voice sounded on the phone, deep and soothing. "Dr Marcus here. To whom am I speaking?"

"I'm Melanie's... It's... I..." He waited patiently. "Look, Dr Marcus, can I come and see you? I can't really do this on the phone. I'm very sorry. I—"

"Four-thirty this afternoon?"

"Er, yes. Yes! Thank you. I mean... Thank you! I'll be there on time," I said and hung up. Suddenly, I felt stupid: why on earth did I say I'd be on time?

I had realised, lucidly enough in the circumstances, that Melanie had never given me any details regarding her family. There was no address written down anywhere, as far as I could see, and I couldn't find her phone. Dr Marcus was the only point of contact I had, and I wasn't even sure if he was a relative or not.

By the time I arrived at the clinic, I was a wreck. I hadn't been able to stop blubbering on the way, and now the receptionist had obviously noticed that I was trembling badly. Dr Marcus led me into his office immediately, sat me down and waited for me to speak.

I took a deep breath. "Melanie died last night." I still couldn't believe I was saying those words.

"Oh, no. That's awful. She was such a sweet girl. What on earth happened?"

"She was pregnant—seven months—and she had a miscarriage. They couldn't do anything." I started crying again.

"And you're the father?"

I nodded. "If it wasn't for me, she'd still be alive, wouldn't she?"

"You can't blame yourself." That soothing voice again.

"I don't know what I'm going to do. I don't think I can live without her." I broke down completely and huddled up in the chair.

After a while, Dr Marcus spoke again. "Can I get you anything?"

"Yes, please. I want Melanie." Such was my current state of mind, I was almost laughing when I said this, but the doctor watched me in deadly earnest. "She told me you could do miracles..."

He opened a desk drawer and took out a form. "I can help you with the pain, if you want." I must have looked confused. "The emotional pain, I mean. I can help you."

"How?"

"Melanie might have told you I practise hypnotism. I think you might be amenable to it, and you look as though you need a way to deal with this situation. My technique involves combining hypnosis with some powerful drugs. I've had remarkable results."

Although I was vaguely aware that this didn't feel like normal procedure—I wasn't his patient, after all—I was too overwrought to think this through objectively. "I just want her back."

"I can sense your pain. Melanie wouldn't have wanted to see you go through this suffering. In memory of her, let me do this for you." He slid the form across the desk. "You just need to sign, and I'll take care of it."

"Anything... " I said dejectedly while scribbling my signature.

Within a few minutes, he had given me an injection and was already speaking to me in a way that felt reassuring, even though I couldn't really make out the words. The last thoughts I remember having were that I hadn't yet got around to asking him for Melanie's parents' address.

After a fitful sleep, I woke up early and switched off the alarm. I found myself tiptoeing around the bedroom, and I wasn't sure why I was doing that. In the gloom, I looked at the bed, and my heart leapt: Melanie was lying there, sleeping peacefully. What had happened? Was the last twenty-four hours just a bad dream? Still feeling confused, I wanted to jump on the bed, wake her up and give her a big hug. But I couldn't. For some inexplicable reason, I continued to quietly get ready to go to work. Just as I was leaving the room, she suddenly rolled over in the bed. "Hmmm?"

"Don't worry, darling. I'm just off to catch the 7:38. I've got a pile of paperwork waiting for me." What was I doing? Why was I saying this?

"Don't I get a goodbye kiss, then?"

"No time, sweetheart. I'll blow you a kiss, instead. Must go."

Despite shutting the door quietly behind me, I desperately wanted to go back in and speak to Melanie but, instead, I ran all the way to the station.

All day long, I mulled over what was happening to me but somehow carried on with my office tasks as normal. The dream had been so vivid, and I even remembered dealing with the exact same paperwork as I was doing now.

Late in the afternoon, the phone rang: it was the hospital, and the nurse sounded worried. "Yes, she's in the emergency room right now, and the doctors are doing everything they can..."

The pit of my stomach churned. No, I can't go through this again, I thought.

I even recognised the passengers sitting opposite me on both trains. And when I arrived at the hospital, sure enough, they told me they were still operating on Melanie.

Once the consultant came out to see me, I already knew what had happened, but I still could not help asking, "Is the baby all right?"

The doctor shook his head as before and informed me that they couldn't save the baby and then that Mel had died, too. The exact details all over again, the haemorrhaging, the loss of strength...

Even though I recognised everything that was going on, I still felt the same physical sensations. My throat constricted: this was no dream.

Eventually, I walked over to the window and watched the fireworks again. Why was I being punished like this?

When I woke up, Melanie was in bed next to me. As soon as I got up, I realised that it was now the day before Melanie died. She was still with me, and I could still love her, but only as long as it was in exactly the same way as before. No deviation. I was powerless to alter the tiniest detail.

Was this how Dr Marcus was treating me? Helping me relive my experiences so that I could find closure? If so, when would I wake up, and would I be better for it?

The same few fireworks were being set off when we went to bed. "Why can't they wait for Guy Fawkes Night tomorrow?" I heard myself muttering again.

My life was apparently moving backwards. On the six-month anniversary of Mel's pregnancy, I again raised my glass of wine to her, and she told me once more how Dr Marcus had helped her give up smoking. She gave me his dog-eared business card: "I recommend him highly—he can work miracles."

Time moved on. I think.

Now I was sitting on the sofa listening to *Tosca*, and I knew the exact moment the stylus was about to jump on the record.

Then it was our wedding again in Gretna Green. "Happy?" I asked.

"You always ask me that," she said. "Yes, very."

After our wedding, Melanie proposed to me, suggesting we elope and, back in *La Pergola*, she told me she was pregnant.

Rome, the night before returning to England. We had made love, and now I was awake at three o'clock in the morning. I knew she had left the apartment to walk to Castel Sant'Angelo, and yet I still had to stretch out my arm to caress Mel's hair. All the anxiety flooded through me when I found the bed was empty; I silently told myself to go back to sleep, but my body wouldn't let me. I threw on my clothes, headed downstairs and watched Melanie's silhouette walking towards me, as I knew she would, glowing beneath the street lights.

She still didn't throw the coin in the fountain, and she cried when she saw the airline tickets in the envelope. I moved into her flat. We had the silly argument about my cappuccino.

"Morning, John. Would you like some coffee? I'm doing some bacon sandwiches if you'd like some."

As we talked over breakfast, following my night on the sofa on New Year's Day, I was suddenly overwhelmed by the realisation that there was only one day left of the time I'd had with Melanie. What was going to happen next? Was this the end of my treatment? Would I suddenly wake up? Or was I going to continue living backwards and eventually regress to childhood? I carried on my conversation with Melanie while I continued pondering these questions.

Maybe this was not just hypnotism? Maybe I was actually reliving my whole life through some strange, mystical phenomenon, and I was going back to the womb. Is this how you die? Am I dead already?

Eros. Anteros. The crowd chanting the countdown to midnight. The long kiss one second later. Our trudge through the rain to Mel's flat. Drinking more wine. Curling up on the sofa.

Was this it?

I awoke to the smell of sizzling bacon. After a brief moment of disorientation, relief surged through me. Melanie was cooking breakfast in the kitchen—I hadn't lost her. Then I remembered I was on the sofa, and I had only ever slept on it once, on the morning of New Year's Day.

She walked into the room. "Morning, John. Would you like some coffee? I'm doing some bacon sandwiches if you'd like some."

"It smells amazing. Yes, please."

I was still unable to say anything else. So, what was happening now? The days seemed to be going forwards again: did this mean I was being given a second chance? My consciousness was floating above everything around me, detached from reality but acutely—supernaturally, even—aware of what was going to happen next, down to the tiniest detail. But I couldn't change anything; I couldn't even wiggle my little finger if it hadn't been pre-ordained. So, what was the point of all this? If there even was one...

Melanie was explaining to me how small the kitchen was.

Inexorably, we were both heading once more towards that fateful night in the hospital. We argued about the cappuccino again—*Clever-Posh-Pants*—and I unpacked my box of LPs in her flat. Rome came and went, we married once more at the anvil, and the record jumped. I blew Melanie a kiss before I ran off to the station, and my heart was in my mouth as I waited in the office for the call. The phone rang, and I sat in the hospital listening to the bad news from the doctor. I just could not believe I was having to go through this yet again.

I saw Dr Marcus the next day, and I wanted to tell him not to give me the injection, but I was blubbering and begged him to let me have Melanie back.

I woke up early and tiptoed around the bed, trying not to wake Melanie. I waited in the office for the call from the hospital...

We were moving towards our first meeting in Piccadilly Circus, and nothing ever changed. I didn't want to see her eyes watching me through the crowd, and I didn't want to escort her back to her flat. We shouldn't have made love the night she walked to Castel Sant'Angelo. One single change would have made everything different. The butterfly effect. But only my thoughts changed; my words, my actions, everything around me remained exactly the same.

And so it continued, again and again. I felt like a tide being pulled between two shores; I often lost track of whether my time was going backwards or forwards. Was I in a coma? Had the hypnosis treatment gone terribly wrong? Would I ever wake up?

"They know what I'm like: a bit unpredictable."
"Don't I get a goodbye kiss, then?"
"I was starting to think it would never happen to me. And then I became afraid that this might not last."
"You see, I can do surprises, as well."
"Morning, John. Would you like some coffee?"
"I'll be there on time."
"Take it, John. You never know when it might come in handy." No! Don't take it!
"She told me you could do miracles…"
"I can help you."
"Happy?"
"You always ask me that. Yes, very."
"And when baby arrives, you'll be able to play nursery rhymes on it, too."
"My name's Melanie, by the way."
"I'll never leave you."

I didn't touch the cup of tea. I stood up and walked over to the window in the hospital. After the red firework burst, I knew the next one would be blue, just as it always was. And then gold. And then green. And then red. As always.

"So, what is he? The god of ant-eaters?"

"See! You *don't* know it all, Clever-Posh-Pants!" I wished she would stop calling me that. It wasn't funny anymore. After all these times, I couldn't stand the damn pet name. In fact, I hated it. But I had to laugh.

As always.

They say true love never dies. More's the pity.

Tomorrow, I will see Dr Marcus, and I know exactly what I'm going to say.

***

About the Author

terencewaeland.co.uk
Coming later this year!

By trade, Terence is a graphic designer and photographer, living in Kent. Although we have the pleasure of being his first short story publisher, his previous submissions have reached the top thirty of the London Short Story Prize an the semi-finals of the Screencraft Cinematic Short StoryC ompetition. He has also written two full-length thrillers.

Other Works From This Author Links
Flash Fiction submitted to Sensorially Challenged Volume 3

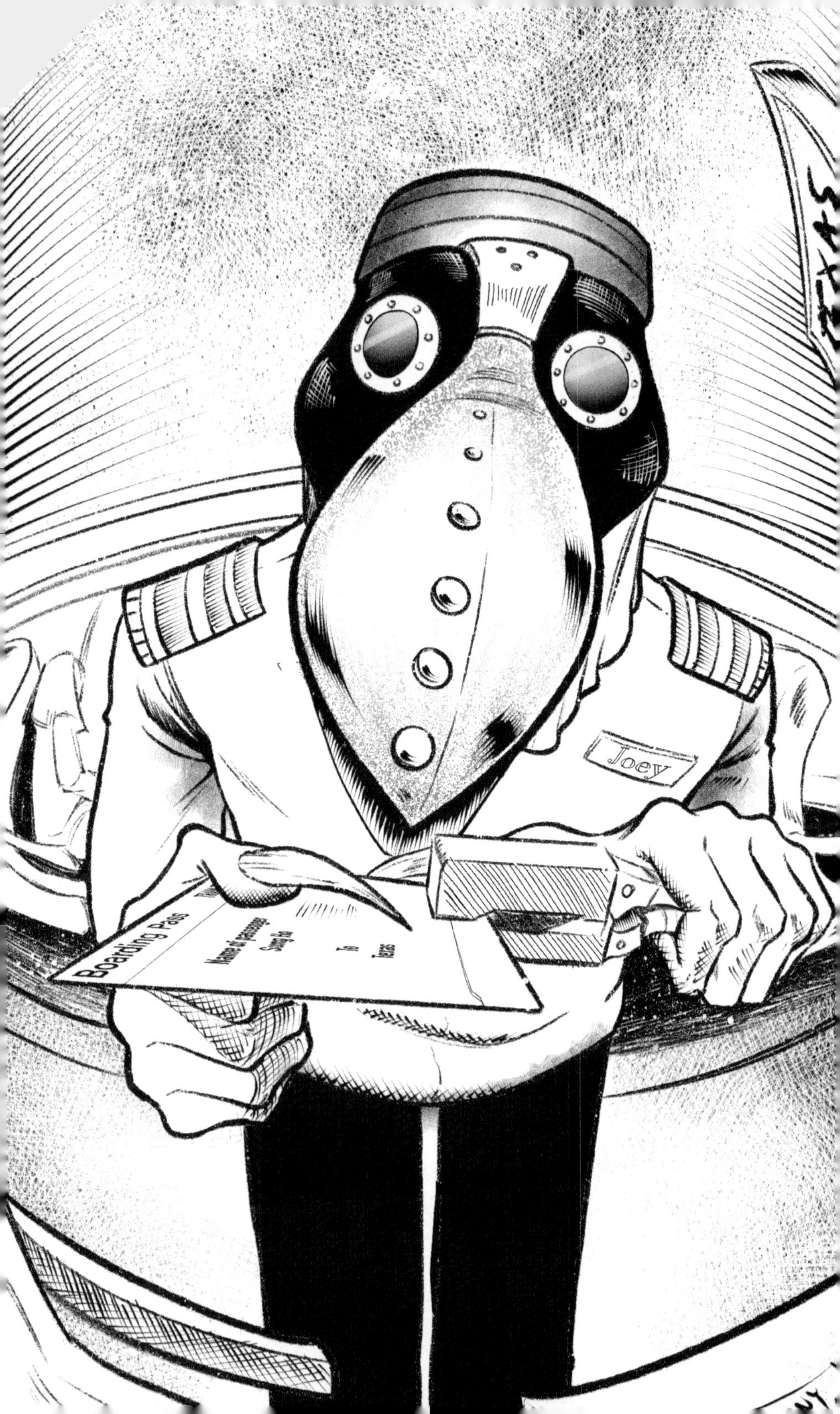
Joey
Boarding Pass
Name of passenger
To
Texas

Without You

by Clarence Carter

Footsteps on the platform clattered and thumped as Areum stood in the corner with her hands clasped over her ears. Loud noises had always been an issue. Once she'd owned a pair of noise-cancelling headphones. Those, like most of her belongings, were gone. Closing her eyes did nothing to reduce the anxiety.

Her son, Sung-ho, stood by her side patiently. Opening her eyes, those big, beautiful browns were staring back. He had a curiosity about him well beyond his age. Although he spoke well for nine, he'd never overcome a terrible shyness.

The ticket in her pocket read Texas, and she was grateful to escape the cold. New England winters had never grown on her. What little she remembered of Korea didn't impress her either. Besides, the way her mother spoke about it made her miss it less.

Every few seconds, Areum checked over her shoulder, expecting someone to be there. Walking through the crowd brought on another level of paranoia. Their greedy eyes searched her as if inspecting a piece of meat.

Men in suits passed, bumping elbows with denizens of the station. Overflowing trash cans stunk of yesterday's garbage. The cement benches in the center were riddled with graffiti, some of the images phallic in nature. Litter blew in the breeze.

An old man sat on the floor, drumming a rhythm on an overturned bucket. This had drawn Sung-ho's attention. With that mature curiosity, he watched as the man slapped his drumsticks, creating a beat.

In the corner of the platform sat a vendor cart. A dingey-looking thing, once white, beaten down by age. A smiling black man stood behind it, serving hot dogs for a dollar a piece. Sung-ho tugged at her sleeve and pointed to the cart, which she'd been eyeballing herself. They hadn't eaten all day.

Tied to the side of the cart were a handful of balloons meant to draw in children. As Areum stepped up to it, she observed the selection. There were only hot dogs and a few options for soda. And balloons.

Sung-ho tugged at her sleeve and pointed at them.

She nodded.

They ordered two hot dogs and a balloon. Areum smothered her dog in everything, hoping the toppings would add caloric value. They didn't have much money, and Texas was still far.

There weren't any available seats on the benches, which didn't bother her. They were going to be sitting for several hours anyway. Ketchup had already covered Sung-ho's mouth. That boy never could keep clean. Areum pointed at it, to which he shrugged. With a napkin, she wiped his face, making him squirm.

The dog was surprisingly good, considering she'd gotten it off a cart and only for a dollar. Tying the balloon around his wrist proved to be difficult because he wouldn't stay still. They made short work of lunch. Tossing the trash away, she wondered if the balloon would survive the trip.

The green balloon bounced up and down as Sung-ho ripped it out of the air and slapped it. Repeatedly he did this with an obnoxious whap. To be a kid again, she thought distantly. To entertain herself as an adult was expensive, but a cheap balloon could keep him occupied for hours.

A strong blast of the horn warned of the train's arrival, followed by a rattle that shook the station. As they gathered in small lines, Areum followed their lead. They'd clearly done this before.

Whack, whack. Sung-ho slapped the balloon, missing a bald-headed man by inches. Another disapproving look stopped him, temporarily. Palming the balloon like a basketball, he moved his fingers on it, creating a squelch.

An elderly woman with an expensive purse had been looking at her. Ever since childhood, she'd shied away from strangers' looks. As the vibrations of the train shook her legs, she wondered why the woman had been staring.

The metallic screech of the brakes sent shockwaves that pierced her eardrums. She winced against the pain. The headphones would have done wonders. As if Sung-ho could read her mind, he gave her hand a gentle squeeze.

How'd I get so lucky? she thought.

The crowd bumped and pushed onto the train. Clinging tightly to Sung-ho, desperate not to lose him, she boarded. People trickled into their seats. Verifying with the ticket, she found theirs in the third car. They had no luggage to store. Sung-ho took the window, leaving her with the aisle.

On the platform, the drummer stood and took a bow. A couple of people clapped, and he began gathering his things.

A man in a blue suit with long gangly fingernails walked up the aisle. He stopped at each seat, asking for the tickets. The metal hole punch crunched with each one. He worked diligently, asking the occasional passenger a question or two. He feigned interest, but Areum sensed danger.

As he got closer, she wondered what it was that gave her that feeling. He looked like any ordinary transit employee, blue suit, hat, shiny shoes, and a pin. Everything looked normal aside from his long nails. Perhaps it was the confidence with which he took authority or the smile that said, I'm fooling all of you, and you're too stupid to realize.

The tremble in her hands wouldn't stop as she extended the ticket to him. A devious smile crossed his face, and she imagined him using those crooked teeth to bite off children's fingers. Pain erupted in her mouth as she bit into her tongue. Entertaining those thoughts could be detrimental.

The hole punch crunched. "Are you going to Texas for business or pleasure?" he asked in a slow, monotone.

After imagining that, she found it difficult to look him in the face. "My mother has fallen ill."

With lips much too wet, the smile faded. "Sorry to hear that." He returned the stub and moved to the next seat. "Business or pleasure?" his voice continued.

The crunching hole punch and the visual of him biting fingers paired into one terrifying experience. Deep in her imagination, she imagined the spittle on his lips as blood.

This is how it starts.

After the door swished open, she immediately regretted what she'd said. Her superstitious mother wouldn't forgive her for such a lie. She, like many Koreans, had the Han. Areum did not inherit her mother's beautiful green eyes, but she did inherit that awful feeling of dread and grief.

The lie festered beneath her skin like an infection, and each returning thought made it more gangrenous. *I wouldn't have said it under ordinary circumstances.* Now that she'd put it out there, she hoped it wouldn't come true. Their family had been through enough.

An image of her mother floating through the kitchen came to mind. Her hips swung to music from the old country, and oven mitts covered her hands. A smile shone on her face. A beautiful vision if ever she'd had one. The smile faded. A wet, choking sound escaped her lips. Her hands rushed to her throat as rivulets of blood spattered the mitts.

My mother has fallen ill.

Sung-ho's hand fell on top of hers, startling her from the vision. A worried look covered his face. He said nothing, only held her hand in silence. At times, he read her like a book, and she always wondered how.

Even with the comfort of her son, Areum struggled to shake off the hallucination. Thunderous gallops of her heart eased as she settled further into the seat. Using the breathing techniques Dr. Maverick taught her, Areum calmed herself. If things got intolerable, she could always take the pills.

The lump in her pocket assured her. The safety net.

They had time to kill and nothing to do. A cell phone would have been great entertainment if she'd had one.

The train clattered on the tracks, and trees flashed by the window. Sung-ho looked bored. The balloon had since been forgotten. With a closed fist, she held it out to him. Kai, bai, bo.

At first, Sung-ho looked at her as if she were crazy. Then she bounced her fist a couple of times, and he got the gist. The first round, she'd gone paper, and he'd gone rock. Second round, he did paper, and she'd switched to scissors. Then third round, she kept scissors, and he'd gone paper.

They went on like this until the sun knelt behind the trees. Eventually, Sung-ho leaned his head on her shoulder and watched out the window as she ran her fingers through his hair. It didn't take long before a light snore filled the silence.

Once, she'd heard something about idle hands. Her hands weren't the problem, but her idle mind was.

The thought of her ill mother returned. She envisioned her bent over, spattering blood from her mouth, and painting the kitchen floor. After she'd said it, it became a possibility. Her hand crept over the pill bottle, but she refused. A little longer, she told herself. In the depth of this vision, someone found her mother's body. They, too, became infected.

In an effort to occupy her imagination, Areum observed the train car. Across the aisle sat an older black man with a newspaper. The light barely lit it, and she could tell he'd given up. It sat in his lap more as a decoration than anything. She thought about his backstory. Searching for clues, checking his shoes and his clothes, she guessed approximately how much money he made. It all seemed rather boring. What she'd accessed to be a teacher or an accountant wasn't good enough.

Instead, she imagined him to be a deacon or a religious leader of sorts. Her public school education and nonreligious parents had left her incapable of differentiating between the many denominations in the Boston area. Lutheran, Baptist, Presbyterian. For a while, she imagined him giving a sermon and the cadence of his voice, the one she'd projected on him, brought her comfort.

Ahead three rows sat a beautiful blonde who periodically stole glances to her right. Areum imagined it to be an equally attractive man, muscular and well-dressed. They'd been giving googly eyes the whole time.

The mind games were fun. By the time the train had gone dark, she'd made up backstories for everyone in sight. She'd even come up with a story for the eerie ticket man. He wasn't a man at all but the bringer of death. It was his job to escort people to either heaven or hell.

My mother has fallen ill.

She imagined her mother lying on the floor, blood dripping from her mouth. Those beautiful green eyes wide open, staring at her, knowing. Perhaps the ticket man would collect her. If Areum could, she'd have called her mother and confessed. She'd have begged for forgiveness and only then purged herself of the guilt.

The door to the next car swooshed open, and she saw something. It took her a long time to determine what she'd seen, or what she thought she saw. In the next car stood a man dressed in black, holding what looked like a cane. He'd been prodding someone with it. Perhaps poking them while they slept. The thought made her chuckle based on its sheer lunacy.

To her left, the man coughed. An uneasy feeling raised gooseflesh on her skin. The vision of her mother hacking blood on the floor was still fresh in her memory. Although a coincidence, she didn't like it. Then she thought about the spread.

Her foot tapped repeatedly against the floor. Sung-ho rustled off her shoulder and leaned against the window. His eyelids flickered as if he were in the depths of a fascinating dream. Once, she'd even sworn he made a noise, like a kitten. The balloon hovered freely above his head.

The man coughed again.

Areum turned to him, hoping he was alright. What she saw instead was an increase of coughs, deeper and wetter. With a hand to his mouth, his eyes bulged. Desperation and confusion covered his face.

A few rows ahead, more coughs erupted. The blonde woman who'd stole glances at the hunk came next. A hand covered her mouth. A heinous chorus of croaks and gags filled the interior of the train car.

A million bizarre thoughts ran through her mind, one of them being that it, whatever it could be, might be coming from the window. For whatever reason, the cough had skipped her and Sung-ho.

The door swished open again. On the far side, she saw him.

A bird-like mask with goggles hid his face. He used the cane to push at someone on the floor. They weren't sleeping. They were dead.

Just before the door whirred closed, he looked at her.

Her breath caught in her throat.

The pulse in her temples quickened.

Guilt poured over her, knowing that she'd brought this hell upon herself. Quickly she pulled the orange bottle from her pocket and stared at the pills. It would have been so easy to take them, to give in. Instead, she returned them to her pocket and closed her eyes.

When they opened, the ticket man stepped through the door. There wasn't anyone behind him. No bird-like mask, no goggles, and no cane. Simply the ticket man asking, "Business or pleasure?"

Their eyes met, momentarily. The uneasy feeling remained. Something about him rose her defenses. The image of him biting off children's fingers returned, and the sound echoed through her mind.

Areum clasped her hands over her ears and tried the breathing techniques again. Dr. Maverick had talked her through meditations many times before. Focusing on her breath, Areum tried to think of nothing else.

As her thoughts cleared, the man to her left stopped coughing. He'd reclined his seat the allotted three inches and rested his hands across his potbelly. With his eyes closed, he looked peaceful.

She thanked her lucky stars that it wasn't reality, but only some dimension of hell she'd imagined. Riddled with anxiety, she couldn't wait until they arrived in Texas. There she could call her mother. There she could set things straight.

Sung-ho moaned in his sleep, shuffling uncomfortably. She stroked his head a couple of times, easing the nightmare.

The train jostled and blasted its horn. Much to her surprise, her son didn't wake. He didn't even stir. Out the window, scattered trees blew in the wind, judging by the descending speed they were approaching another station. More than anything, she wanted to wake Sung-ho and get off, but they were a long way from Texas still.

Although no one entered her car, their luggage clattered on board. Their voices carried through the automatic door. The windows did nothing to muffle the sounds from the platform. There were fewer people, probably because it was night. Their tired faces reflected her own.

With more energy, she might have given them backstories or observed their belongings to guess their careers. Her mind had grown too tired for that. The fight to keep her eyelids open intensified.

The train blasted its horn again as it chugged to life. The people on the platform disappeared, giving way to more trees. Occasionally they'd let up, and she'd see an intersection with a car or two, or a handful of buildings. Otherwise, it remained the same.

Her eyelids had grown heavy, and she longed for sleep, but that lingering fear kept her awake. If she closed them, Areum feared horrible dreams awaited. Her mother lying on the floor in a pool of blood. The passengers with their bodies slumped over in the seats, or worse, all over the floor. She imagined this thing spreading, infecting people by the millions.

Also, she knew he'd be there, lurking deep in the recessions of her nightmare. Wearing all black with that bird mask, tagging along with a cane. He would be there, and he might never leave.

Another station and tons of miles passed. Over time she'd regained control. Above, what little she could see from craning her neck, showed a pallet of brightly illuminated stars. They were beautiful.

That old nursery rhyme came to mind. Star light. Star bright. Areum found herself wishing upon a star that the hallucinations would end.

With his hand in hers, she felt as if the good within him balanced out the evil she imagined in the world. Sung-ho could bring balance where the chemicals in her brain couldn't. Without him, she had no purpose. No reason to live.

Darkness cast upon the train as they entered a long tunnel. The walls outside were only lit by a periodic lantern. The lining of the ceiling had two strips of bulbs that barely illuminated the car. Outside the window, she saw nothing but stone walls.

The chugging deepened from the echo of the tunnel.

Ahead the unseen hunk coughed.

Not again.

The door swished open, and the man stumbled in. *Thump, thump, tap.* With the tip of the cane, he touched the unseen man. His leather-gloved hand raised to the mask, adjusted, and returned to his side. *Thump, thump, tap.*

Areum's heart pounded against the walls of her ribs.

The man had collapsed into the aisle. The masked man prodded him with the cane again, poking his sides. Lying on the floor with outstretched arms, he wheezed. His hands stretched for the masked man but didn't reach him.

Coughs sounded from the car behind her, loud ones.

He must have heard them because he moved again. *Thump, thump, tap.*

The leather seat pressed against her face as she hid from him.

A wet, obnoxious cough came from beside her. Her eyes grew wide in disbelief as she turned and looked at Sung-ho. His face had gone pale, and his eyes dark. Sweat stood out on his forehead. In the pits of his shirt were stains probably caused by a fever.

With a finger pressed to her lips, she silenced him. More than the illness itself, she feared he would come. With her eyes, she pleaded for his silence, begged for it.

Sung-ho clasped a hand over his mouth.

Maneuvering around the seat, she stole another glance at the front of the car. The man in black had moved on to the beautiful blonde, who'd slumped over with her head dangling from the armrest. Her head swiveled in response to his cane. Unpleasant groans left her lips, but she was too tired to protest.

Areum tried to suppress a whimper, but she was too late.

The masked man's head spun, eyes peering in her direction.

She sunk behind the seat. Had he seen her?

Thump, thump, tap.

The noise intensified in both volume and proximity.

Thump, thump, tap.

Even if she could run, there was nowhere to go.

Eyes clenched tightly, she started chanting, "You're not real. You're not real."

For a long time, she didn't dare open them. She imagined him standing there, waiting to scare her.

Only in her imagination, she smelled leather and death. When she dared open her eyes, he wasn't there. After checking the aisle, she concluded it wasn't real.

The fear of these delusions intensified. Every time she imagined him, he got closer. Instinctively her hand clasped over the mound in her pocket. The safety net.

Sung-ho looked fine. He'd jostled in his sleep again but didn't look feeble and pale as he had in the vision. Fog from his breath pattered the window.

Every muscle in her body ached from tension. Exhaustion clung to her like a wet blanket. She couldn't wait to get off the train and resume the next chapter of her life.

Desperately, she clung to reality. If she allowed her imagination to wander, things would get worse. Areum didn't know exactly what would happen if he reached her. For a second, she imagined staring into the black mask of death and shuddered.

Luckily the man across the aisle had closed his eyes. Otherwise, he'd have witnessed her panic and called the police. Then they'd find her and drag her back there.

Within those walls, she wasn't allowed to see Sung-ho. They made sure of it.

After talking herself off the ledge, an ounce of comfort swept over her. The hallucinations wouldn't last forever. They never did. Once she reached a pay phone, she was certain they'd go away.

Within the stillness of the train, Areum's head nodded. The battle to keep her eyes open was coming to an end. Several times she told herself to stay awake, to be vigilant.

The masked man wasn't real, of that she was certain, but she knew her imagination could be her worst enemy. All sorts of horrific scenarios ran through her mind, sometimes indistinguishable from reality. As a young girl, that imagination had been her best friend. Before she'd grasped English, she'd had no friends except those in her head.

A light sleep came over her, but no nightmares waited. A couple hours passed, and her eyes opened to the orange glow of dawn. With the sun came a sense of ease. Less bad things happened in the daylight.

Much to her surprise, Sung-ho was awake. He'd taken her hand in his and stared out the window, as he'd done before. He, too, looked mesmerized by the sunrise. The balloon drifted above his head, forgotten.

A gurgling erupted in her stomach. The hot dogs had worn off, and she was hungry again. There had been a café car somewhere on the train, and she wondered if she could find it. As she shuffled through her pockets, she concluded there wasn't enough money. They'd have to wait.

Off the edge of his seat, Sung-ho kicked his feet. This made her smile. With a boy as painfully shy as him, she'd learned to pick up on his body language. Much like she'd done with English, she studied him carefully.

That nap did nothing to repair the exhaustion. They could sleep when they arrived.

The brakes screeched again, followed by the blaring horn. Ahead was another train station. Outside, she watched as people walked freely about the city. They looked happy, most of them. The train hissed as it stopped, and she saw them on the platform, waiting to board.

Thump, thump, tap.

As if in slow motion, the doors sprung open. People boarded. He stood at the front of the car with his hands resting on the brass notch of the cane.

To her right, she looked out the window at the platform. The people waiting in line had changed. They weren't happy morning commuters anymore.

The flesh around their mouths had split and dangled. The skin hung loosely from their bones like lepers. The life that had once shone from their faces had been replaced by an emotionless, peeling mask. These people brushed past the man in black as they boarded. With them came the pungent odor of rotting flesh.

Their feet dragged as they crept toward their seats. Maggots squirmed within the gaping holes of their skin. Parts of their bones and organs were visible through the deterioration.

Sung-ho's hand overlapped hers.

She turned and looked at him.

Sung-ho rose and stole a glance over the seat and into the aisle. When he returned to his seat, he spoke. "Why don't you take your medicine?"

The train jerked to life. Its powerful engine chugged.

Closing her eyes, she embraced another hallucination. Tears burned in her ducts. She shook her head.

He squeezed her hand tighter, encouraging her. "If you take your medicine, the monsters will go away."

Again, she shook her head.

"Why not?"

With a trembling hand, Areum wiped away a tear. "If I take them, you'll go away too."

***

About the Author

ClarenceCarterAuthor.com

Clarence is a Maine based author who has been writing for nearly a decade. He loves fiction, both reading and writing. He's an active member of the HWA Horror Writers Association, is currently serving as a juror for the Bram Stoker Awards, and has attended their winter courses Horror University.

Other Works From This Author Links

The Latchkey Kids
Shadows & Keyholes
A girl named Mishka

Acknowledgments

We would like to express our deepest gratitude to our staff editors, **Rachael Swanson** and **Kasey Kubica**, for their tireless efforts in reviewing submissions, proofreading, and overall helping us stay on track throughout the creation of this anthology. Their dedication to this project and attention to detail have been invaluable.

We also want to thank **Dany Rivera** for her beautiful story art, which has added a new layer of meaning to the stories we've collected. Her talent and creativity have truly enhanced this project. You can find her at danycomicsarts.com

We are also grateful to our volunteer submission readers, **Suhas Sridhar**, **rklep13**, and **Blake Pingleton**, who generously shared their time and expertise to help us sort through the many submissions we received. Their feedback and insights were crucial in helping us identify the most compelling stories for this anthology.

A special thank you to our Anthology Contributors: **Brandon Ebinger, Clarence Carter, David Lee Zweifler, Gordon Grice, Stuart Freyer, Thomas Bales, Thomas Stewart, M.

W. Irving, Christopher Beck, Christopher Yusko, Dustin Reade, Terence Waeland, Susan L. Lin, Paul Melhuish

Finally, we want to extend our appreciation to all the authors who submitted to this anthology. We recognize the time, effort, and passion that goes into writing and submitting work for consideration, and we were grateful for the opportunity to read and appreciate each submission.

Thank you to everyone who has contributed to this project in any way.

We could not have done it without you!

If you liked any of our stories, take a moment to stop by our Amazon page and leave a review!

Coming Soon!

Our next anthology, **The Devil Who Loves Me**, will begin preorders on May 5th, with the full release scheduled for June 23rd. The anthology will take you on a dark journey through an old-world kind of love and chivalry that will **Make. You. Feel.** Expect a cover reveal in mid to late April. Visit our website and join our mailing list to get updates on sales, author interviews, and art sneak peeks!

Printed in Great Britain
by Amazon